SILENCE

SHUSAKU ENDO

Silence

by SHUSAKU ENDO

Translated by
William Johnston

Taplinger Publishing Company
New York

Seventh Paperback Printing

First published in paperback in 1980

Copyright © 1969 by Monumenta Nipponica

Translated from the Japanese *Chinmoku*
This translation first published in 1969
by Monumenta Nipponica, Tokyo

For information, address inquiries to

Taplinger Publishing Company
132 West 22nd Street
New York, New York 10011

Library of Congress Catalog Card Number 78-27168
ISBN 0-8008-7186-3

Contents

Translator's Preface

SHUSAKU ENDO has been called the Japanese Graham Greene. If this means that he is a Catholic novelist, that his books are problematic and controversial, that his writing is deeply psychological, that he depicts the anguish of faith and the mercy of God—then it is certainly true. For Mr. Endo has now come to the forefront of the Japanese literary world writing about problems which at one time seemed remote from this country: problems of faith and God, of sin and betrayal, of martyrdom and apostasy.

Yet the central problem which has preoccupied Mr. Endo even from his early days is the conflict between East and West, especially in its relationship to Christianity. Assuredly this is no new problem but one which he has inherited from a long line of Japanese writers and intellectuals from the time of Meiji; but Mr. Endo is the first Catholic to put it forward with such force and to draw the clear-cut conclusion that Christianity must adapt itself radically if it is to take root in the 'swamp' of Japan. His most recent novel, *Silence*, deals with the troubled period of Japanese history known as 'the Christian century'—about which a word of introduction may not be out of place.

I

CHRISTIANITY was brought to Japan by the Basque Francis Xavier, who stepped ashore at Kagoshima in the year 1549 with two Jesuit companions and a Japanese interpreter. Within a few months of his arrival, Xavier had fallen in love with the Japanese whom he called 'the joy of his heart'. 'The people whom we have met so far', he wrote enthusiastically to his companions in Goa, 'are the best who have as yet been discovered, and it seems to me that we shall never find . . . another race to equal the Japanese.' In spite of linguistic difficulties ('We are like statues among them,' he lamented) he brought some hundreds to the Christian faith before departing for China, the conversion of which seemed to him a necessary prelude to that of Japan. Yet Xavier never lost his love of the Japanese; and, in an age that tended to relegate to some kind of inferno everyone outside Christendom, it is refreshing to find him extolling the Japanese for virtues which Christian Europeans did not possess.

The real architect of the Japanese mission, however, was not Xavier but the Italian, Alessandro Valignano, who united Xavier's enthusiasm to a remarkable foresight and tenacity of purpose. By the time of his first visit to Japan in 1579 there was already a flourishing community of some 150,000 Christians, whose sterling qualities and deep faith inspired in Valignano the vision of a totally Christian island in the north of Asia. Obviously, however, such an island must quickly be purged of all excessive foreign barbarian influence; and Valignano, anxious to entrust the infant Church to a local clergy with all possible speed, set about the founding of seminaries, colleges and a novitiate—promptly despatching to Macao Francisco Cabral, who strongly opposed the plan of an indigenous Japanese Church. Soon things began to look up: daimyos in Kyushu embraced the Christian faith, bringing with them a great part of their subjects; and a thriving Japanese clergy took shape. Clearly Valignano had been building no castles in the air: his dream was that of a sober realist.

It should be noted that the missionary effort was initiated in the Sengoku Period when Japan, torn by strife among the warring daimyos, had no strong central government. The distressful situation of the country, however, was not without advantages for the missionaries who, when persecuted in one fief, could quickly shake the dust off their feet and betake themselves elsewhere. But unification was close at hand; and Japan was soon to be welded into that solid monolith which was eventually to break out over Asia in 1940. The architects of unity (Nobunaga, Hideyoshi and Ieyasu) were all on intimate terms with the Portuguese Jesuits, motivated partly by desire for trade with the black ships from Macao, partly (in the case of Nobunaga and Hideyoshi) by a deep dislike of Buddhism, and partly by the fascination of these cultured foreigners with whom they could converse without fear of betrayal and loss of prestige. Be that as it may, from 1570 until 1614 the missionaries held such a privileged position at the court of the Bakufu that their letters and reports are now the chief source of information for a period of history about which Japanese sources say little. All in all, the optimism of Valignano seemed to have ample justification.

Yet Japan can be a land of schizophrenic change; and just what prompted the xenophobic outburst of Hideyoshi has never been adequately explained. For quite suddenly, on July 24th 1587, while in his cups, he flew into a violent rage and ordered the missionaries to leave the country. 'I am resolved', ran his message, 'that the padres should not stay on Japanese soil. I therefore order that having settled their affairs within twenty days, they must return to their own country.'[1] His anger, however, quickly subsided; most of the missionaries did not leave the country; and the expulsion decree became a dead letter. So much so that C. R. Boxer can observe that within four short years there was 'a community of more than 200,000 converts increasing daily, and Hideyoshi defying his own prohibition by strolling through

1   See C. R. Boxer, *The Christian Century in Japan*, University of California Press, 1951, p. 148.

the gilded halls of Juraku palace wearing a rosary and Portuguese dress.'[2]

Nevertheless the writing was on the wall; and ten years after the first outburst, Hideyoshi's anger overflowed again. This time it was occasioned by the pilot of a stranded Spanish ship who, in an effort to impress the Japanese, boasted that the greatness of the Spanish Empire was partly due to the missionaries who always prepared the way for the armed forces of the Spanish king. When this news was brought to Hideyoshi he again boiled over and ordered the immediate execution of a group of Christian missionaries. And so twenty-six, Japanese and European, were crucified on a cold winter's morning in February 1597. Today, not far from Nagasaki station, there stands a monument to commemorate the spot where they died.

Yet missionary work somehow continued with the Jesuits apprehensive but still in favour at the royal court; and it was only under Hideyoshi's successor Ieyasu, the first of the Tokugawas, that the death sentence of the mission became irrevocable. From the beginning, Ieyasu was none too friendly toward Christianity, though he tolerated the missionaries for the sake of the silk trade with Macao. But here things were changing: for the English and the Dutch had arrived. Nor was it long before the role of interpreter and confidant was transferred from

2 Boxer, p. 153.

the Portuguese Jesuits to the English Will Adams—who lost no time in assuring the Shogun that many European monarchs distrusted these meddlesome priests and expelled them from their kingdoms. Ieyasu evinced the greatest interest in the religious conflict that was rending Europe, questioning the English and the Dutch about it again and again. At the same time his apprehension grew as he observed the unquestioning obedience of his Christian subjects to their foreign guides.

And so finally in 1614 the edict of expulsion was promulgated declaring that 'the Kirishitan band have come to Japan . . . longing to disseminate an evil law, to overthrow true doctrine, so that they may change the government of the country, and obtain possession of the land. This is the germ of a great disaster, and must be crushed.'[3] This was the death blow. It came at a time when there were about 300,000 Christians in Japan (whose total population was about twenty million) in addition to colleges, seminaries, hospitals and a growing local clergy. 'It would be difficult', writes Boxer, 'if not impossible, to find another highly civilized pagan country where Christianity had made such a mark, not merely in numbers but in influence.'[4]

Even now, however, a desperate underground missionary effort was kept alive until, under Ieyasu's successors, the hunt for Christians and priests became so systemati-

3   *Ibid.* p. 318.
4   *Ibid.* p. 321.

cally ruthless as to wipe out every visible vestige of Christianity. Especially savage was the third Tokugawa, the neurotic Iemitsu—'neither the infamous brutality of the methods which he used to exterminate the Christians, nor the heroic constancy of the sufferers has ever been surpassed in the long and painful history of martyrdom.'[5]

At first the most common form of execution was burning; and the Englishman, Richard Cocks, describes how he saw 'fifty-five persons of all ages and both sexes burnt alive on the dry bed of the Kamo River in Kyoto (October 1619) and among them little children of five or six years old in their mothers' arms, crying out, "Jesus receive their souls!"'.[6] Indeed, the executions began to be something of a religious spectacle, one of which Boxer describes as follows:

> This ordeal was witnessed by 150,000 people, according to some writers, or 30,000 according to other and in all probability more reliable chroniclers. When the faggots were kindled, the martyrs said *sayonara* (farewell) to the onlookers who then began to intone the *Magnificat*, followed by the psalms *Laudate pueri Dominum* and *Laudate Dominum omnes gentes*, while the Japanese judges sat on one side 'in affected majesty and gravity, as in their favorite posture'. Since it had rained heavily

5 *Ibid.* p. 337.
6 *Ibid.* p. 349.

the night before, the faggots were wet and the wood burnt slowly; but as long as the martyrdom lasted, the spectators continued to sing hymns and canticles. When death put an end to the victims' suffering, the crowd intoned the *Te Deum Laudamus*.[7]

But the Tokugawa Bakufu was not slow to see that such 'glorious martyrdoms' were not serving the desired purpose; and bit by bit death was preceded by torture in a tremendous effort to make the martyrs apostatize. Among these tortures was the 'ana-tsurushi' or hanging in the pit, which quickly became the most effective means of inducing apostasy:

The victim was tightly bound around the body as high as the breast (one hand being left free to give the signal of recantation) and then hung downwards from a gallows into a pit which usually contained excreta and other filth, the top of the pit being level with his knees. In order to give the blood some vent, the forehead was lightly slashed with a knife. Some of the stronger martyrs lived for more than a week in this position, but the majority did not survive more than a day or two.[8]

A Dutch resident in Japan declared that 'some of those who had hung for two or three days assured me that the

7 *Ibid.* p. 342–3.
8 *Ibid.* p. 354.

pains they endured were wholly insufferable, no fire nor no torture equalling their languor and violence.'[9] Yet one young woman endured this for fourteen days before she expired.

From the beginning of the mission until the year 1632, in spite of crucifixions, burnings, water-torture and the rest, no missionary had apostatized. But such a record could not last; and finally the blow fell. Christovao Ferreira, the Portuguese Provincial, after six hours of agony in the pit gave the signal of apostasy. His defection being so exceptional might seem of little significance; but the fact that he was the acknowledged leader of the mission made the shock a cruel one—all the more so when it became known that he was collaborating with his former persecutors.

The next setback for Christianity was the Shimabara Rebellion. Caused by the merciless taxation and oppression of the magistrate of Nagasaki, it later became a manifestation of Christian faith, the insurgents carrying banners with the inscription, 'Praised be the Most Holy Sacrament,' and shouting the names of Jesus and Mary. The uprising was put down with ruthless cruelty, and the Tokugawa Bakufu, convinced that such a rebellion could only have been possible with help from outside, decided once for all to cut their ties with Portugal and seal off their country from the world.

9   *Ibid.* p. 354.

Nevertheless some missionaries tried to enter. There was Marcello Mastrilli who came partly to make amends for Ferreira and of whom Inoue, the Lord of Chikugo, boasted that he died 'an agonizing death, yammering and screaming in the pit.' And finally in 1643 came a group of ten (European, Chinese and Japanese) among whom was Giuseppe Chiara—Mr. Endo's Sebastian Rodrigues. Quickly captured, they all apostatized after long and terrible tortures; though most, perhaps all, later revoked their apostasy. Even the Dutch eye-witnesses were moved to compassion by the awful state of their Papist rivals who 'looked exceedingly pitiful, their eyes and cheeks strangely fallen in; their hands black and blue, and their whole bodies sadly misused and macerated by torture. These, though they had apostatized from the Faith, yet declared publicly to the interpreters that they did not freely apostatize, but the insufferable torments which had been inflicted upon them forced them to it.'[10] Chiara died some forty years after his apostasy, stating that he was still a Christian. As for Christovao Ferreira, about his subsequent life and death not much is known. His grave can still be seen in a temple in Nagasaki, but the record of his burial was burnt in the atomic holocaust of 1945. Chinese sailors at Macao testified that prior to his death he had revoked his apostasy, dying a martyr's death in that pit which had pre-

10   *Ibid.* p. 393.

viously conquered him. But the Dutch residents in Japan say nothing of this; and so his death, as much of his life, must forever remain a mystery.

Yet Christianity's roots had gone too deep to be eradicated. Besides the martyrs (estimated at some five or six thousand for the period 1614–40 alone) thousands of crypto-Christians kept their faith. Through the secret organization described by Mr. Endo, the faith was handed down; baptism was administered; catechism was taught. They gave their names, of course, to their Buddhist temple; they complied with the order to trample on the sacred image; and today at Ueno Museum in Tokyo one can still see those *fumie* rubbed flat and shining by the hundreds of feet that ached with pain (if I may borrow Mr. Endo's phrase) while they trampled on someone whom their hearts loved. Handed down, too, was the tradition that the fathers would return; and in 1865, when Japan was reopened, the crypto-Christians came out from their hiding, asking for the statue of Santa Maria, speaking about Christmas and Lent, recalling the celibacy of the priests.

They are still there in their thousands, in Nagasaki and the offshore islands, clinging tenaciously to a faith that centuries of ruthless vigilance could not stamp out. Some of them are united with the world-wide Church; others are not. In their prayers remain smatterings of the old Portuguese and Latin; they preserve pieces of the soutanes and rosaries and disciplines that belonged to the fathers whom they loved; they retain their devotion to Santa Maria. And it was while living among them that Shusaku Endo wrote *Silence*.

II

I HAVE outlined the historical background, without which *Silence* might not easily be understood. But now it becomes necessary to add that the interest this novel evoked in Japan was less historical than contemporary. The two foreign apostates were immediately taken as symbols of a Christianity which has failed in Japan because it is so stubbornly Western. 'Father, you were not defeated by me,' says the victorious Inoue. 'You were defeated by this swamp of Japan.' It is precisely the swamp of Japan that cannot absorb the type of Christianity that has been propagated in these islands.

Graham Greene has well pointed out that to interpret novels in this way can lead to dangerous error; and Mr. Endo, too, in the course of discussions on his book, often protested that he was writing literature, not theology. Yet on these occasions many of his remarks showed that he was not indifferent to the theological implications of what he wrote and one is left with the impression that the novel is in some way the expression of a conflict between his Japanese sensibility and the Hellenistic Christianity that has been given to him. For example, in an interview recorded in the magazine *Kumo* he said:

I received baptism when I was a child . . . . . in

other words, my Catholicism was a kind of ready-made suit . . . . . I had to decide either to make this ready-made suit fit my body or get rid of it and find another suit that fitted . . . . . There were many times when I felt I wanted to get rid of my Catholicism, but I was finally unable to do so. It is not just that I did not throw it off, but that I was unable to throw it off. The reason for this must be that it had become a part of me after all. The fact that it had penetrated me so deeply in my youth was a sign, I thought, that it had, in part at least, become coextensive with me. Still, there was always that feeling in my heart that it was something borrowed, and I began to wonder what my real self was like. This I think is the 'mud swamp' Japanese in me. From the time I first began to write novels even to the present day, this confrontation of my Catholic self with the self that lies underneath has, like an idiot's constant refrain, echoed and reechoed in my work. I felt that I had to find some way to reconcile the two.[11]

'The mud swamp Japanese in me' . . . . . Japan is a swamp because it sucks up all sorts of ideologies, transforming them into itself and distorting them in the process. It is the spider's web that destroys the butterfly, leaving only

11 Translation by F. Mathy; see: Shusaku Endo. Japanese Catholic Novelist, *Thought*, Winter 1967.

the ugly skeleton. Mr. Endo has, on other occasions, referred to the fact that many of the so-called Christian intellectuals since Meiji were, in fact, Buddhist or nihilist underneath and ended up by sloughing off their Christianity in time of crisis. This was because the 'mud swamp Japanese' had not allowed them to take into the depths of their being the Christianity that was presented to them. If this Christianity had been less incorrigibly Western, things might have been different. Elsewhere Mr. Endo speaks poignantly of this very struggle in his own heart, calling it the peculiar cross that God has given to the Japanese:

> For a long time I was attracted to a meaningless nihilism and when I finally came to realize the fearfulness of such a void I was struck once again with the grandeur of the Catholic Faith. This problem of the reconciliation of my Catholicism with my Japanese blood . . . has taught me one thing: that is, that the Japanese must absorb Christianity without the support of a Christian tradition or history or legacy or sensibility. Even this attempt is the occasion of much resistance and anguish and pain, still it is impossible to counter by closing one's eyes to the difficulties. No doubt this is the peculiar cross that God has given to the Japanese.[12]

12 Translation by F. Mathy, *Ibid.*

In short, the tree of Hellenized Christianity cannot simply be pulled out of Europe and planted in the swamp of a Japan that has a completely different cultural tradition. If such a thing is done, the fresh young sapling will wither and die.

Yet this does not mean that the Christian cause is doomed. For Christianity has an infinite capacity for adaptation; and somewhere within the great symphony of Catholicism is a strain that fits the Japanese tradition and touches the Japanese heart. A different strain this from that evoked by the cultures of Greece and Rome, a strain perhaps so intimately blended with the whole that its gentle note has never yet been heard by the Christian ear. But it is there, and it must be found:

> But after all it seems to me that Catholicism is not a solo, but a symphony . . . . . If I have trust in Catholicism, it is because I find in it much more possibility than in any other religion for presenting the full symphony of humanity. The other religions have almost no fullness; they have but solo parts. Only Catholicism can present the full symphony. And unless there is in that symphony a part that corresponds to Japan's mud swamp, it cannot be a true religion. What exactly this part is—that is what I want to find out.[13]

Anyone familiar with modern theology in the West will

13   Translation by F. Mathy, *Ibid.*

quickly see that Mr. Endo's thesis is more universal than many of his Japanese readers have suspected. For if Hellenistic Christianity does not fit Japan, neither does it (in the opinion of many) suit the modern West; if the notion of God has to be rethought for Japan (as this novel constantly stresses), so has it to be rethought for the modern West; if the ear of Japan is eager to catch a new strain in the vast symphony, the ear of the West is no less attentive—searching for new chords that will correspond to its awakening sensibilities. All in all, the ideas of Mr. Endo are acutely topical and universal.

III

FINALLY, in all fairness to existing Japanese Christianity, I must add that Mr. Endo's book and his thesis have been extremely controversial in this country, and one can scarcely take his voice as that of Christian Japan. Shortly after the publication of *Silence* I myself was in Nagasaki where I found some indignation among the old Christians, who felt that Mr. Endo had been less than fair to the indomitable courage of their heroic ancestors. Criticism also came from the Protestant Doshisha University where Professor Yanaibara protested vigorously that these two priests had no faith from the beginning. It was not the swamp of Japan that conquered them; it was simply that their sociological faith, nourished in Christian Portugal, evaporated beneath the impact of a pagan culture. 'The martyrs heard the voice of

Christ', he wrote in the *Asahi Journal*, 'but for Ferreira and Rodrigues God was silent. Does this not mean that from the beginning those priests had no faith? And for this reason Rodrigues' struggle with God is not depicted.' As for the failure of Christianity, Professor Yanaibara is not convinced:

> Obviously the belief of Ferreira and Inoue that Japan is a swamp which cannot absorb Christianity is not a reason for apostasy. It was because he lost his faith that Ferreira began to think in this way . . . . . In that Christian era there were many Japanese who sincerely believed in Christ, and there are many who do so today. No Christian will believe that Christianity cannot take root in Japan. If the Japanese cannot understand Christianity, how has it been possible for Mr. Endo to write such a novel?[14]

Indeed, the very popularity of Mr. Endo's novel would seem to proclaim a Japan not indifferent to Christianity but looking for that form of Christianity that will suit its national character.

Much could be said about the nature of a Japanese Christianity, but I have usurped more space than is normally allotted to a mere translator; so, with a word of thanks to Professor M. Himuro of Waseda University who helped with the Nagasaki dialect and translated

14 *Asahi Journal*, 1966, 5, 8.

the two documents at the end of the book, I leave the reader in the hands of Shusaku Endo.

William Johnston
Sophia University, Tokyo

SILENCE

SHUSAKU ENDO

Prologue

NEWS reached the Church in Rome. Christovao
Ferreira, sent to Japan by the Society of Jesus in
Portugal, after undergoing the torture of 'the
pit' at Nagasaki had apostatized. An experienced missionary held in the highest respect, he had spent thirty-
three years in Japan, had occupied the high position of
provincial and had been a source of inspiration to priests
and faithful alike.

He was a theologian, too, of considerable ability, and
in the time of persecution he had secretly made his way
into the Kamigata region to pursue his apostolic work.
From here the letters he sent to Rome overflowed with
a spirit of indomitable courage. It was unthinkable that
such a man would betray the faith, however terrible the
circumstances in which he was placed. In the Society of
Jesus as well as the Church at large, people asked themselves if the whole thing were not just a fictitious report
invented by the Dutch or the Japanese.

Not that the Church at Rome was ignorant of the

straitened circumstances in which the Japanese mission was situated. Letters from the missionaries had left no room for doubt. From 1587 the regent Hideyoshi, reversing the policy of his predecessor, had initiated a frightful persecution of Christianity. It first began when twenty-six priests and faithful were punished at Nishizaka in Nagasaki; and following on this Christians all over the country were evicted from their households, tortured and cruelly put to death. The Shogun Tokugawa pursued the same policy, ordering the expulsion of all the missionaries from Japan in the year 1614.

Reports from the missionaries tell of how on the 6th and 7th October of this same year, seventy priests, both Japanese and foreign, were herded together at Kibachi in Kyushu and forced to board five junks bound for Macao and Manila. Then they sailed into exile. It was rainy that day, and the sea was grey and stormy as the ships drenched by the rain made their way out of the harbor, passed beside the promontory and disappeared beyond the horizon.

Flaunting this severe decree of exile, however, thirty-seven priests refused to abandon their flock and secretly remained hiding in Japan. And Ferreira was one of these underground priests. He continued to inform his superiors by letter of the capture of the missionaries and the Christians, and of the punishment to which they were subjected. Today there is still extant a letter he wrote from Nagasaki on March 22nd 1632 to the Visitor

8

Andrew Palmeiro giving an exhaustive description of the conditions of that time:

In my former letter I informed Your Reverence of the situation of Christianity in this country. And now, I will go on to tell you of what has happened since then. Everything has ended up in new persecution, new repression, new suffering. Let me begin my account with the story of five religious who from the year 1629 were apprehended for their faith. Their names are Bartholomew Gutierrez, Francisco de Jesus, Vicente de San Antonio of the Order of Saint Augustine, Antonio Ishida of our own Society, and a Franciscan, Gabriel de Santa Magdalena.

The magistrate of Nagasaki, Takenaka Uneme, tried to make them apostatize and to ridicule our holy faith and its adherents, for he hoped in this way to destroy the courage of the faithful. But he quickly realized that words alone would never shake the resolution of these priests; so he was forced to adopt a different course of action; namely, immersion in the hell of boiling water at Unzen.

He gave orders that the five priests be brought to Unzen and tortured until such time as they should renounce their faith. But on no account were they to be put to death. In addition to the five priests, Beatrice da Costa, wife of Antonio da

Silva, and her daughter Maria were to be tortured, since they, too, in spite of all attempts at persuasion, had refused to give up their faith.

On December 3rd the party left Nagasaki for Unzen. The two women were carried in litters, while the five men were mounted on horses. And so they bade farewell. Arriving at the port some distance away, their arms and hands were bound, their feet were shackled, and they were put on board a ship and tightly tied to its side.

That evening they reached the harbor of Obama at the foot of Unzen; and the next day they climbed the mountain where the seven, one by one, were thrust into a tiny hut. Day and night they remained there in confinement, their feet shackled and their arms bound, while around them guards kept watch. The road to the mountain, too, was lined with guards; and without formal permission from the officials no one was permitted to pass that way.

The next day the torture began in the following way. One by one the seven were taken apart from the surrounding people, brought to the edge of the seething lake and shown the boiling water casting its spray high into the air—and then they were urged to abandon the teaching of Christ or else they would experience in their very bodies the terrible pain of the boiling water which lay before them. The cold weather made the steam arising from the bubbling lake look terrible indeed, and the very sight of it would make a strong man faint, were it not for the grace of God. But everyone of them, strengthened by God's grace, showed remarkable courage and even asked to be tortured, firmly declaring that they would never abandon their holy faith. Hearing this dauntless reply, the officials tore off the prisoners' clothes, bound them hand and foot to posts, and scooping up the boiling water in ladles, poured it over their naked bodies. These ladles were perforated and full of holes so that this process took a considerable time and the suffering was prolonged.

The heroes of Christ bore this terrible torment without flinching. Only the young Maria, overcome with the excess of her suffering, fell to the ground in agony. 'She has apostatized! She has apostatized!' they cried; and carrying her to the hut they promptly sent her back to Nagasaki. Maria denied that she had wished to apostatize. Indeed, she even pleaded to be tortured with her mother and the rest. But they paid no attention to her prayers.

The other six remained on the mountain for thirty-three days. During that time the priests Antonio and Francisco, as well as Beatrice, were each tortured six times in the boiling water.

Father Vicente was tortured four times; Fathers Palmeiro and Gabriel twice. Yet in all this not one of them so much as breathed a groan or a sigh.

Fathers Antonio and Francisco as well as Beatrice da Costa, in particular, undaunted by tortures, threats and pleadings of all kind, displayed a courage worthy of a man. In addition to the torture of the boiling water, she was subjected to the further ignominy of being obliged to stand for hours upon a small rock, exposed to the jeering and insults of the crowd. But even when the frenzy of her persecutors reached its zenith, she did not flinch.

The others, being weak in health, could not be punished too severely since the wish of the magistrate was not to put them to death but to make them apostatize. Indeed, for this reason he went so far as to bring a doctor to the mountain to tend their wounds.

At last, however, Uneme realized that he would never win. On the contrary his followers, seeing the courage of the priests, told him that all the springs in Unzen would run dry before men of such power could be persuaded to change their minds. So he decided to bring them back to Nagasaki. On January 5th he confined Beatrice to a house of ill fame, while the priests he lodged in the local prison. And there they still are.

This whole struggle has had the effect of spreading our doctrine among the multitude and of strengthening the faith of our Christians. All has turned out contrary to the intentions of the tyrant.

Such was Ferreira's letter. The Church at Rome could not believe that this man, however terrible the torture, could be induced to renounce his faith and grovel before the infidel.

In 1635 four priests gathered around Father Rubino in Rome. Their plan was to make their way into a Japan in the throes of persecution in order to carry on an underground missionary apostolate and to atone for the apostasy of Ferreira which had so wounded the honor of the Church.

At first their wild scheme did not win the consent of their Superiors. Though sympathizing with the ardor and apostolic zeal which prompted such a plan, the Church authorities felt reluctant to send any more priests to such a country and to a mission fraught with such peril. On the other hand, this was a country in which from the time of Francis Xavier the good seed had been most abundantly sown: to leave it without leaders and to abandon the Christians to their fate was something unthinkable. Furthermore, in the Europe of that time the fact that Ferreira had been forced to abandon his faith in this remote country at the periphery of the world was not simply the failure of one individual but a humiliating defeat for the faith itself and for the whole of Europe. Such was the way of thinking that prevailed; and so, after all sorts of troubles and difficulties, Father Rubino and his four companions were finally permitted to set sail.

In addition to this group, however, there were three other priests planning to enter Japan secretly in the same way—but these were Portuguese and their reason was different. They had been Ferreira's students and had studied under him at the ancient monastery of Campolide. For these three men, Francisco Garrpe, Juan de Santa Marta and Sebastian Rodrigues, it was impossible to believe that their much admired teacher Ferreira, faced with the possibility of a glorious martyrdom, had grovelled like a dog before the infidel. And in these sentiments they spoke for the clergy of Portugal.

They would go to Japan; they would investigate the matter with their own eyes. But here, as in Italy, their Superiors were slow to give consent. At length, however, overcome by the ardent importunity of the young men, they agreed to this dangerous mission to Japan. This was in the year 1637.

Consequently, the three young priests set about preparing their long and arduous journey. It was customary at that time for the Portuguese missionaries who went to the Orient to join the fleet which went from Lisbon to India; and the departure of this Indian fleet was one of the most exciting events of the year in Lisbon. Before the eyes of the three men there arose in vivid colors the spectacle of an Orient which was literally the end of the earth and of a Japan which was its uttermost limit. As one opened the map one saw the shape of Africa, then India, and then the innumerable islands and countries of Asia were all spread out. And then, at the north-east extremity, looking just like a caterpillar, was the tiny shape of Japan. To get to this country one must first go to Goa in India, then over miles and miles of sea; for a period of weeks and months one must go on and on. From the time of Saint Francis Xavier, Goa had been the gateway to all missionary labor in the East; it had two cominaries where students from all parts of Asia studied and where the European missionaries learned about conditions in the country for which they were bound. Here missionaries sometimes had to wait for six months or even a year for a ship that would take them to the country to which they were destined.

The three priests strove with all their might to learn what they could about conditions in Japan. Fortunately there were many reports sent from Japan by Portuguese missionaries from the time of Luis Frois and these told of how the new Shogun Iemitsu had adopted a policy of repression even more cruel than that of his father or grandfather. Especially in Nagasaki, from the year 1629 the magistrate Takenaka Uneme had inflicted upon the Christians the most inhuman and atrocious sufferings, immersing them in pools of boiling water and urging them to renounce their faith and change their religion. It was said that in one single day the number of victims sometimes reached no less than sixty or seventy. Since it was Ferreira himself who had sent this news there could be no mistake about its reliability. In any case the new missionaries realized that they must have from the beginning the realization and conviction that the end of their arduous journey might bring them up against a fate more terrible than any of the sufferings they had endured on the way.

Sebastian Rodrigues, born in 1610 in the well-known mining town of Tasco, entered religious life at the age of seventeen. Juan de Santa Marta and Francisco Garrpe, both friends of Rodrigues, also studied with him at the seminary of Campolide. From their early days at the minor seminary they had spent their days sitting at their desks in study, and they all had vivid memories of their old teacher Ferreira from whom they had learned theology.

And this same Ferreira was now somewhere in Japan. Had that face with its clear blue eyes and soft radiant light—had it been changed by the hands of the Japanese torturers? This was the question they asked themselves. They could not believe that this face could now be distorted because of insults heaped on it; nor could they believe that Ferreira had turned his back on God and cast away that gentle charity that characterized his every action. Rodrigues and his companions wanted by all means to get to Japan and learn the truth about the fate of Ferreira.

On March 25, 1638, the Indian fleet sailed out from the river Tagus to a salvo of guns from the fortress of Belem. On board the Santa Isabella were the three missionaries who, after receiving a blessing from the Bishop, Joao Dasco, had boarded the commander's ship. As they reached the mouth of the brown river and plunged into the blue noonday sea, they leaned against the side of the ship watching the promontory and the mountain gleaming like gold. There were the red walls of the farm houses. The Church. From the church-tower the tolling of the bell which bade farewell to the departing ships was carried out into the sea.

Now for their journey around Africa to India. Three days after departure they hit up against a terrible storm on the West coast of Africa.

On April 2nd they reached the island of Porto Santo; some time later Madeira; on the 6th they arrived at the Canary Islands where they encountered ceaseless rain pouring down from a sky which contained no breath of wind. In the utterly windless calm, the heat was unbearable. And then, in addition to everything, disease broke out. On the Santa Isabella alone more than one hundred victims lay moaning on the deck and in the bunks below. Rodrigues and his companion together with the crew hastened around tending the sick and helping to bleed them.

July 25th, the feast of Saint James, the ship at last rounded the Cape of Good Hope. On this day a violent wind again arose so that the mast of the ship was broken and crashed down on the deck with a rending sound. Even the sick and Rodrigues and his companions were summoned up to rescue the foresail from the same peril. But scarcely had they succeeded in their attempt when the ship ran on a rock. If the other ships had not been there to help, the Santa Isabella would probably have sunk there and then.

After the storm the wind again calmed down. The sail lay lifeless; only its pitch black shadow fell upon the faces and bodies of the sick who lay like dead men on the deck. And so the days passed one by one with the glaring heat of the sun beating down upon a sea which had not so much as a swell of the waves.

All these mishaps prolonged the journey so that food and water became scarce; but at last on October 9th they reached their destination: Goa.

After arrival they were able to get more detailed news about Japan than had been possible at home. They were told that since January of the year in which they had set sail, thirty-five thousand Christians had caused an insurrection at Shimabara; and in the ensuing bloody conflict with the forces of the Bakufu the rebels had been butchered to the last man—men and women, young and old, all alike had been slain. As a result of the war, the whole district was so desolate that scarcely a human shadow could be seen, while the remnants of the Christians were being hunted down one by one. The news, however, which gave the greatest shock to Rodrigues and his companions was that as a result of this war Japan had cut all trade relations and intercourse with their country. Portuguese ships were forbidden to enter the harbors of Japan.

It was with the realization that they could not be brought to Japan in a Portuguese ship that the three priests reached Macao. They felt desperate.

The town of Macao, in addition to being the base of Portuguese operations in the Far East, was a base for trade between China and Japan. Consequently, if they waited here there was the possibility that some stroke of good fortune might help them on their way.

Immediately on arrival they received clear-cut advice from the Visitor Valignano who was in Macao at that time. Missionary work in Japan, he said, was now out of question nor had he any intention of sending missionaries to a country fraught with such dangers. From the time of the outbreak of persecution in Japan, it should be said, the whole administration of the Japanese Province of the Society of Jesus had been entrusted to this Superior, Valignano, who ten years before had founded at Macao a College for the formation of missionaries bound for China and Japan.

In regard to Ferreira whom the three men intended to seek out after arrival in Japan, Valignano gave the following report: From the year 1633 all news from the underground mission had come to an abrupt and drastic end. Dutch sailors returned to Macao from Nagasaki related that Ferreira had been taken and tortured in the pit. After that the whole matter was obscure and investigation of the true facts was impossible. This was because the Dutch had left on the very day that Ferreira had been suspended in the pit. The only thing that could be said with certainty was that Ferreira had been cross-examined by the newly-appointed magistrate Inoue, the Lord of Chikugo. In any case, the Macao mission could in no way agree to priests travelling to a Japan in such conditions. This was the frank opinion of Valignano.

Today we can read some of the letters of Sebastian Rodrigues in the library of the Portuguese 'Institute for the Historical Study of Foreign Lands'. The first of these begins at the time when he and his companions heard from Valignano about the situation in Japan.

Chapter 1

(*Letter of Sebastian Rodrigues*)

Pax Christi. Praised be Christ.

I HAVE already told you about how we arrived at
Goa last year on October 9th, and now on May 1st
we have reached Macao. Amidst all the difficulties
and privations of the journey Juan de Santa Marta became utterly exhausted and it looked as if he was getting
malaria, so only Francis Garrpe and myself are working
with all our strength at the missionary college here.
We certainly received a wonderful welcome.

The problem is, however, that Father Valignano,
Rector of the college, who has been here for ten years, has
been utterly opposed to our journey to Japan. In his room
overlooking the bay he spoke to us at length and this is
the gist of what he said: 'I am obliged to refuse to send
any more missionaries to Japan. The sea journey is extremely dangerous for Portuguese ships and you will
encounter all sorts of obstacles before even setting foot
in the country.'

His opposition is not altogether unreasonable, in view of the fact that since 1636 the Japanese government, suspecting that the Portuguese were in some way connected with the Shimabara rebellion, has completely cut all commercial relationship with them. Not only this, but in the journey from Macao the seas neighbouring on Japan are infested by English and Dutch warships which open fire on our trading ships.

'And yet our secret mission could with God's help turn out successful,' said Juan de Santa Marta, blinking his eyes fervently. 'In that stricken land the Christians have lost their priests and are like a flock of sheep without a shepherd. Some one must go to give them courage and to ensure that the tiny flame of faith does not die out.'

At these words a shadow passed over Valignano's face, and he remained silent. No doubt to this very day he was deeply troubled by the dilemma of his duty as a Superior and the fate of the unfortunate, persecuted Christians. And so the old man said no word, resting his forehead on his hands.

From his room the harbor of Macao could be seen in the distance. The sea was red in the evening sun. Black junks floated on the water, scattered here and there like black smudges.

'And one more point. We have an added duty: we want to find out the truth about our teacher Ferreira.'

'About Ferreira we have had no further news. The reports about him are vague. Anyhow, at present we don't have any plans for investigating the truth or falsity of what has been said about him.'

'Is he alive?'

'Even that we don't know. . . . . ' Valignano raised his head and heaved a deep sigh as he spoke. 'The reports he sent me regularly from the year 1633 have come to a sudden end. Whether he unhappily got sick and died, whether he is lying in the prison of the infidel, whether (as you are imagining) he won a glorious martyrdom, or whether he is still alive trying to send some report but unable to do so—about this at present we can say nothing.'

Valignano did not so much as utter a word about rumors that Ferreira had succumbed beneath the torture of his enemies. Like us, he was loth to attribute such fanciful charges to his old friend.

'Moreover. . . .' And now Valignano spoke with some emphasis, 'In Japan there has now appeared a person who is indeed a terror for the Christians. His name is Inoue.'

This was the first time we had heard the name of Inoue. Valignano went on to say that in comparison with the savagery of Inoue someone like Takenaka, the former magistrate of Nagasaki who had butchered so many Christians, was no more than a simple-minded person.

And so to imprint on our memories the name of this Japanese whom we would undoubtedly meet after landing in Japan, we repeated the unfamiliar sounds again and again: I-NO-U-E.

From the last report sent by the Christians in Kyushu, Valignano had a good deal of knowledge about this man. Since the rebellion of Shimabara he had become for all practical purposes the architect of the Christian persecution. Quite unlike his predecessor Takenaka, he was cunning as a serpent so that the Christians who until now had not flinched at threats and tortures succumbed one by one to his cunning wiles.

'And the sad fact', went on Valignano, 'is that he was formerly of our faith. He is even baptized.'

About this persecutor I will probably be able to give you more information later on, but what I want to tell you just now is that Valignano, prudent Superior though he is, was finally moved by our pleading—especially by that of Garrpe—and consented to our secret mission to Japan. So now the die is cast. For the conversion of Japan and the glory of God we have somehow made our way to the East; now we face a future which is certainly fraught with even greater perils and hardships than that sea journey around Africa and across the Indian Ocean. But 'if you are persecuted in one town, flee to another'; and within my heart there constantly arise the words of the *Apocalypse* that honor and glory and power belong to God alone.

As I have already told you, Macao is at the mouth of the great river Chu-Kiang. It is built on one of the many islands with which the entrance to the bay is studded, and like all the towns of the East there is no wall surrounding it, so that it is impossible to say where the city boundaries are. The Chinese houses stretch out like dust. But anyhow, no matter how many towns and cities of our country you imagine you can never get a picture of what it is like. The population is said to be about twenty thousand, but this number is almost certainly false. The only things here that might recall our own country are the governor's palace, the Portuguese warehouses and the cobbled roads. A fortress with cannons stands facing out into the bay, but fortunately until this day the cannons have never had to go into action.

The greater part of the Chinese show no interest in our teaching. On this point Japan is undoubtedly, as Saint Francis Xavier said, 'the country in the Orient most suited to Christianity'. However, ironically enough, as a result of the Japanese government's forbidding ships of its own country to go to foreign lands, the monopoly of the silk trade in the whole Far East has now fallen into the hands of the Portuguese merchants in Macao so that the total income of this import is expected to rise to four hundred seraphim as opposed to one hundred seraphim last year and the year before.

Today I have wonderful news for you. Yesterday we at last succeeded in meeting a Japanese. Formerly it seems that quite a number of Japanese religious and merchants came to Macao, but with the closing of their country such visits were brought to an end and even the few who were here returned to their own country. Even when we asked Valignano we got the answer that there were no Japanese in this town. And yet, quite by chance we found that there was a Japanese living in the midst of the Chinese in this town. Let me tell you how we came to meet him.

Yesterday—an awfully rainy day—we visited the Chinese sector of the town to see if we could somehow get a ship bound secretly for Japan. We wanted to find a captain and sailors. Macao in the rain. . . . The rain makes this wretched town even more wretched. The whole place was shrouded in ashen grey, while the Chinese, huddled in little houses that looked like dog-kennels, left the dirty streets so deserted that there was not a shadow of life in them. As I look at such streets I think (I wonder why?) of the mystery of human life—and then I grow sad.

Going to the house of the Chinese to whom we had an introduction we spoke about our business, and he promptly told us that there was here in Macao a Japanese who wanted to return to his native country. In answer to our request his little boy went in search of the Japanese.

What am I to say about this man, this first Japanese I ever met in my life? Reeling from excess of alcohol, a drunken man staggered into the room. About twenty-eight or nine years of age, he was dressed in rags. His name was Kichijiro. When finally he answered our questions we learned that he was a fisherman from the district of Hizen near Nagasaki. Before the famous Shimabara insurrection he had been adrift on the sea and had been picked up by a Portuguese ship. Whether or not it was due to his drunkenness I do not know, but there was a crafty look on his face, and as he spoke he would roll his eyes.

'Are you a Christian?' The question came from Garrpe. But the fellow suddenly shut up like a clam. We could not understand why Garrpe's question should make him so unhappy. At first he did not want to talk at all; but at length, yielding to our entreaties, he began bit by bit to tell the story of the Christian persecution in Kyushu. And here it is. In the village of Kurasaki in Hizen he had witnessed the spectacle of twenty-four Christians being subjected to the water punishment by the local daimyo. Wooden stakes were fixed in the sea at the water's edge and the Christians were bound to them. When the tide came in, the water would reach up to a certain mark, and then recede. The Christians gradually became utterly exhausted and after about a week they died in the most terrible agony. Did even Nero of Rome devise such a cruel method of death?

As our conversation went on, we noticed a strange thing. While Kichijiro described this hair-raising spectacle, his face became distorted; then suddenly he lapsed into silence. He shook his hand as though some terrible memory rose up from the past to haunt him. I wonder if among those twenty or so Christians who underwent the water torture there were some of his friends and acquaintances. Perhaps we had put our finger on an open wound which should not have been touched.

'Well, anyhow you are a Christian, aren't you?' Again Garrpe put the question persistently. 'You are. Aren't you?'

'I'm not,' said Kichijiro shaking his head. 'No, I'm not.'

'Anyhow, you want to go back to Japan. We have money to buy a ship and to get together a captain and sailors. So if you would like to return to your country. . .'

At these words those Japanese eyes, drunken and dirty yellow, flashed craftily and, remaining squatting on his knees in a corner of the room, with trembling voice as though he were speaking in self-defence he begged to be allowed to return to his own country if only to see again his beloved relatives who remained at home.

Thus began our dealings with this jittery fellow. In the dimly lit and dirty room a fly kept buzzing around and around. On the floor lay the empty sake bottles from which he had drunk. But anyhow, it is good to have this fellow. Once we land in Japan we won't know right from left. Someone will have to shelter us. We will have to get in contact with Christians who can protect us. So now we can use this man as our first guide.

For a long time Kichijiro sat facing the wall, clasping

his knees and thinking deeply about the terms we now offered. Then he agreed. For him it is an adventure fraught with danger, but I suppose he feels that if he misses this chance he will never again be able to get back to Japan.

Anyhow, thanks to Father Valignano it looks as if we are going to get hold of a big junk. Yet how frail and passing are the plans of men! Today we got news that the ship is eaten up by white ants. And here it is terribly difficult to get hold of iron and pitch.

Every day I keep writing this report bit by bit, so that it looks like a diary without a date. Please be patient in reading it. A week ago I told you that the junk we had succeeded in getting hold of was almost consumed by white ants; but now, thanks to God, we have found a method of overcoming this difficulty. We are going to seal up the inside and then set sail for Taiwan. Then if this emergency measure looks like holding out longer, we will go straight on to Japan. We ask for God's protection that we do not run into any big storm in the East China Sea.

This time I have bad news for you. I told you that Santa Marta, completely exhausted by the long, painful sea journey, looked like catching malaria. Now once again he has been seized by a severe fever accompanied by shivering all over his body. He is in bed in one of the rooms of the College. You who knew him in his former vigorous health cannot imagine how wretchedly thin and broken-down he has become. His eyes are blood-shot and dim, and if you put a wet towel on his head it becomes warm as though it had been immersed in hot water. To go to Japan in such a condition is simply un-thinkable. Valignano says that unless we leave him here for treatment he cannot give permission for the journey of the other two.

'We go first,' said Garrpe to console Marta. 'We'll prepare the way so that you can come afterwards when you get better.'

But can anyone predict what will happen? Perhaps he will live a safe and happy life, while we like so many other Christians will be captured by the infidel. . . . .

Marta remained silent, his cheeks and chin covered with a thick stubble; and he stared at the window. What was in his mind? You who have known him for so long can certainly understand his feelings. The day when we boarded ship, received the blessing of Bishop Dasco and sailed out of the River Tagus was followed by the long terrible journey. Our ship had been visited by thirst and sickness. And why did we endure all this? Why did we make our way to this crumbling town in the Far East?

We priests are in some ways a sad group of men. Born into the world to render service to mankind, there is no one more wretchedly alone than the priest who does not measure up to his task. Marta in particular since our arrival in Goa had a very special devotion to Saint Francis Xavier. Every day, while praying at the shrine of the saint in India, he had prayed that he might go to Japan.

Every day we keep praying that his health may be restored as soon as possible. But he makes no progress. Yet God bestows upon man a better fate than human knowledge could possible think of or devise. Our departure draws near. Only two weeks remain. Perhaps God in his omnipotence will miraculously make all things well.

The repair of the ship is proceeding rapidly. The new boards we put in after the trouble from the white ants make it look completely different. It looks as if the twenty-five sailors that Valignano found for us will bring us to the sea near Japan. These Chinese look thin and wasted like sick men who have not eaten for months; but the power of their wiry hands is incredible. With these thin arms they can lift the heaviest food boxes with ease. Their arms look like iron pokers. Anyhow, we are only waiting for a suitable wind to set sail.

As for our Japanese, Kichijiro, he mingles with the Chinese sailors, carries baggage and helps with the mending of the sail; but we are missing no chance of watching closely the character of this Japanese upon whom our whole future fate may depend. By now we have come to realize what a cunning fellow he is. And his cunning comes from weakness of character. Listen to what happened the other day. When the eyes of the Chinese overseer were upon him he made a show of working with all his might, but when the overseer went away he immediately began to idle. At first the other sailors said nothing, but at length they were able to put up with it no longer and beat him soundly. That in itself is not too important, but what astonished us was that when he was struck down and severely kicked by three sailors he grew deadly pale and, kneeling on the sand where he had fallen, pleaded for pardon in the most ugly way you could imagine.

Such conduct is pretty far from anything you could call Christian patience, but this weakling's cowardice is just like that. Raising his face that had been buried in the sand he shouted out something in Japanese. His nose and cheeks were covered with sand and a dirty spittle ran down from his mouth. Now we get some idea of why he suddenly shut up like a clam when we first mentioned the Japanese Christians. Perhaps whenever he speaks he has a dreadful fear of his own words. Be that as it may, this one-sided fight was brought to an end when we finally intervened on his behalf, and so all became quiet. Since that time Kichijiro greets us with a servile grin.

'Are you really a Japanese? Honestly, are you?' It was a typical Garrpe question, and not without a touch of bitterness. But Kichijiro, with a look of astonishment, asserted emphatically that he was. Garrpe had too

credulously taken at its face value the talk of so many
missionaries about 'this nation whose people don't even
fear death'. It is true, of course, that there are Japanese
who have endured torture for five days on end without
wavering in their fidelity; but there are also cowardly
weaklings like Kichijiro. And it is to such a man that we
have to entrust ourselves after reaching Japan. He has
promised to put us in touch with Christians who will
give us shelter; but now that I see his way of acting I
wonder how much he can be trusted. But don't think
that because I write in this way we have lost our energy
and enthusiasm. On the contrary, when I reflect that I
have entrusted my future to a fellow like Kichijiro I cannot help laughing. When you come to think of it, Our
Lord himself entrusted his destiny to untrustworthy
people. In any case, in our present circumstances there
is no alternative but to trust Kichijiro. So let's do so.

Only one thing is really disconcerting. He is a terrible
drunkard. After his day's work he uses every penny he
has received from the overseer on sake. His way of acting
when drunk is unspeakable. I can only conclude that he
has some haunting memory, something that he is trying
to forget by drinking.

In the night of Macao there echoes out the sad, long-
drawn-out sound of the bugle from the lips of the soldier
guarding the fortress. Here, as at home, in our monastery
after supper there is benediction in the chapel; and then

the priests and brothers, candles in hand, retire to their rooms in accordance with the rule.

The servants have just marched through the courtyard. In the rooms of Garrpe and Santa Marta the light is extinguished. Truly this is the end of the earth.

Beneath the light of the candle I am sitting with my hands on my knees, staring in front of me. And I keep turning over in my mind the thought that I am at the end of the earth, in a place which you do not know and which your whole lives through you will never visit. A throbbing sensation fills my being, and behind my eyelids arises the memory of that long and terrible sea journey so that my breast is filled with pain. Certainly my being in this utterly remote and unknown Oriental town is like a dream. Or rather, if I begin to reflect that it is not a dream I feel like shouting out that it is a miracle. Is it true that I am in Macao? Am I not perhaps in a dream? I cannot believe this whole thing.

On the wall is a great big cockroach. Its rasping noise breaks the solemn silence of the night.

'Go into the whole world and preach the gospel to every creature. He who believes and is baptized will be saved; he that does not believe will be condemned'. Such were the words of the risen Christ to the disciples assembled for supper. And now as I obey this injunction the face of Christ rises up before my eyes. What did the face of Christ look like? This point the Bible passes over in silence. You know well that the early Christians thought of Christ as a shepherd. The short mantle, the small tunic; one hand is holding the foot of the lamb while the other clasps a staff. This figure is familiar in our countries, for we see it reflected in many of the people whom we know. That was how the earliest Christians envisaged the gentle face of Christ. And then in the eastern Church one finds the long nose, the curly hair, the black beard. All this was creating an oriental Christ. As for the medieval artists, many of them painted a face of Christ resplendent with the authority of a king. Yet tonight for me the face is that of the picture preserved in Borgo San Sepulchro. There still remains fresh in my memory the time when I saw this picture as a seminarian for the first time. Christ has one foot on the sepulchre and in his right hand he holds a crucifix. He is facing straight out and his face bears the expression of encouragement it had when he commanded his disciples three times, 'Feed my lambs, feed my lambs, feed my lambs. . .' It is a face filled with vigor and strength. I feel great love for that face. I am always fascinated by the face of Christ just like a man fascinated by the face of his beloved.

At last our departure is only five days away. We have absolutely no luggage to bring to Japan except our own hearts. We are preoccupied with spiritual preparation only. Alas, I feel no inclination to write about Santa Marta. God did not grant to our poor companion the joy of being restored to health. But everything that God does is for the best. No doubt God is secretly preparing the mission that some day will be his.

Chapter 2

(Letter of Sebastian Rodrigues)

The peace of God.

Glory to Christ.

WITHIN the space of one short letter I don't know how to speak about the innumerable events that have crowded into my life in the past two months. Moreover, in my present state I do not even know if this letter will ever reach you. But my mood is such that I just cannot keep from writing; for I feel the duty of leaving you something written down.

For eight days after leaving Macao our ship was blessed with extraordinarily fine weather. The sky was clear and blue; the sail bellied out in the wind; we could see the shoals of flying fish gleaming like silver as they leapt out of the waves. Every morning Garrpe and I offered Mass on board ship, giving thanks to God for our safe passage, but it was not long until we hit up against our first storm. It was May 6th when a strong wind began to blow from the southeast. The sailors were men of

37

experience. They took down the sail and put up a smaller one in the front of the ship. But now it was dead of night, and the only thing possible was to abandon our ship to the winds and the waves. Meanwhile in the front of the ship a great rift was opened and the water began to pour in. For almost the whole night long we worked at stuffing cloth into the rift and bailing out the water.

Just as dawn was breaking the storm ceased. The sailors, as well as Garrpe and myself, in utter exhaustion could only throw ourselves down between the bales of luggage and stare up at the thick black rainclouds floating off to the east. There arose in my heart the thought of Saint Francis Xavier. He also, in the calm which followed such a storm, must have looked up at the milky sky. And then for the next eighty years how many missionaries and seminarians had sailed around the coast of Africa, passed by India, and had crossed over this very sea to preach the gospel in Japan. There had been Bishop Cerqueira; there had been Organtino, Gomes, Lopez, Gregorio. . . . . .

If one began to count them there was no limit. And among them there were some, like Gil de Mata, who met their fate in a sinking ship with their eyes fixed on Japan. Now I have some idea of the tremendous emotion that filled their breasts and enabled them to endure this awful suffering. All these great missionaries gazed at both the milky clouds and the thick black rain clouds floating away to the east. What thoughts filled their minds at such times? This also I can well imagine.

Beside the ship's baggage was Kichijiro. I could hear his voice. During the storm this pitiful coward made almost no attempt to help the sailors and now, wretchedly pale, he lay between the baggage. Splashed all around him was white vomit; and he kept muttering something in Japanese.

With the sailors we looked at the fellow with contempt. We were too exhausted to be interested in his stammering Japanese. But quite by accident jumbled in with his sentences I caught the words 'gratia' and 'Santa Maria'. This fellow who was just like a pig that buried its face in its own vomit had without a doubt uttered twice the words, 'Santa Maria'.

Garrpe and I exchanged glances. Was it possible that he was of our faith—this wretch who all through the journey not only failed to help but was even a positive nuisance. No. It was impossible. Faith could not turn a man into such a coward.

Raising up a face filthy with his own vomit, Kichijiro turned on us a glance of pain. And then with his usual cunning he made a pretence of not understanding the questioning looks we fixed on him. He smiled his cowardly smile. He has the most fawning, obsequious laugh you could possibly imagine. It always leaves a bad taste in our mouths.

'I am asking a question,' said Garrpe raising his voice.

'Give me a clear answer. Are you, or are you not, a Christian?'

Kichijiro shook his head vigorously. The Chinese sailors from their place between the bales of luggage looked at the whole affair with a mixture of curiosity and contempt. If Kichijiro were a Christian, why did he go so far as to conceal the whole affair even from us priests? My guess was that this cowardly fellow was afraid lest on returning to Japan we might give him over to the officials, revealing the fact that he was a Christian. On the other hand, if he was not really a Christian how explain the terror with which the words 'gratia' and 'Santa Maria' rose to his lips. Anyhow, the fellow intrigues me. I feel sure that bit by bit I will come to learn his secret.

Until this day there was no sign of land, no trace of an island. The grey sky stretched out endlessly and sometimes the rays of the sun struck the ship so feebly as to be heavy on the eyelids. Overcome with depression we just kept our eyes fixed on the cold sea where the teeth of the waves flashed like white buds. But God did not abandon us.

Quite suddenly a sailor who had been lying like dead in the stern of the ship raised a loud cry. There from the horizon towards which his finger pointed, a bird came flying. And this tiny bird which flew across the ocean came to rest on the sail, rent and torn by the storm of the previous night. Next, countless twigs came floating along the surface of the water. This indeed was proof that the land for which we longed so ardently was not far away. But our joy quickly changed to alarm. . . If this was really Japan we must make sure not to be seen even by the smallest vessel. The sailors on such a ship would doubtless hasten at once to tell the officials that a junk containing foreigners was drifting on the waves off the coast.

Garrpe and I crouched amidst the luggage like a couple of dogs as we waited for darkness to come. The sailors put up a small sail in front of the ship and they made a brave attempt to keep clear of the pieces of land that looked like mainland.

Midnight came. The ship moved forward noiselessly. Fortunately there was no moon; the sky was jet black; no one found us. The mainland rose up before us. We noticed that we were entering right into a harbor on both sides of which steep mountains arose. And now we could also see clumps of houses huddled together beyond the strand. Kichijiro was the first to wade ashore; next came myself; and last of all Garrpe got into the icy cold water. Was this Japan? or was it an island belonging to some other country? Frankly, none of us had any idea.

We hid silently in a tiny hollow while Kichijiro went off to explore the situation. The sound of footsteps on the sand came near to where we crouched. As we clutched our wet clothes and held our breath, we saw passing just before us the figure of an old woman with a cloth on her head and a basket on her back. She did not notice our presence and went on her way. Her departing footsteps faded into the night, and once again the deadly silence descended on the shore. 'He won't come back! He won't come back!' exclaimed Garrpe tearfully. 'Where has he gone, the weak-minded coward?'

But I was thinking of a more terrible fate. He had not fled. Like Judas he had gone to betray us. Soon he would appear again, and with him would be the guards.

'A band of soldiers went there with lanterns and torches and weapons', said Garrpe, quoting the Scriptures.

We reflected on the night at Gethsemane when Our Lord trusted himself without reserve to the hands of men. But the time dragged on so slowly that my spirit was almost crushed. It was fearful indeed. The perspiration flowed down my forehead and into my eyes. And then came the sound of footsteps. A group of people was approaching. The light of their torches burned dismally in the dark, and they came closer and closer.

Someone thrust a torch forward and in its light there appeared the ugly face, both red and black, of a small old man, while around him five or six young men with frightened eyes looked down on us.

'Padre, Padre!' The old man made the sign of the cross as he uttered the words, and in his voice there was a gentle note of solicitude for our plight. As for us, this 'Padre', spoken in our own beloved Portuguese tongue, was something we had never dreamt of hearing in this place. Needless to say, the old man could not know more Portuguese than this, but before our eyes he made the sign of the cross showing a bond of something that held us together. These indeed were Japanese Christians. All in a whirl I stood up in the sand. At last I had set foot on Japanese soil, and the realization of this fact swept over me with tremendous force.

Kichijiro was cowering behind the others with that servile smile of his. He always looks just like a mouse ready to scamper off at the slightest thing. I bit my lip with shame. Our Lord had entrusted himself to anybody—because he loved all men. And here I was with such a feeling of distrust toward this one man Kichijiro.

'Quickly. Keep walking.' It was the old man who was talking, and he urged us on with a whisper. 'We can't afford to be seen by the gentiles.'

'The gentiles!' Another word from our language now known to the Christians. Our forebears from the time of Xavier taught them these words. What sweat and toil it had taken to plunge the spade into this barren soil, then to fertilize it, to cultivate it until it reached this present stage. Yes, the seed had been sown; it sprouted forth with vigor; and now it was the great mission of Garrpe and myself to tend it lest it wither and die.

That night they kept us in hiding beneath the low ceiling of their house; nearby was a barn from which the stench was carried to where we lay. They assured us, however, that there was no danger. But how had Kichijiro been able to find the Christians so quickly?

The next day, while it was still dark, Garrpe and I changed into peasants' clothes and together with the young men who had met us on the previous day we climbed up a mountain which lay behind the village. The Christians wanted to keep us hidden there; they had a safer place there, a charcoal hut. Thick, thick mist lay over the woods and over the path along which we walked. Eventually this mist turned into light rain.

Arrived at our destination we heard for the first time about the place in which we now found ourselves. It was a fishing village called Tomogi, not too far from Nagasaki. It contained about two hundred households and the greater number of the villagers had already received baptism.

'And how are things now?' I asked.

'Yes, father.' It was Mokichi who spoke, a young man who accompanied us; and looking back at his friend, 'Now we can do nothing,' he went on. 'If it is found out that we are Christians we will all be killed.'

How shall I describe the joy that filled their faces when we gave them crucifixes that we had had around our necks. Both of them bowed to the very ground, and pressing the crucifixes to their foreheads spent a long time in adoration. Apparently they had not had such crucifixes for many, many years.

'Is it possible that we have a priest in our midst?'

44

Mokichi held my hand clasped in his as he spoke. 'And what about brothers?'

Needless to say, these people had met neither priest nor brother for six years. Until six years ago a Japanese priest, Miguel Matsuda, and a Jesuit brother, Mateo de Coros, had secretly kept in contact with this village and its immediate surroundings, but in November 1633, worn out by labor and suffering, they had both passed to their reward.

'But what has happened during these six years? What about baptism and the sacraments?' It was Garrpe who asked the question. And the answer of Mokichi stirred us to the very depths of our being. Indeed I want through you to convey to my Superiors what he said—and not only to my Superiors but to the whole Church in Rome. As he spoke, I recalled the words of the Gospel that some seed fell upon good ground and springing up it brought forth fruit, some tenfold, some thirtyfold, some sixtyfold and some a hundredfold. For the fact is that with neither priests nor brothers and in the throes of a terrible persecution at the hands of the government, they secretly made their own organization for the administration of the sacraments; and so they kept alive their faith.

For example, in Tomogi this organization was set up more or less as follows. From the Christians one of the older men was chosen to play the role of the priest. (I am simply writing to you without any embellishment

what Mokichi said to me.) The old man we met yesterday at the shore (they call him 'Jiisama') holds the
highest post of authority; he leads a blameless life, and
the task of baptizing the children is entrusted to him.
Beneath the Jiisama is a group of men known as 'Tossama' whose job it is to teach the Christians and to lead
them in prayer. Then there are helpers known as 'Mide-
shi'. All are engaged in this life-and-death struggle to
keep the faith alive.

'And all this goes on only in Tomogi. . . . .?' I asked
the question with some enthusiasm. 'I suppose other
villages are preserving their faith in the same way and
with the same kind of organization.'

This time Mokichi shook his head. Only afterwards
did I realize that in this country where blood relationship is of such primary importance the people of one
village, though closely united among themselves like
one family, sometimes go so far as to look with hostility
on the peoples of other villages.

'Yes, father, I can only speak for the people of our own
village. Too much contact with other villages might
end up in accusation before the magistrate.'

But I begged Mokichi and his friends to look for
Christians in the other villages also. I felt that as quickly
as possible word should be sent out that once again a
priest, crucifix in hand, had come to this desolate and
abandoned land.

From that time our life has become more or less as follows. At dead of night we offer Mass, just as they did in the catacombs; and then when morning comes we climb the mountain again and wait in hiding for any of the Christians who may want to visit us. Every day two of them bring to us our ration of food. We hear confessions, give instruction, teach them how to pray. During the day we keep the door of our tiny hut tightly closed and we refrain from making the slightest noise lest anyone passing outside may hear it. Needless to say, it is out of question to build a fire lest any trace of smoke be seen. And then, just in case..... foreseeing every contingency Mokichi and his friend have dug a kind of cave under the very floor of our hut.

It is not impossible that there are still Christians in the villages and islands west of Tomogi, but under the circumstances we cannot so much as stir outside our hut during the day. And yet I am determined, come what may, to seek out and find the lonely and abandoned flock.

Chapter 3

(Letter of Sebastian Rodrigues)

IN this country June marks the beginning of the rainy season. I have been told that the rain falls continuously for more than a month. With the coming of the rain the officials will probably relax their vigilance, so I intend to make use of this opportunity to travel around the neighbourhood and search out the remaining Christians. I want to let them know as quickly as possible that they are not utterly abandoned and alone.

Never have I felt so deeply how meaningful is the life of a priest. These Japanese Christians are like a ship lost in a storm without a chart. I see them without a single priest or brother to encourage and console, gradually losing hope and wandering bewildered in the darkness.

Yesterday rain again. Of course this rain is no more than a herald of the heat that follows. But all day long it makes a melancholy sound as it falls in the thicket which surrounds our hut. The trees shake and tremble as they let fall the drops of rain. And then Garrpe and I, pressing our faces to the tiny cracks in the wooden door, try to peer out into the surrounding world. Seeing nothing but rain and more rain, a feeling like anger rises up within our breasts. How much longer is this life to continue? Certainly both of us become strangely impatient and jittery, so that when either one of us makes even the slightest faux pas the other turns on him a baleful eye. This is only the result of nerves stretched taut like a bowstring day after day after day.

But now let me give you some more detailed information about these people of the village of Tomogi. They are poor farmers who eke out a living by cultivating potatoes and wheat in little fields. They have no ricefields. When you see how the land is cultivated right up into the middle of the mountain facing the sea, you are struck not so much by their indefatigable industry as by the cruelty of the life they have inherited. Yet the magistrate of Nagasaki exacts from them an exceedingly harsh revenue. I tell you the truth—for a long, long time these farmers have worked like horses and cattle; and like horses and cattle they have died. The reason our religion has penetrated this territory like water flowing into dry earth is that it has given to this group of people a human warmth they never previously knew. For the first time they have met men who treated them like human beings. It was the human kindness and charity of the fathers that touched their hearts.

I have not yet met all the people of Tomogi. This is

because from fear of the officials only two villagers can climb up to our little hut each night. Truth to tell in spite of myself I cannot help laughing when I hear the mumbling Portuguese and Latin words in the mouths of these ignorant peasants: 'Deus', 'Angelus', 'Beato' and so on. The sacrament of confession they call 'konshan'; heaven they call 'parais'; hell is 'inferno'. Not only are their names difficult to remember, but their faces all look the same—which causes not a little embarrassment. We confuse Ichizo with Seisuke, and we get Omatsu mixed up with another woman called Saki.

I have already told you something about Mokichi, so I would like now to say a few words about a couple of the other Christians. Ichizo is a man of about fifty who comes at night to our hut—and he always wears on his face an expression which makes you think he is angry. While attending Mass, and after it is over, he says not a word. In fact, however, he is not angry at all; this is just his natural expression. He is extraordinarily curious, and he scrutinizes carefully every movement and gesture of Garrpe and myself with his narrow, wrinkled eyes.

Omatsu, I'm told, is Ichizo's elder sister. Long ago she lost her husband and is now a widow. Twice she has come right up to our place with her niece, Sen, carrying on her back a basket with food for us. Like Ichizo, she too is extremely inquisitive and, together with her niece, scrutinizes Garrpe and me as we eat our meal. And what a meal! You couldn't imagine how wretched it is—a few fried potatoes and water. And while Garrpe and I gulp it down, the two women look on, laughing with evident satisfaction.

'Are we really so queer?' exclaimed Garrpe once, flaring up in anger. 'Is our way of eating so funny?'

They didn't understand a word he said, but burst out laughing, their faces crumpling up like paper.

But let me tell you something more about this secret organization of the Christians. I have already explained about the offices of Jiisama and Tossama, that the Jiisama is responsible for the sacrament of baptism, and that the Tossama have the job of instructing the faithful in prayer and catechism. These Tossama have moreover made a calendar of all the feasts of the Church and teach the faithful accordingly. From what they say, the feasts of Christmas, Good Friday, Easter—all are celebrated by these Tossama. Needless to say, they cannot have Mass on these days since there are no priests; but they secretly set up a holy picture in one of the houses and recite their prayers in front of it (they say their prayers in Latin just like us—'Pater Noster', 'Ave Maria' and so on) and in the intervals between the recitation of their prayers they chat about everything and anything. Nobody knows when the officials may come bursting in; but if that should happen everything is so arranged that the Christians can say they were simply having some kind of meeting together.

Since the rebellion of Shimabara the Lord of this

district has made an extremely thorough effort to hunt down the hidden Christians. Every day the officials go around making a thorough inspection of every village, and sometimes they will make a sudden swoop upon a house when no one is expecting it.

For example, since last year a decree has been issued forbidding anyone to make a fence or hedge between his house and that of his neighbour. They want everyone to be able to see into the house of his next-door neighbour and, if he notices any suspicious behaviour, to report it at once. Anyone who informs on us priests receives a reward of three hundred pieces of silver. For one who informs on a brother the reward is two hundred; and anyone informing on a Christian receives one hundred. I don't need to tell you what a temptation such an amount of money must be for these destitute peasants. Consequently, the Christians have almost no trust in the people of other villages.

I have already told you that Mokichi and Ichizo have expressionless faces, much like puppets. Now I understand the reason why. They cannot register on their faces any sorrow—nor even joy. The long years of secrecy have made the faces of these Christians like masks. This is indeed bitter and sad. Why has God given our Christians such a burden? This is something I fail to understand.

In my next letter I'll tell you about our search for Ferreira and also about Inoue (do you remember? the man who, at Macao, Valignano said was the most to be feared). Please give my respects and my promise of prayers to Father Minister Lucius de Sanctis.

Rain again today. Garrpe and I are lying in the darkness on the straw that serves us for a bed. Tiny little lice are crawling over my neck and back so that sleep is out of question. Japanese lice keep quiet during the day, but at night they walk all over our bodies—brazen, unmannerly wretches!

Until now no one has gone so far as to climb up to our hut on such a rainy night, so we have a chance to rest not only our bodies but also our nerves stretched to breaking point by this daily tension. Listening to the sound of the rain dripping from the trees in the grove my thoughts have turned again to Father Ferreira.

The peasants of Tomogi know absolutely nothing about him. But it is certain that until the year 1633 the father was carrying on an underground apostolate at Nagasaki not too far from where we are. And it was precisely in that year that all communication between himself and Valignano at Macao was cut like a cord. I wonder if he is still alive. Could it be true, as the rumor goes, that he grovelled like a dog before the infidels and cast away everything to which he had hitherto devoted his life? And supposing he is alive, is he too listening to the depressing sound of this rain? and with what feelings?

Suddenly I turned to Garrpe who was fully engaged in

his battle with the lice, and unburdened myself: 'If one of us could go to Nagasaki we might find some Christians who know Father Ferreira.'

In the darkness Garrpe stopped his twisting and turning and coughing. Then he commented: 'If we were caught it would be the end. This is not just a problem for the two of us. The danger extends to these peasants around us. Anyhow, don't forget that we are the last stepping-stones of the Gospel in this country.'

I uttered a deep sigh. He raised his body from the straw and as he peered intently at me I could gauge his way of thinking. The faces of Mokichi, Ichizo and the youngsters of Tomogi came before my eyes one by one. But could no one go to Nagasaki in our place? No. That wouldn't do either. These people had relatives and dependents. Their position was quite different from that of the priest without wife and children.

'What about asking Kichijiro?' I ventured.

Garrpe laughed a dry laugh. And I also recalled to mind the scene on the ship—the cowardly figure of Kichijiro with his face buried in the filth, clasping his hands and begging for mercy from the sailors.

'Crazy!' remarked my companion. 'You can't trust him an inch.'

Then we lapsed into a long silence. The rain pattered rhythmically on the roof of our little hut like the trickling of sand through an hour-glass. Here night and solitude are identical.

54

'And we, too, will we be caught like Ferreira?', I murmured.

'I'm more worried about these insects crawling all over my body,' retorted Garrpe.

Since coming to Japan he has always been in good spirits. Perhaps he feels that with good-nature and humor he can give courage to both of us. To tell you the truth, my own feeling is that we will not be captured. Man is a strange being. He always has a feeling somewhere in his heart that whatever the danger he will pull through. It's just like when on a rainy day you imagine the faint rays of the sun shining on a distant hill. I cannot picture myself at the moment of capture by the Japanese. In our little hut I have a feeling of eternal safety. I don't know why this should be. It's a strange feeling.

At last the rain has stopped, after three days of incessant falling. We can only judge this from the white ray of sunlight that penetrates a crack in the wooden door of our hut.

'Let's go out for a moment,' I said.

Garrpe nodded approval with a smile of joy.

As I pushed open the wet door, the song of the birds broke in from the trees like the rising of a fountain. Never before had I felt so deeply the sheer joy of being alive. We sat down near the hut and took off our kimonos. In the seams of the cloth the firmly entrenched lice looked just like white dust, and as I crushed them one by one with a stone I felt an inexpressible thrill of delight. Is this what the officials feel when they capture and kill the Christians?

Some fog still lingered within the wood, but faintly through it could be seen the blue sky and the distant shimmering sea. After the long confinement in our hut, I now stood again in the open, and giving up battle with the lice I gazed greedily at the world of men.

'Nothing to be afraid of!' Garrpe's white teeth flashed as he smiled with good humor and exposed his golden-haired chest to the rays of the sun. 'I don't know why we've been so jittery. In the future we must sometimes at least allow ourselves the pleasure of a sunbath.'

And so day after day the cloudless skies continued; and as our self-confidence grew we gradually became bolder. Together we would walk along the slopes in the wood filled with the smell of fresh leaves and wet mud. The good Garrpe would call our charcoal hut 'the monastery'. When we went for a stroll he would say with a laugh, 'Let's go back to the monastery and have a meal of warm bread and good, thick soup. But we'd better say nothing about it to the Japanese!' We were recalling the life we led with you in the monastery of Saint Xavier's at Lisbon. Needless to say, we don't have here a bottle of wine nor a piece of meat. The only food we get is the fried potatoes and the boiled vegetables that the peasants of Tomogi bring us. But the conviction grows deeper and deeper in my heart that all is well and that God will protect us.

One evening an interesting thing happened. We were sitting as usual chatting on a stone between our hut and the wood. All of a sudden in the rays of the darkening sky a huge bird flew out of the trees and, tracing a great black arc in the sky, winged off towards the distant hills.

'Somebody is watching us!' Garrpe spoke breathlessly, his eyes fixed on the ground, his voice sharp but hushed. 'Don't budge! Remain just as you are!'

From a hill bathed in the dying sunlight and slightly removed from the thicket from which the bird had sprung up just now, two men stood looking in our direction. We realized immediately that they were not the peasants of Tomogi whom we knew so well. We sat stiff like stones without moving a muscle, uttering a prayer that the western sun would not reveal our faces.

'Is anybody there?' The two men from the top of the hill raised their voices and shouted aloud. 'Is anybody there?'

Were we to answer or to keep quiet? A single word might well betray us. So from fear we said nothing.

'They're descending the hill and coming here,' whispered Garrpe in a low voice, remaining seated as he was. 'No, they aren't. They are going back the way they came.'

They went down into the valley growing smaller and smaller as they receded into the distance. But the fact was that two men had stood on the hill in the light of the western sun, and whether or not they had seen us we did not know.

That same night Ichizo came up the mountain and with him a man named Magoichi who was one of the Tossama. As we explained what had happened in the evening Ichizo's eyes narrowed and he scrutinized every inch of the hut. At length he stood up silently and after a word to Magoichi the two men began to tear up the floor boards. A moth flew round and round the oil lamp as they worked. Taking a spade that was hanging on the wooden door, Ichizo began to dig up the soil. The silhouettes of the two men as they wielded the spades floated on the opposite wall. They dug a hole big enough to hold both of us, and in it they put some straw; then they closed it up again with boards. This, it seems, is to be our future hideout in case of emergency.

From that day we have taken the utmost precautions, trying not to show ourselves outside the hut at all, and at night we don't make use of any light whatever.

The next event took place five days after the one I have recorded. It was late at night and we were secretly baptizing a baby that had been brought along by Omatsu and two men belonging to the Tossama. It was our first baptism since coming to Japan, and of course we had no candles nor music in our little hut—the only instrument for the ceremony was a broken little peasants' cup which we used for holy water. But it was more touching than the liturgy of any cathedral to see that poor little hut with the baby crying and Omatsu soothing it while one of the men stood on guard outside. I thrilled with joy as I listened to the solemn voice of Garrpe as he recited the baptismal prayers. This is a happiness that only a missionary priest in a foreign land can relish. As the water flowed over its forehead the baby wrinkled its face and yelled aloud. Its head was tiny; its eyes were narrow; this was already a peasant face that would in time come to resemble that of Mokichi and Ichizo. This child also would grow up like its parents and grandparents to eke out a miserable existence face to face with the black sea in this cramped and desolate land; it, too, would live like a beast, and like a beast it would die. But Christ did not die for the good and beautiful. It is easy enough to die for the good and beautiful; the hard thing is to die for the miserable and corrupt—this is the realization that came home to me acutely at that time.

When they departed I lay down in the straw, exhausted. The smell of the oil the three men had brought still lingered in the hut. Once again the lice crawled slowly over our backs and legs. I don't know how long I slept; but after what seemed a short time I was wakened by the snoring of the optimistic Garrpe who was fast asleep. And then—some one was pushing at the door of the hut, trying little by little to open it. At first I thought it might only be the wind from the valley below blowing through the trees and pressing against the door.

59

Quietly I crawled out of the straw and in the darkness put my fingers on the floor-boards underneath which was the secret hiding-place dug by Ichizo.

The pushing against the door now stopped, and a man's voice could be heard, low and plaintive: 'Padre, Padre. . . . . .'

This was not the signal of the peasants of Tomogi. They had agreed to give three gentle knocks on the door. Now at last Garrpe too was awake and without the slightest movement he strained his ears for the next sound.

'Padre!' The plaintive voice made itself heard again. 'There's nothing wrong. Don't be afraid of us.'

In the pitch darkness we held our breath in silence. What sort of crazy official was laying a trap like this?

'Won't you believe us? We are peasants from Fukazawa. For a long time we have been longing to meet a priest. We want to confess our sins.'

Dismayed by our silence they had now given up pushing at the door, and the sound of their receding footsteps could be heard sadly in the night. Grasping the wooden door with my hands I made as if to go out. Yes, I would go. Even if this was a trap, even if these men were the guards, it didn't matter. 'If they are Christians, what then?' said a voice that beat wildly in the depths of my heart. I was a priest born to devote my life to the service of man. What a disgrace it would be to betray my vocation from cowardly fear.

'Stop!' cried Garrpe fiercely. 'You idiot. . . . '

'I'm no idiot. This is my duty.'

As I tore open the door, the pale white rays of the moon bathed the great earth and the trees in silver light. What a night it was!

Two men dressed in rags as though they were beggars crouched there like dogs. Looking up at me they murmured: 'Father, won't you believe us!'

I noticed that the feet of one of them was covered with blood where he had cut himself while climbing the mountain. Both of them were faint and ready to collapse with exhaustion. Nor was this surprising. They had made their way here from the Goto Islands twenty leagues away, a two-day journey.

'We were on the mountain a while ago. Five days ago we hid over there and looked across in this direction.' One of them pointed at the hill beyond our hut. So it was these men that had been watching us that evening.

We brought them inside, and when we gave them the dried potatoes that Ichizo had brought us they seized them greedily with both hands and thrust them into their mouths like beasts. It was clear that they had not eaten for two days.

And then we began to speak. Who on earth had told them that we were here—that was our first question.

'Father, we heard it from a Christian of our village. His name is Kichijiro.'

'Kichijiro?'

'Yes, father.'

Still they crouched like beasts in the shadow of the oil lamp with the potato clinging to their lips. One of the fellows had practically no teeth, but he would stick out the one or two he had and laugh like a child. The other seemed stiff and tense in the presence of two foreign priests.

'But Kichijiro is not a Christian,' I said finally.

'Oh, he is, father. Kichijiro is a Christian.'

This was an answer we had not quite expected. Yet we had half wondered at times if the fellow were not after all a Christian.

But now the whole situation was gradually beginning to change. Now it was clear enough: Kichijiro was a Christian who had once apostatized. Eight years before, he and his whole family, all Christians, had been betrayed through envy by an informer and had been brought up for questioning. Ordered to tread on the picture of Christ, his brothers and sisters had firmly refused to do so. Only Kichijiro, after a few threats from the guards, had yelled out that he would renounce his faith. His brothers and sisters were immediately brought off to prison but Kichijiro himself, though set free, did not return to his native village.

On the day of the burning at the stake, his cowardly face was observed in the crowd that surrounded the place of execution. And then this face, covered with mud and looking like a wild dog, unable to endure the sight of the martyrdom of his brethren, immediately withdrew and disappeared from sight.

From these men we heard astonishing news. In the district known as Odomari, the villagers had succeeded in escaping the vigilance of the officials, and they were still Christians to a man. And not only Odomari. The neighbouring district and villages of Miyahara, Dozaki and Egami, although to outward appearances they were Buddhist, were in fact Christian—a fact which was barely kept hidden. For a long, long time they had been awaiting the day when we priests would once again come across the distant sea to help them and give them a blessing.

'Father, we have not been to Mass. We have not confessed our sins. We have only said our prayers.' It was the man with the blood-stained feet who spoke.

'Come quickly to our village. Father, we teach our little children their prayers. They are waiting for the day you will come.' The fellow with the yellow teeth, opening a mouth that yawned like an enormous cave, nodded approval. The fish oil burned and crackled. Garrpe and I could not refuse such a plea. We had been too cowardly until now. It was embarrassing to think of our weakness in comparison with the courage of these Japanese peasants who had slept in the mountains and lacerated their feet in order to come to us.

The sky was white. The air of the milky morning blew into our hut. In spite of all our urging they refused to get into the straw and rest; instead they slept squatting down with their arms around their knees. And then at last the rays of the morning sun pierced the cracks between the boards of our hut.

Two days later we discussed with the Christians of Tomogi the question of our going to Goto. Finally it was decided that Garrpe should remain while I would try to contact the Christians of Goto for a period of five days. They were not too enthusiastic about the plan. Some even ventured the suggestion that the whole thing was a dangerous plot to ensnare us.

The appointed day came. It was night; and they secretly came to meet me at the beach. I was wearing the clothes of a Japanese peasant, and Mokichi with one other man came to see me off in the ship they had prepared at the shore. It was a moonless night; the sea was jet black; and the only sound that could be heard was the rhythmic movement of the oars. But the man who plied them spoke not a word. As we sailed into the open sea the waves swelled and the ship rocked.

Suddenly I was seized with a terrible fear, doubt, suspicion. Was not this fellow here to sell me? The people of Tomogi had warned me; and they were right. Why had the fellow with the bloodstained feet not come?— and the other with no teeth? I looked at the Japanese face in front of me. It was impassive and expressionless like a Buddha; and my feelings became all the more apprehensive. Yet go I must. I had said I would.

The black sea stretched out everywhere in the night; while the sky held not a single star. Then, after travelling for two hours through the darkness I sensed the black shape of an island moving slowly beside us. This, my companion told me, was Kabashima, an island close to Goto.

Reaching the shore, I felt dizzy with seasickness, exhaustion and tension. Three fishermen were waiting for us, and as I looked up at them there in the center was the face of Kichijiro with the same old cringing, servile smile. In the village there was no light, but somewhere a dog was howling frantically.

The toothless fellow had not exaggerated in his description of how eagerly the peasants and fishermen of Goto were waiting for a priest. Even now I am completely overwhelmed with work. I don't even have time for sleep. They come to my house one after another, completely ignoring the ban on Christianity. I baptize the children and hear the confessions of the adults. Even when I keep going all day long I don't get through them all. They remind me of an army marching through the parched desert and then arriving at an oasis of water— this is the way they come to me, thirsty and longing for refreshment. The crumbling farm house that I use for a chapel is jammed tight with their bodies, and so they confess their sins, their mouths close to my ear and emitting a stench that almost makes me vomit. Even the sick crawl in here to meet me.

'Father, won't you listen to me?'. . . . . 'Father, won't you listen to me?'. . . . . And so it goes on.

But the funniest thing of all is Kichijiro. No longer the same man, now he is the hero of the village, extolled to the skies; and he walks around with his head in the air. Anyhow, I suppose it is alright for him to put on airs because without him I could not have come here at all. But his past—his apostasy and so on—seems to be completely forgotten. I wonder if this drunk has exaggerated to the Christians the whole story of Macao and our sea journey. Perhaps he has made out that the arrival of the two priests in Japan is all his work.

And yet I have no inclination to scold him. I hate his glib talk, but I cannot deny that I am greatly in his debt. I urged him to go to confession, and with great humility he confessed all the sins of his past life.

I ordered him always to keep in mind the words of Our Lord: 'He who confesses my name before men, him also will I confess before my Father who is in heaven; but he who denies my name before men him also will I deny before my Father who is in heaven.'

At this Kichijiro grovelled like a whipped dog and struck his forehead with his hand in token of repentance. This fellow is by nature utterly cowardly and seems quite unable to have the slightest courage. He has good will, however; and I told him in no uncertain terms that if he wanted to overcome this weakness of will and this cowardice that made him tremble in face of the slightest violence, the remedy was not in the sake he kept drinking but in a strong faith.

My hunch from some time back was not wrong. What are the Japanese peasants looking for in me? These people who work and live and die like beasts find for the first time in our teaching a path in which they can cast away the fetters that bind them. The Buddhist bonzes simply treat them like cattle. For a long time they have just lived in resignation to such a fate.

Today I baptized thirty adults and children. And not only from here; for the Christians make their way through the mountains from Miyahara, Kuzushima and Haratsuka. I then heard more than fifty confessions. After Sunday Mass for the first time I intoned and recited the prayers in Japanese with the people. The peasants stare at me, their eyes alive with curiosity. And as I speak there often arises in my mind the face of one who preached the Sermon on the Mount; and I imagine the people who sat or knelt fascinated by his words. As for me, perhaps I am so fascinated by his face because the Scriptures make no mention of it. Precisely because it is not mentioned, all its details are left to my imagination. From childhood I have clasped that face to my breast just like the person who romantically idealizes the countenance of one he loves. While I was still a student, studying in the seminary, if ever I had a sleepless night, his beautiful face would rise up in my heart.

Anyhow, whatever about this, I realize how dangerous these gatherings are. Sooner or later the whole movement may get to the ears of the officials.

Here also there is no word of Ferreira. I met two Christians, old men, who had seen him. The upshot of our conversation was that Ferreira had set up a house at a place called Shinmatsu, near Nagasaki, for abandoned infants and the sick. This was, of course, before the persecution became intense; but just from listening to their talk, the countenance of my old teacher rose up before my eyes—the chestnut-colored beard, the slightly hollowed eyes. . . I began to wonder if he had mingled with these destitute Japanese Christians in the same way as he had with us students, putting his hand on their shoulders with the same friendly warmth.

Quite deliberately I asked a pointed question: 'Was the father of a severe nature?'

One of the old men looked up at me and earnestly shook his head in disagreement. 'No, no, no, I have never met such a kind and gentle person in my life', was what his trembling lips seemed to say.

Before returning to Tomogi I instructed these people as to how to form the organization I have already described to you. I mean the one that the people of Tomogi had devised secretly when they were completely deprived of priests. So I taught them how to choose their Jiisama and to make their Tossama. In their present circumstances this is the only way they can continue to teach catechism to their young people and to their children. Indeed, they take to this method with great enthusiasm, and when they come to decide on their Jiisama and

Tossama they begin to wrangle with one another like the people of Lisbon at election time. Amongst them, of course, Kichijiro keeps stubbornly putting himself forward for any post of honor.

One more interesting point. The peasants here, just like those at Tomogi, kept pressing me for a small crucifix or medal or holy picture or some such thing. And when I replied that I had left all these things behind, they looked quite crushed. Finally, I had to take my rosary and, unfastening the beads, give one to each of them. I suppose it is not a bad thing that the Japanese Christians should reverence such things; but somehow their whole attitude makes me uneasy. I keep asking myself if there is not some error in their outlook.

Six days later, in the evening, I once again secretly boarded the little ship and we rowed our way back through the dark sea in the night. I listened to the monotonous sound of the oars plied through the water and to the sea as it washed the sides of the ship, while Kichijiro stood in the stern singing softly to himself. Five days previously, when I had crossed over to the island in this same ship, an inexplicable fear had suddenly seized me; and now as I recalled this foolish panic I could not help smiling. Anyhow, all was well now. Such were my thoughts.

In fact, since coming to Japan everything had worked out beyond my wildest expectations. We had not been obliged to undertake any dangerous adventure; we had succeeded in finding new groups of Christians; to date the officials knew nothing of our existence. I went so far as to think that Father Valignano in Macao had been altogether too afraid of persecution from the Japanese. Feelings of joy and happiness suddenly filled my breast: the feeling that my life was of value and that it was accomplishing something. I am of some use to the people of this country at the ends of the earth, I reflected—a people and a country which you can never understand.

Perhaps it was because of this feeling of well-being that the return journey seemed so much shorter than the journey out. So when the ship grated on the shore I could scarcely believe that we had already reached Tomogi.

Hiding on the shore I waited alone for Mokichi and his friend. Even this precaution, I felt suddenly, was quite meaningless; and I kept reflecting on the night when Garrpe and I had arrived in this country.

Footsteps on the shore. 'Father......'

Overcome with joy I jumped up to clasp the other with my sand-covered hand.

'Father, flee! Quickly, quickly, go away!' Mokichi spoke with great rapidity, pushing me in front of him. 'The guards are in the village.'

'The guards.....?'

'Yes, father, the guards. The news has reached them.'

'And they know about us?'

Mokichi shook his head quickly. 'They haven't noticed yet that we have been keeping you in hiding.'

70

And so I ran in the opposite direction, away from the district, with Mokichi and Kichijiro pulling my hands. Into the fields we went, trying to keep ourselves hidden as we made our way through the wheat to the place where our little hut was.

Drizzle was falling gently. Japan's rainy season had begun.

Chapter 4

(A Letter of Sebastian Rodrigues)

SO once again I can send you a letter. I have already told you about my return from Goto and how the government officials were ransacking the village. I cannot but be grateful to God for the safety of Garrpe and myself.

Fortunately, before the officials reached the place, the Tossama got everyone to hide away with all speed their holy pictures, crucifixes and any object that might arouse suspicion. In these circumstances the 'cordia' organization was splendid. When the officials arrived, all kept working in the fields with innocent faces, and the Jiisama answered the questions simply and nonchalantly. The wisdom of peasants shows itself in their ability to pretend that they are fools. After a long period of interrogation the exhausted officials were satisfied and went away.

Ichizo and Omatsu told us this story with evident pride, and as they described the details they pushed out their teeth and laughed with glee. What cunning showed itself in their features!

Yet one puzzling problem remains: did someone betray us? Surely it could not be one of the villagers; and yet little by little they themselves have become suspicious of one another. I begin to get anxious lest there be a split among them.

Apart from this, however, now that I am back again in the village I am completely at peace. Our hut is full of light; I can hear the cock crow from the foot of the hill; the red flowers are in bloom, spread over the earth like a beautiful carpet.

Since coming back to Tomogi, Kichijiro is very popular here too. He swaggers around visiting the houses and talking big about conditions in Goto. He tells them what a welcome I got there and how he himself was much appreciated because he brought me there—and when he goes on with this talk, the people of the village give him food and even sometimes offer him sake.

One time he arrived at our hut completely drunk with two or three of his young comrades. His face was flushed as he shouted: 'I am with you. . . If I am with you, you have nothing to fear.' His companions looked at him with respect, and he began to sing with even more enthusiasm. 'I am with you. If I am with you, you have nothing to fear,' he shouted when he had finished singing. And then stretching out his legs he fell fast asleep.

Is it that he is a good fellow at heart? or is it that he is agreeable? Anyhow, I just can't hate him.

Now let me tell you some more about the life of the Japanese. Needless to say, I am telling you about the peasants of Tomogi whom I have seen. I'm just passing on to you what they said. Don't conclude that the whole of Japan is just like this.

The first thing you must realize is that the poverty and squalor in which these peasants live is beyond anything you have ever seen in Portugal. Even the more wealthy among then, the upper class, only get the taste of rice about twice a year. Their usual fare is potatoes and radishes and such-like vegetables, while their only drink is warm water. Sometimes they dig up roots and eat them. They have a queer way of sitting—completely different from ours. Their knees are on the ground or the floor, and then they sit back on their heels. For them this posture is restful; but until we got used to it, it was terribly painful. The roofs of the houses are made of thatch. The houses are filthy, and their stench is unbearable. In Tomogi there are only two households that have a cow or horse.

The feudal lord has unlimited power over his people, much more than any king in a Christian country. The yearly tax is bitterly high, and those who fail to pay it are punished mercilessly. Indeed, the Shimabara rebellion was a terrible reaction against the unbearable sufferings imposed by this taxation. For example, here in the village of Tomogi, they tell the story of how, five years ago, the wife and children of a man called Mozaemon were seized as hostages and put in the water prison simply because he did not pay his tax of five bags of rice. The peasants are the slaves of the samurai, and above them stand the landowners. The samurai make much of weapons and, irrespective of rank, they all carry a dagger and a sword once they reach the age of thirteen or fourteen. The landowner has absolute power over the samurai, and he can kill at will anyone he does not like and confiscate all his property.

The Japanese go bareheaded both in winter and in summer, and the clothing they wear leaves them exposed to the cold. Generally they cut off their hair so as to be completely bald, only leaving one long tress of hair hanging down their back. The bonzes shave their heads completely, and there are others also, not bonzes, among the samurai, who do likewise. . . .

. . . this is a sudden break.
I'm going to write to you as accurately as possible what happened on June 5th, though this report may well end up by being very brief. In our present plight we cannot say when the danger will come upon us. It may be that I will not have a chance to write to you at length and in detail.

On the 5th, around noon, I had a feeling that something

75

strange was going on in the village down below. Through the trees we could hear the incessant barking of dogs. On quiet days, of course, when the weather is fine, it is not unusual for the bark of dogs and even the clucking of hens to be carried faintly up here—and indeed the sound is something of a consolation in our confinement; but today we felt somehow uneasy about it. Suspecting that something ominous might be in the wind, we went to the east side of the copse to look down and see what was going on. From here we could get the best view of the village at the foot of the mountain.

The first thing that caught our attention was a cloud of white dust on the road which skirted the sea and led into the village. What could this be? A bare-backed horse was galloping wildly out of the village at the entrance of which stood five men (clearly they were not our peasants) firmly barring the way so that no one could escape.

We realized immediately what had happened: the guards had come to search the village. Garrpe and I, falling over ourselves in haste, rushed back to our hut and, grabbing everything that might betray us, buried it in the hole dug by Ichizo. That done we plucked up courage and decided to go down through the trees and have a clearer view of what was going on in the village.

Not a sound could be heard. The white noonday sun beat mercilessly down on the road and on the village. All we could clearly see was the shadow of the farmhouses lying black on the road. Why was there no sign of life? Even the barking of the dogs had suddenly come to an end, and Tomogi was like an ancient, abandoned ruin. Yet I could sense the awful silence that enveloped the whole place. Earnestly I prayed to God. Well I knew that we should not pray for the happiness and good fortune of this world; yet I prayed and prayed that this awful noonday silence might forever be taken away from the village over which it hung so ominously.

Again the dogs began to bark as the men who had formed a block at the entrance to the village rushed out. Mingled with them we could see the form of the Jiisama—that poor old man—bound tightly with ropes. From his horse a samurai, wearing a black umbrella-like hat, shouted out an order and they all formed a single file behind the old man and then moved forward. Another samurai brandishing a whip led the way alone, with his own cloud of white dust, and as he rode he kept glancing backwards. The memory of the whole thing still remains vividly in my mind: the horses lifting high their legs as they galloped along, the old man reeling and staggering as he was dragged off by his captors. And so the procession advanced along the road in the white heat of the sun, just like a line of ants. Then it was lost from sight.

That night we heard the details from Kichijiro and Mokichi. The guards had appeared before noon. This time the people had no warning of their arrival. And so the samurai rode in, shouting orders to their men, galloping around the village and peering into every corner, while the people fled helter skelter in confusion.

No trace of anything Christian was found. Yet this time they did not give up in despair and withdraw. Instead, the samurai herded the peasants together in one place and declared that unless they made a clean breast of the whole thing a hostage would be taken. Yet no one spoke a word.

'We do not neglect to pay our taxes; and we do our duty to the State.' It was the Jiisama who spoke up to the samurai. 'And our burials, too—they are performed in the temple.'

To this the samurai made no answer. Instead, with his whip he pointed to the Jiisama and immediately his men, who were standing in a group behind, threw a rope around the old man and bound him tightly.

'Be careful! I want no back chat. We're not here for discussion. An informer has recently told us that amongst you there are secret adherents of this forbidden Christian sect. If anyone will say frankly who these people are he will receive one hundred pieces of silver. But if you don't confess, you must accept the consequences. After three days we will come for another hostage. Think it over!'

The peasants stood erect, silent. Men, women, children—all were silent. And so the seconds passed. It was as if enemies were staring at one another. Looking back on it now, I realize that it must have been precisely at this time when everything became silent that we looked down on the village from the mountain.

The samurai turned his horse toward the entrance and brandishing his whip rode off. The old Jiisama, bound and trailed along behind the horses, fell, stood up, then fell again. The men would grab hold of him trying to make him stand up as he was dragged along.

Such was the incident of June 5th just as we heard it.

'No, father, we didn't say a word about you,' said Mokichi, hands on knees, 'and if they come again, we'll still say nothing. No matter what happens we'll stand by you.'

He probably said this because he noticed the shadow that passed over our faces, a momentary fear and apprehension. If that was so, how ashamed I feel. Yet even Garrpe, good-natured in the face of the most terrible difficulties, fixed upon Mokichi a glance that was filled with anguish. 'But if this goes on, you'll all end up as hostages,' he finally said.

'Yes, father. It might turn out that way. But even so, we'll say nothing.'

'But this is impossible. Rather than such a calamity it is better for the two of us to get away from this mountain altogether.' As he spoke, Garrpe turned to Mokichi and myself and to the terrified Kichijiro who sat beside us. 'Can't we take refuge in this man's island?'

At these words a spasm of fear crossed the face of Kichijiro, but he said not one word. Looking back on the situation I see that this cringing weak-willed fellow, having brought us here and being embroiled in the whole m tter, was in an awful fix. On the one hand he did not want to lose his reputation as a good Christian; and yet in his little head he was thinking furiously of a way to preserve his life. And so his cunning eyes flashed as he rubbed his hands just like a fly. He said that the same problem would then arise in Goto since it would be searched also. Then he kept trying to prove that it would be better to go to some place further removed. But anyhow no decision was reached that night, and the two men stealthily descended the mountain.

The next day the people of Tomogi were all excited and nervous. Far be it from me to make any criticism of them, but I want to tell you just what Mokichi reported to me. They were split into two factions: one faction insisted that the two of us should move off to a different location, the other said that the village ought to shelter us, come what may. There were even some who said that Garrpe and myself were responsible for the evil that had befallen the village. In the midst of all this Mokichi, Ichizo and Omatsu displayed an unwavering faith. No matter what happened they would protect the priests—such was their stand.

This confusion gave the authorities the chance they were looking for. On June 8th they adopted a new approach. This time it was not a ferocious-looking samurai on horseback who came but an old samurai with smiling face, accompanied by four or five followers. He advised the people to weigh the matter carefully, thinking of the pros and cons of the whole thing. He indicated that whoever would honestly reveal the names of the adherents of this Christian sect would obtain a reduction in taxation in the coming years. For these destitute farmers the thought of a tax reduction must have been alluring indeed; yet they overcame the temptation.

'If you take such a firm stand, I suppose there is nothing for me but to believe you,' said the old man as he laughingly looked back at his followers. 'And yet I must ask my Superiors which is right—your statement or that of our informer. So we need a hostage. From your number please select three men and send them to Nagasaki tomorrow. Since I am quite confident that you are doing nothing wrong, there is nothing to worry about.'

In his voice there was not the slightest hint of intimidation, but everyone knew that it was a trap. And so the men of Tomogi spent that night debating fiercely as to who should be sent to the magistrate's headquarters at Nagasaki. The men selected might never return. Small wonder that even the Tossama and the others who held office flinched. Gathering together in a dark farm house the peasants scrutinized one another keenly. Each seemed to be asking himself secretly how he could escape this terrible role.

The name of Kichijiro was mentioned. Probably the reasons for this were, firstly, that he was in a sense a stranger—not a native of Tomogi; and secondly many harbored the deep feeling that the whole catastrophe had occurred just because of him. Poor weakling! When he saw what was happening he fell into the most terrible confusion and began to cry. Finally he broke into abusive language against everyone around. But the others argued that they would have to abandon their wives and children. 'You don't belong to this village,' they said. 'The officials won't cross-examine you so severely. Please go in our place.' With clasped hands they entreated him, until finally from sheer weakness he could no longer refuse. So it was decided that he should go.

'Let me go too.' It was Ichizo who suddenly spoke up. Everyone gasped in amazement. Could this be the silent, stubborn Ichizo they knew so well?

And then it was Mokichi's turn. He would join the other two, he said.

9th. From morning a light, drizzling rain had kept falling. The trees in front of our hut could scarcely be seen, wrapped as they were in the grey mist. The three climbed up to the wood. Mokichi seemed a little excited. Ichizo, his eyes narrowed as always, was sullen and silent. Behind the other two was Kichijiro looking like a whipped dog, pitifully glaring at me with eyes that seemed filled with resentment.

'Father, if we are ordered to trample on the *fumie*. . . .' Mokichi, head hanging, mumbled the words as though he was talking to himself. 'It's not only a matter that concerns us. If we don't trample, everyone in the village will be cross-examined. What are we to do?'

At this, such a feeling of pity welled up within my breast that without thinking I gave an answer that I know you would never give. I thrust from my mind the memory of how Father Gabriel, during the persecution at Unzen when dragged before the *fumie* had cried out: 'I had rather this foot were cut off than that I should trample on this image. . . . . .' I know that many Japanese Christians and fathers have manifested such feelings when the holy picture was brought before their feet. But was it possible to demand this from these three unfortunate men?

'Trample! Trample!' I shouted. But immediately I realized that I had uttered words that should never have been on my lips. Garrpe looked at me reproachfully.

Kichijiro was still snivelling. 'Why has Deus Sama given us this trial? We have done no wrong,' he cried.

We were silent. Mokichi and Ichizo also remained silent; their eyes seemed fixed on a speck in the empty sky.

So all together we joined in a last prayer; and when we had finished, the three men descended the mountain. Garrpe and I watched the figures as they disappeared into the mist and were lost from sight. Never again was I to meet Mokichi and Ichizo.

Again it is a long time since I wrote to you. I have

already described how the officials descended upon Tomogi; but I had to wait until now to be able to continue with the details about the cross-examination of the·three Christians at Nagasaki. We multiplied our prayers to Heaven that they, together with the Jiisama, might be restored to us in safety. Night after night the people of the village offered up their prayers for this intention.

I do not believe that God has given us this trial to no purpose. I know that the day will come when we will clearly understand why this persecution with all its sufferings has been bestowed upon us—for everything that Our Lord does is for our good. And yet, even as I write these words I feel the oppressive weight in my heart of those last stammering words of Kichijiro on the morning of his departure: 'Why has Deus Sama imposed this suffering upon us?' And then the resentment in those eyes that he turned upon me. 'Father', he had said, 'what evil have we done?'

I suppose I should simply cast from my mind these meaningless words of the coward; yet why does his plaintive voice pierce my breast with all the pain of a sharp needle? Why has Our Lord imposed this torture and this persecution on poor Japanese peasants? No, Kichijiro was trying to express something different, something even more sickening. The silence of God. Already twenty years have passed since the persecution broke out; the black soil of Japan has been filled with the lament of so many Christians; the red blood of priests has flowed profusely; the walls of the churches have fallen down; and in the face of this terrible and merciless sacrifice offered up to Him, God has remained silent. This was the problem that lay behind the plaintive question of Kichijiro.

Anyhow, let me simply tell you about the fate that befell us after this.

The three men were summoned to the magistrate's office at a place called Sakuradai. For two days they were left lying in the prison at the back of the place, until finally they were brought out for questioning. For some reason or other the questioning began with a strangely mechanical question and answer.

'You know that Christianity is an outlawed religion?'

Mokichi, spokesman for the others, nodded his assent.

'A report has been sent in that you are practising this outlawed religion. What have you to say?'

All three answered that they were convinced Buddhists living in accordance with the teaching of the monks at the Danna Temple.

The next step was: 'If that is so, trample on the *fumie*.'

A board to which was attached an image of the Virgin and Child was placed at their feet. Following my advice, Kichijiro was the first to place his foot on the image; after him Mokichi and Ichizo did likewise. But if they thought that only by this would they be pardoned, they were greatly mistaken. Slowly there appeared on the faces of the watching officials faint smiles. What had caught their attention was not the actual fact of the Christians placing their foot on the *fumie* but the expressions on their faces as they did so.

'You think you can deceive us like that?' said one of the officials, an old man. And now for the first time the three recognized him as the old samurai who'd ridden into Tomogi some days before. 'Do you think we are fools? Do you think we didn't notice how heavy and nervous your breathing became. . . . ?'

'We are not excited,' Mokichi exclaimed earnestly. 'We are not Christians.'

'Well, let us try one more way,' came the answer.

And with this the order was given that they should spit on the crucifix and declare that the Blessed Virgin was a whore. Only afterwards did I hear that this was a plan thought out by Inoue, the man whom Valignano had spoken of as being the most dangerous of all. This Inoue, who had at one time received baptism to get advancement in the world, knew well that these poor peasants honored the Virgin above all. Indeed, I myself since coming to Tomogi have been a little worried seeing that the peasants sometimes seem to honor Mary rather than Christ.

'Come now. Won't you spit on it? Won't you repeat the words as you are told?'

Ichizo grasped the *fumie* in both hands and, as the officials prodded him on from behind, he tried to spit on it; but somehow he was powerless. He could not do it. Kichijiro, too, hung back, making no movement.

'What's the matter with you?'

At the fierce urging of the officials, a white tear overflowed from the eye of Mokichi and rolled down his cheek. Ichizo, too, shook his head as though caught in the throes of pain. Then both of them at last confessed openly that they were Christians. Only Kichijiro, overcome by the threats, gasped out the required blasphemy against the Virgin.

'Now spit!' came the order.

At the command he let fall on the *fumie* the insulting spittle that could never be effaced.

Following upon this investigation, Mokichi and Ichizo were imprisoned for ten days in the prison of Sakuradai. As for the apostate Kichijiro, he was set free and, with that, he disappeared from sight. Since that time he has not returned here. It would be impossible for him to come back.

We have now entered the rainy season. Every day the fine drizzle falls unceasingly. Now for the first time I come to see what a gloomy pest this rain is—a pest that destroys everything both on the surface and at the root. This district is like a country of the dead. No one knew what fate would overtake our two Christians. Fear that they too would eventually be subjected to the same investigation gripped the people, and almost no one went into the fields to work. And beyond the dreary fields how black the sea was!

20th. Once again the officials rode into the village, this time with a proclamation. Here, on the beach of Tomogi, Mokichi and Ichizo would be subjected to the water punishment.

22nd. A procession, looking like a long line of peas, could be seen approaching from the distance along the rain-blanketed ashen road. Slowly the tiny figures grew in size. In the midst of the group, their arms bound fast and their heads hanging low, surrounded by guards rode Ichizo and Mokichi. The people of the village did not venture out from behind the barred doors of their houses. Behind the long procession were a number of stragglers who had joined from the neighbouring villages to view the spectacle. The whole scene could be observed from our hut.

Arriving at the shore, the officials ordered a fire to be lighted so that Ichizo and Mokichi could warm their bodies drenched by the rain. And then (as I have been told) with an unwonted sense of pity, someone gave them a cup of sake to drink. When I heard this I could not help thinking of how one of the soldiers gave to the dying Christ some vinegar on a sponge.

Two trees, made into the form of a cross, were set at the water's edge. Ichizo and Mokichi were fastened to them. When it was night and the tide came in, their bodies would be immersed in the sea up to the chin.

They would not die at once, but after two or even three days of utter physical and mental exhaustion they would cease to breathe. The plan of the authorities was to let the people of the village of Tomogi as well as the other peasants get a good view of this prolonged suffering so that they would never again approach the Christian faith. It was already past noon when Mokichi and Ichizo were fastened to the trees and the officials, leaving four guards to watch, withdrew on horseback. The onlookers also, who had at first come in great numbers to watch the spectacle, now gradually departed.

The tide came in. The two forms did not move. The waves, drenching the feet and lower half of their bodies, surged up the dark shore with monotonous roar, and with monotonous roar again receded.

In the evening, Omatsu together with her niece brought food to the guards and asked if they might give the two men something to eat. Receiving this permission, they now approached in a small boat.

'Mokichi! Mokichi!', cried Omatsu.

'What is it?', Mokichi is said to have replied.

Next, 'Ichizo! Ichizo!' she said. But the aged Ichizo could make no answer. Yet that he was not dead was clear from the occasional slight movement of his head.

'You are suffering terribly; but be patient. Padre and all of us are praying. You will both go to Paradise.'

Such were Omatsu's words of earnest encouragement; but when she tried to put the potato she had brought into Mokichi's mouth he shook his head. If he must die anyway, he seemed to feel, he would like to escape as quickly as possible from this torment. 'Give it to Ichizo,' he said. 'Let him eat. I can endure no more.'

Omatsu and her niece, distraught and tearful, returned to the shore; and here, drenched by the rain, they raised their voices and wept.

Night came. The red light of the guards' blazing fire could be seen faintly even from our mountain hut, while the people of Tomogi gathered on the shore and gazed at the dark sea. So black were the sea and the sky that no one knew where Mokichi and Ichizo were. Whether they were alive or dead no one knew. All with tears were praying in their hearts. And then, mingled with the sound of the waves, they heard what seemed to be the voice of Mokichi. Whether to tell the people that his life had not yet ebbed away or to strengthen his own resolution, the young man gaspingly sang a Christian hymn:

> We're on our way, we're on our way
> We're on our way to the temple of Paradise,
> To the temple of Paradise. . . . .
> To the great Temple. . . . .

All listened in silence to the voice of Mokichi; the guards also listened; and again and again, amid the sound of the rain and the waves, it broke upon their ears.

24th. The drizzle continued all day, while the people of Tomogi, again huddled together, stared from afar at the stakes of Mokichi and Ichizo. The shore, enveloped by rain, stretched out wearily like a sunken desert. Today there came no 'gentile' spectators from the neighbourhood. When the tide receded there only remained in the distance the solitary stakes to which were fastened the two men. It was impossible to distinguish between the stakes and the men. Mokichi and Ichizo adhered to the stakes in such a way that they became part of them. The only indication that they were still alive was the dark moaning of a voice which sounded like that of Mokichi.

The moaning sometimes ceased. Mokichi had not even the strength to encourage himself with a hymn like that of yesterday. Yet after an hour of silence the voice was again brought to the ears of the people by the wind. Hearing this sound, like that of an animal, the peasants trembled and wept. In the afternoon the tide gradually comes in again; the black, cold color of the sea deepens; the stakes seem to sink into the water. The white foaming waves, swirling past the stakes, break on the sand, a white bird, skimming over the surface of the sea, flies far, far away. And with this all is over.

They were martyred. But what a martyrdom! I had long read about martyrdom in the lives of the saints—how the souls of the martyrs had gone home to Heaven, how they had been filled with glory in Paradise, how the angels had blown trumpets. This was the splendid martyrdom I had often seen in my dreams. But the martyrdom of the Japanese Christians I now describe to you was no such glorious thing. What a miserable and painful business it was! The rain falls unceasingly on the sea. And the sea which killed them surges on uncannily—in silence.

In the evening the officials again arrived on horseback. At their command, the guards gathered damp pieces of wood and, removing the bodies of Mokichi and Ichizo from the stakes, began to burn them. This they did to prevent the Christians from bringing home the remains for veneration. When the bodies were reduced to ashes, they threw them into the sea. The flame they had kindled flared red and black in the breeze; the smoke flowed over the sandy beach while the people, without the slightest movement, vacantly watched its undulations. When all was over, heads hanging like cows, they shuffled back to their homes.

Today, while writing this letter, I sometimes go out of our hut to look down at the sea, the grave of these two Japanese peasants who believed our word. The sea only stretches out endlessly, melancholy and dark, while below the grey clouds there is not the shadow of an island.

There is no change. But I know what you will say: 'Their death was not meaningless. It was a stone which in time will be the foundation of the Church; and the Lord never gives us a trial which we cannot overcome. Mokichi and Ichizo are with the Lord. Like the numerous

Japanese martyrs who have gone before, they now enjoy everlasting happiness.' I also, of course, am convinced of all this. And yet, why does this feeling of grief remain in my heart? Why does the song of the exhausted Mokichi, bound to the stake, gnaw constantly at my heart:

> We're on our way, we're on our way,
> We're on our way to the temple of Paradise,
> To the temple of Paradise. . . . .
> To the great Temple. . . . .

I have heard from the people of Tomogi that many Christians when dragged off to the place of execution sang this hymn—a melody filled with dark sadness. Life in this world is too painful for these Japanese peasants. Only by relying on 'the temple of Paradise' have they been able to go on living. Such is the sadness which fills this song.

What do I want to say? I myself do not quite understand. Only that today, when for the glory of God Mokichi and Ichizo moaned, suffered and died, I cannot bear the monotonous sound of the dark sea gnawing at the shore. Behind the depressing silence of this sea, the silence of God. . . . . the feeling that while men raise their voices in anguish God remains with folded arms, silent.

This may well be my last report. This morning we got word that the guards are getting ready to comb the mountains. Before this search can get under way we have

93

got the hut back to its original condition and have done away with every trace of our hiding there. So now we leave the hut. And where will we go? Neither Garrpe nor I have yet decided. For a long time we talked the thing over wondering if we should flee together or separate. Finally we decided that even if one became a prey of the gentiles it was better that the other should remain. In other words, we would part company. And yet why on earth do we remain in this country at all? We did not make that long journey around Africa, across the Indian Ocean, on to Macao and then to Japan just to flee like this from one hiding place to another. It was not to hide in the mountains like fieldmice, to receive a lump of food from destitute peasants and to be confined in a charcoal hut without being able even to meet the Christians. What had happened to our glorious dream?

Yet one priest remaining in this country has the same significance as a single candle burning in the catacombs. So Garrpe and I vowed to one another that after our separation we should strive might and main to stay alive.

Anyhow, if my report now comes to an abrupt end (for all I know you may not even to date have received it), do not think that we are necessarily dead. It is just that in this barren land we must leave one small spade to till the ground. . . . .

All around me is the black sea; it is impossible to tell

where the blackness of the night begins. I cannot see whether or not there are islands around me. The only thing that tells me I am on the sea is the heavy breathing of the young man who rows the boat behind me—the sound of the oars in the water, the lapping of the waves against the edge of the boat.

One hour ago Garrpe and I parted. We clambered on board separate little ships and left Tomogi—he went off in the direction of Hirado. In the pitch darkness I could not even see him; we did not even have time to say goodbye.

Left all alone, I trembled from head to foot—it seemed that my body was outside the control of my will. Were I to say that this moment was not filled with dread I would be telling a lie. No matter how strong one's faith, physical fear can overwhelm one completely. When I was with Garrpe we could at least share our fear as one shares bread, breaking it in two; but now I was all alone in the black sea of the night and must take upon myself the cold and the darkness and everything else. (Have all the Japanese missionaries felt such terror? I wonder about them.) And then somehow or other the mouse-like face of Kichijiro, filled with terror, rose up in my imagination. Yes, that cowardly wretch who had trampled on the *fumie* at Nagasaki and fled. Were I an ordinary Christian, not a priest, would I have fled in the same way? What kept me going now might be my self-respect and my priestly sense of duty.

I called out to the young man at the oars, asking him for water; but he made no answer. I began to understand that ever since that martyrdom the people of Tomogi regarded me as a foreigner who had brought disaster to them all—a terrible burden to them. Probably this young man would like to be relieved of the task of rowing me across the waters. To dampen my parched tongue I began to suck my fingers, wet with sea water, and I thought of Christ nailed to the Cross and the taste of vinegar in his mouth.

As the ship slowly changed its direction, I could hear the sound of waves breaking against rocks. It was just like the sound of a black drum, and it had been the same at the time of my last crossing. From here the sea went into a deep inlet where it washed the strand of the island. But the whole island was wrapped in thick, thick darkness nor could I see where the village was.

How many missionaries had crossed over to this island on a tiny boat just as I had done! And yet how different were their circumstances from mine! When they came to Japan, fortune smiled gaily upon their every venture. Everywhere was safe for them; they found houses in which they could rest at ease and Christians who welcomed them with open arms. The feudal lords vied with one another to give them protection—not from any love of their faith but out of a desire for trade. And the missionaries did not fail to use this chance to extend their apostolic work. For some reason or other I called to mind the words of Valignano at Macao: 'At one time we seriously discussed the question as to whether our religious habit should be made of silk or of cotton.' As these words suddenly came into my mind, I looked out into the darkness and clasping my knees I laughed softly. Don't misunderstand me. I have no intention of looking down on the missionaries of that time. The only thing is that it seems so ludicrous that this fellow, sitting in an insect-infested little ship, dressed in the peasant clothing of Mokichi from Tomogi—that this fellow should be a priest just like them.

Gradually the black cliffs drew near. From the shore the smell of rotten seaweed was carried to our nostrils, and when the sand began to grate on the bottom of the ship my young companion jumped out into the sea and with both hands began to pull the ship up on to the beach. I, too, got into the shallow water, and breathing deeply of the salty air I made my way up on to the beach.

'Thank you,' I said. 'The village is above, isn't it?'

'Father, I. . . . .'

Even though I could not see his face, the tone of his voice told me that he did not want to have anything more to do with me. We shook hands and, deeply relieved, he ran into the sea. The dull sound of his feet as he jumped aboard the ship echoed in the darkness.

With the sound of the receding oars echoing in my ears, I thought of Garrpe. Where was he now?

As I walked along the shore I spoke to myself like a

mother soothing her child. What was I afraid of? I knew the way. If I went straight I should come into the village which had welcomed me. In the distance I heard something like a low groaning. It was the mewing of a cat. But the only thing I could think of was how to rest my weary limbs and how to put even a little food into my empty stomach.

Arriving at the entrance to the village, the low mewing of the cat became even more distinct. Into my nostrils the wind blew an awful stench which almost made me vomit. It was like rotten fish. But when I set foot in the village I found myself surrounded by a fearful, eerie silence. Not a single person was there.

I will not say it was a scene of empty desolation. Rather was it as though a battle had recently devastated the whole district. Strewn all over the roads were broken plates and cups, while the doors were broken down so that all the houses lay open. The low mewing of the cat from the empty hut seemed somehow impudent, as though the animal was brazenly stalking around the village.

For a long time I stood silent and dazed in the middle of the village. Strange to say, I now felt no anxiety, no fear. The only thing that kept repeating itself quietly in my mind was: Why this? Why?

I walked the village from corner to corner in the deadly silence. Thin, scraggly wild cats wandered all over the place, though where they came from I cannot imagine.

They would brush past my legs and glare at me with blazing eyes. Parched and famished I made my way into an empty house in search of food, but in the end the only thing I got was a bowl of water.

As I stood there, the day's fatigue got the better of me, and leaning against a wall like a camel, I slept. In the middle of my dreams I could feel the wild cats walking around my body and tearing at the stinking, dry fish as they seized it. At other times as I opened my eyes I could see through the broken-down door the thick black sky that held no star.

With the cool gust of morning air I began to cough. Now the sky was white and the mountains that formed the background to the village could be seen faintly from the hut where I was. It was dangerous to stay here. I would get up; I would go out into the road and leave this desolate place. As on the previous night, the ground was strewn with cups and plates and shreds of clothing.

But where was I to go? At any rate, rather than going along by the sea where I would surely attract attention, it seemed safer to take to the hills. Somewhere or other there must be Christians secretly living their life of faith as these people had been doing a month before. I would look for them, and find out what had happened here; and after that I would determine what ought to be done. But then quite suddenly the thought of Garrpe rose up in my mind and I wondered what had befallen him.

And so I took a last look around the village, going into the houses. In that desolation, so complete that at times there was scarcely a place to put one's feet, I finally found a little dried rice. This I wrapped in some of the rags lying on the ground, and carrying it with me I headed for the mountains.

I got to the top of the first mountain, the mud sodden with the drizzle clinging to my feet, and gradually I began to climb along the rice paddies. How poor were the Christians! With what painstaking care they had tilled the plain soil, dividing the fields with fences of stone. Yet with only this narrow strip of land that ran along beside the sea it was impossible to live and at the same time pay taxes. Everywhere was the stench of manure on the poor wheat and chestnuts, while swarms of flies attracted by the smell filled the air and sometimes settled on my face, to my intense annoyance. At last, as dawn broke and the mountains began to stand out in the sky like the blade of a sword, I could see the flocks of crows cawing raucously as they flew in circles among the white clouds.

At the top of the hill I stopped to look down at the village beneath. A brown clump of earth; a cluster of straw roofs; huts made of mud and wood; not a sign of life on the road nor on the black shore. Leaning against a tree I looked down on that valley silvered by the rain. Only the morning sea was beautiful. This sea, holding in its embrace a number of small islands, flashed like a needle in the faint sunlight, while the waves biting at the shore foamed white with froth. I recalled how many missionaries had come and gone across this sea and had been received by the Christians: Xavier, Cabral, Valignano and the rest. Certainly Xavier when he came to Hirado had passed this way. And then Torres, that great and noble Japanese missionary, he too had visited these islands. Yet these men had been loved so deeply by the people, had received such a welcome, had had churches which, though small, were beautiful and decorated with flowers. They had had no need to fly to the mountains for hiding like haunted men. When I reflected on my own condition a strange desire to laugh rose up within my heart.

Today again the sky was clouded. It looked as if it was going to be hot. Crows circled over my head persistently; and when I stopped for a moment their darkly ominous cawing would cease; but when I began to walk they would come after me again. Sometimes one of them would settle on the branch of a nearby tree and, fluttering its wings, it would watch me. Once or twice I threw stones at the cursed birds.

About noon I reached the foot of the crescent-shaped mountain. I kept choosing a road from which I would not lose sight of the sea and the coast; I wondered if there were any villages on those islands in the sea. In the murky sky, rainclouds flowed slowly along like huge ships. I sat down in the grass and began to chew the dried rice I had stolen from the village and cucumbers I had picked up along the way. The juice of these cucumbers restored my strength and courage somewhat. The wind was blowing over the fields; and then, when I closed my eyes, I sensed the smell of something burning. I stood up.

It was the remains of a fire. Someone had passed this way before me and had gathered twigs to light a fire. I put my fingers into the ashes and found some sense of warmth remaining at the heart.

For a long time I pondered. Should I go back or go on? I had spent but one day without meeting a single person, wandering through that desolate village and these brown mountains. It had only been a day, yet now I seemed to have lost my energy and courage. Any man at all—if only he was a man—I would like to meet him. Such was my first thought, followed by a realization of the dangers that such a course of action would bring. But at last, after long reflection, I yielded to the temptation. Even Christ, I reflected, could not overcome this temptation; for he descended from the mountain and called men to his side.

I could tell immediately the direction in which the man who lit the fire had gone. Only one route was possible—the opposite direction from that along which I had come. Looking up at the sky I saw the white sun flashing in the murky clouds in which the crows were cawing with raucous voices.

Carefully I hastened my steps. Over the plain were scattered all kinds of trees. Sometimes they took on the shape of a man and I, all confused, would come to a standstill, while the hoarse cawing of the pursuing crows kept arousing in me an ominous and ugly presentiment. To distract my attention I kept on walking, looking carefully at the various trees as I passed. From childhood I have loved botany and, since coming to Japan, I have been able to distinguish immediately all kinds of trees that I know. There are some trees which God has planted in every country; but here I found others of a kind I had never set eyes on until now.

In the afternoon, the sky brightened a little, reflecting tiny clouds in the pools of blue and white water which remained on the ground. Squatting down I stirred the water to dampen my neck, now bathed in sweat. The clouds disappeared from the water and instead there appeared the face of a man—yes, there reflected in the water was a tired, hollow face. I don't know why, but at that moment I thought of the face of yet another man. This was the face of a crucified man, a face which for so many centuries had given inspiration to artists. This man none of these artists had seen with his own eyes, yet they portrayed his face—the most pure, the most beautiful that has claimed the prayers of man and has corresponded with his highest aspirations. No doubt his real face was more beautiful than anything they have envisaged. Yet the face reflected in this pool of rainwater was heavy with mud and with stubble; it was thin and dirty; it was the face of a haunted man filled with uneasiness and exhaustion. Do you realize that in such circumstances a man may suddenly be seized with a fit of laughing? I thrust my face down to the water, twisted my lips like a madman, rolled my eyes, and kept grimacing and making ludicrous faces in the water.

Why did I do such a crazy thing? Why? Why?

In the woods a cicada was singing hoarsely. Everywhere else was silent. The sun gradually grew weak; the sky clouded again, and as the shadows lengthened on the plain I gave up hope of ever catching up with the man who had built the fire. 'Weary it proved, the reckless way of ruin, lonely were the wastes we travelled. . . . .' Only the words of the Scripture arose in my heart; and I sang them to myself as I dragged my feet along. 'The sun rises and the sun goes down, and hastens to the place where it rises. The wind blows to the south, and goes round to the north; round and round goes the wind. . . . . All streams run to the sea, but the sea is not full. . . All things are full of weariness; a man cannot utter it; the eye is not satisfied with seeing, nor the ear filled with hearing.'

But now there arose up within my heart quite suddenly the sound of the roaring sea as it would ring in my ears when Garrpe and I lay alone in hiding on the mountain. The sound of those waves that echoed in the dark like a muffled drum; the sound of those waves all night long, as they broke meaninglessly, receded, and then broke again on the shore. This was the sea that relentlessly washed the dead bodies of Mokichi and Ichizo, the sea that swallowed them up, the sea that, after their death, stretched out endlessly with unchanging expressions. And like the sea God was silent. His silence continued.

No, no! I shook my head. If God does not exist, how can man endure the monotony of the sea and its cruel lack of emotion? (But supposing. . . of course, supposing, I mean.) From the deepest core of my being yet another voice made itself heard in a whisper. Supposing God does not exist. . . . .

This was a frightening fancy. If he does not exist, how absurd the whole thing becomes. What an absurd drama become the lives of Mokichi and Ichizo, bound to the stake and washed by the waves. And the missionaries who spent three years crossing the sea to arrive at this country—what an illusion was theirs. Myself, too, wandering here over the desolate mountains—what an absurd situation! Plucking the grass as I went along I chewed it with my teeth, suppressing these thoughts that rose nauseatingly in my throat. I knew well, of course, that the greatest sin against God was despair; but the silence of God was something I could not fathom. 'The Lord preserved the just man when godless folk were perishing all around him. Escape he should when fire came down upon the Cities of the Plain.' Yet now, when the barren land was already emitting smoke while the fruit on the trees was still unripe, surely he should speak but a word for the Christians.

I ran, slipping down the slope. Whenever I slowed down, the ugly thought would come bubbling up into consciousness bringing an awful dread. If I consented to this thought, then my whole past to this very day was washed away in silence.

I felt a drop of water on my cheek, and looking up saw a huge black cloud like a finger floating across the surface of a sky that had now become leaden and murky. The drops became more numerous until at last a blanket of rain enveloped the whole plain like the strings of a harp. Catching sight of a copse of trees quite near -to me I ran into them with all speed. Out flew a number of birds like an arrow from the bow and sped off in search of shelter. The rain struck the leaves where I stood, making a noise like pebbles pattering on a roof. My peasant clothes were completely drenched; the tree-tops, swaying in the silver rain, looked just like sea-weed. And then, far beyond those swaying branches on the shore I caught sight of a hut. Probably the villagers had built it as a place for cutting wood.

The rain stopped as suddenly as it had started. Once again the plain became white and the birds began to sing as though wakened from sleep. Great drops of rain continued to fall from the leaves of the trees and I, wiping from my forehead the water which was flowing down into my eyes, approached the hut. As soon as I looked inside the door I was greeted with a foul stench, and I saw a cloud of flies swarming around the entrance. They were clustering around some human excrement.

I realized immediately that not too long before a man had been here, had rested, and had gone on his way. But truth to tell I felt angry at the fellow who had been so uncivilized as to use the only shelter in such a way. But the situation had its ludicrous side, too; and I burst out laughing. My apprehension about this fellow grew less.

Stepping further inside I saw that the wood was still smoldering. I was glad that there was a remnant of fire before which I could dry out my drenched clothing. Even if I spent some time here, I felt, it would not be too difficult to catch up with the fellow in front; for obviously he was not travelling fast.

When I left the hut, the plain and the trees that had sheltered me were bathed in golden light, while the leaves of the tree, now dry like sand, were filled with song. Picking up a withered branch I used it as a staff and proceeded on my way until finally I arrived at the slope from which could be seen the coast line down below.

There was no change in the languid sea, sparkling like a needle and biting at the curved strand like the huge arc of a bow. One part of the coast held milk-white sand, while another formed an inlet of black rocks. Within the inlet was a tiny landing place where three or four fishing boats were pulled up on the sand. To the west was a fishing village surrounded by trees. It was the first sign of a community I had seen since morning.

Sitting down on the slope I clasped my knees and looked intently at the village with the bold stare of a wild dog. Perhaps the fellow who had left the firewood in the hut had gone down into this village; and I also could run down the slope following in his footsteps. But was this a Christian village? I strained my eyes for any sign of church or cross.

Valignano and the other missionaries at Macao had warned us not to imagine that the churches in this country were the same as those at home. The feudal lords had told the priests to use as churches the mansions and temples that were already there. Indeed it sometimes happened because of this that the peasants confused Christianity with Buddhism, thinking that they were the same thing. Even Xavier, because of the mistake of an interpreter, came near to failure on this point. Some Japanese, hearing his sermons, thought that our God was the sun which the people of this country had revered for many generations. Consequently, the fact that I saw no buildings with spires attached did not mean that there were no churches here. Among the mud cabins down below there might well be one that was a church. And it might well be that the poverty-stricken Christians were hungering for a priest to administer the Blessed Sacrament, hear their confessions and baptize their children. In this desert from which missionaries and priests had been expelled the only one who could give the water of life to this island tonight was myself. Yes, only myself, dressed in these dirty, tattered rags with my arms clasping my legs. 'Lord, everything that You have created is good. How beautiful are your dwellings!'

Violent emotion surged up within my breast, as supporting my body with my staff I slithered down the slope still wet from the rain and ran toward my parish—yes, this was my parish, this was the charge Our Lord had entrusted to me. But as I ran, suddenly from one corner of the village surrounded by pine trees there came the voice of a man. It seemed to rise up from the depths of the earth. Staff in hand I stopped in my traces only to see clearly the dull red flame of a fire. Instinctively realizing that something had happened I ran back up the slope down which I had been sliding so fast. There on the far side of the slope what did I see but the figure of a man dressed in grey peasant clothing and fleeing from me with all his might. Then the fellow looked in my direction and came to a standstill. The hollow terrified face looked at me with something of relief: 'Father!' He waved his hand as he shouted the word. Then again screaming something he pointed to the village. He was signalling to me with his hand to conceal myself. Running up the hill as fast as I could, I tried to hide myself like a wild animal in the shadow of a great rock. I was panting and trying to control my breathing. I heard the sound of footsteps; and then from between the rocks beyond appeared the dirty, mouse-like little eyes of the fellow watching me.

I went to wipe away the perspiration that was rolling down my face; but when I looked at my hand I saw that it was not perspiration but blood. I had struck up against something while jumping down.

'Father!' From the shadow of the rock the little eyes were peering at me. 'Father, how glad I am to see you. . .'

The servile laugh. The attempt to curry favor. The stubble sticking out from the chin. 'It's dangerous here,' he said. 'But I'll look after you.' Silently I looked into that face. Kichijiro, the whipped dog, was smiling at me with furtive eyes. Plucking the grass, pushing it into his mouth and biting it with his yellow teeth, 'It's terrible,' he muttered as he looked down at the village.

As I looked at him, it dawned on me that this was the fellow who had lit that fire in the terraced fields, the fellow who had dirtied the hut. But why was he roaming through the mountains just like me? He had trampled on the *fumie*; what had he to fear?

'Father, why have you come to this island? This is a dangerous place. But I know a village where there are some hidden Christians.'

I kept staring at him in silence. Every village this fellow passed through had been surprised by the government officials. Suspicions from the past came crowding into my mind. Perhaps he was no more than a decoy. I had heard previously that apostates were used as puppets by the government; and the apostates willingly collaborated as though they felt they could justify their own ugly crime by adding one more to their number. Their way of thinking is akin to that of the fallen angels when they allure people into sin.

Evening began to enfold the surrounding mountains but in the village a red flame of light began to move silently around. Yet there was only silence. The village itself as well as its inhabitants seemed to be accepting its suffering without protest. Long inured to suffering, the people could no longer even weep and cry in their pain.

For me to abandon the village and go on my way was as painful as tearing the scab off a wound that had just begun to heal. Within my heart a voice cried out: 'You are weak; you are a coward!' Only to be answered by another telling me not to be carried away by a moment of excitement and sentimentality: 'You and Garrpe are probably the only priests in this whole country. If you die, the Japanese church dies with you. You and Garrpe must live, no matter how great the injuries and sufferings that this life entails.'

Yet I wondered if this were just the voice of my own weakness. There arose in my mind a story I had heard while still in Macao. It was about a Franciscan priest who, escaping a martyr's death, had carried on an underground apostolate—but then he had given himself up at the castle of the feudal lord, Omura. Because of his momentary rashness, the whole underground work of the mission was impaired and the safety of the Christians was jeopardized. This story was well known. Its moral was that a priest does not exist in order to become a martyr; he must preserve his life in order that the flame of faith may not utterly die when the church is persecuted.

Kichijiro followed after me like a wild dog. When I stopped he would stop too. 'Don't walk so fast,' he would shout, 'I'm sick. Tell me where you are going. The magistrate says that the man who finds a father will get three hundred pieces of silver.'

'So my price is three hundred pieces of silver.' These were my first words to Kichijiro, and as I spoke them a bitter laugh crossed my face. Judas had sold Our Lord for thirty pieces of silver; I was worth ten times as much.

'It's dangerous to go alone,' he said. As though somewhat relieved, he caught up with me and kept beating the bushes with the branch of a tree as he walked along by my side. The crying of the birds broke through the darkness of the evening.

'Father, I know a place where there are Christians. It's safe there. Let's go. Tonight we can sleep here; tomorrow we'll set out.'

Without waiting for my answer, he squatted down, cleverly picked up twigs that were not damped by the evening mist, took out a flint-stone from his pouch and lit a fire.

'You must be hungry,' he said; and he took from his

pouch a few dried fish. When my starving eyes caught sight of them, the saliva began to flow freely in my mouth. Since morning I had had nothing to eat except a little uncooked rice and cucumber, so that the food Kichijiro waved before my eyes was tempting indeed. As the fire broke into flame and the salted fish was slowly roasted, an unbearably delicious scent was wafted to my nostrils.

'Won't you eat?'

Baring my teeth, I greedily seized upon the dried fish. One slice was enough to make me compromise with Kichijiro. With a look half of satisfaction and half of contempt he stared at me as I ate ravenously. And all the time he kept chewing grass as though it were tobacco or something like that.

The surrounding country was now wrapped in darkness; the mountains began to grow chilly; the misty rain seemed to penetrate my body. I lay down beside the fire as though to sleep. But sleep was out of question; for if I once lost consciousness, Kichijiro would steal away. He would sell me as he had sold his companions. Perhaps he would do so tonight. For a penniless beggar like himself, three hundred pieces of silver was surely a tantalizing temptation. As I closed my eyes, behind my wearied eyelids there arose vividly the picture I had seen from the plateau, the picture of the sea and the islands: the sea glistening like a needle, the islands spread out over its surface. I had crossed over this beautiful sea blessed by so many missionaries. I recalled the days when the churches had been decorated with flowers, when the Christians had brought gifts of fish and rice. At that time there had been a seminary here where the students sang in Latin just as we had done in Portugal. Valignano had told us that there was even a time when they played on the harp and the organ, much to the delight of the feudal lords.

'Father, are you awake?'

I made no answer, but from half-opened eyes I looked at my companion. If he were to steal off somewhere in the night, it would surely be to summon the government officials. He was watching my sleeping breath, and then little by little he began to move off. I watched him move stealthily away like an animal. This would be his chance to go away; but to my surprise he returned to the fire with a sigh. With both hands he kept piling fresh dry wood on the ashes, and all the time he kept sighing as though in anguish. The red flame of the fire fell upon his cheeks and I could see his silhouette in the night. And then overcome with the day's exhaustion I fell asleep. Sometimes I would open my eyes, and always there was the figure of Kichijiro sitting beside the fire.

The next day we continued to walk under the merciless rays of the sun. White steam rose up from the earth still sodden from yesterday's rain, and beyond the mountain a cloud was glittering brightly. For some time I had been suffering from a headache and a parched throat. Whether or not Kichijiro noticed the pain in my face I do not know; but sometimes he would slowly cross the road, pierce with his staff a snake hidden in the bushes, and put it into his dirty bag. 'We peasants eat these big snakes as medicine,' he said, showing his yellow teeth and laughing.

Why did you not sell me last night for three hundred pieces of silver?, I thought. And there arose in my mind that terribly dramatic scene at the Supper when Christ turned to Judas with the words: 'What thou dost, do quickly.' Priest though I am, I find it difficult to grasp the full meaning of these words. Dragging my feet wearily along beside Kichijiro amidst the rising steam, I kept turning them over in my mind. What emotion had filled the breast of Christ when he ordered away the man who was to betray him for thirty pieces of silver. Was it anger? or resentment? Or did these words arise from his love? If it was anger, then at this instant Christ excluded from salvation this man alone of all the men in the world; and then Our Lord allowed one man to fall into eternal damnation.

But it could not be so. Christ wanted to save even Judas. If not, he would never have made him one of his disciples. And yet why did Christ not stop him when he began to slip from the path of righteousness? This was a problem I had not understood even as a seminarian. I asked many priests about it. Certainly I must have asked Father Ferreira also, but I cannot recall what his answer was. This very fact indicates that he gave no real solution.

'These words were not uttered in anger or hatred. They were words of disgust,' someone had said. But what kind of disgust? Were they disgust for everything in Judas? Did Christ at that moment cease to love him? 'By no means,' came the answer. 'Take the example of a husband betrayed by his wife. He continues to love her; but he never forgives the fact that she, his wife, should betray him. This is the feeling of the husband who loves his wife but feels disgust at such behaviour. . . . . and Christ's attitude toward Judas was something like that.'

This conventional answer failed to satisfy me even as a young man. In fact, even now I cannot understand. If it is not blasphemous to say so, I have the feeling that Judas was no more than the unfortunate puppet for the glory of that drama which was the life and death of Christ. 'What thou dost do quickly.' Yet I could not say such words to Kichijiro, one reason being that I wanted to protect my own life, the other that I hoped ardently that he would not heap betrayal upon betrayal.

'This path is narrow. It's difficult to walk here,' said my companion.

'Is there a river anywhere?' I asked.

The parched, dry feeling in my throat was now unbearable. With the hint of a laugh Kichijiro looked me over: 'Do you want water? You ate too much of that dried fish.'

Like the previous day, crows were flying around, forming an enormous crescent in the sky. Looking up, a flash of white light struck my eyes almost blinding me. I began to regret my compromise and my weakness. For a piece of dried fish I had made an irrevocable failure. I searched for the marsh, but in vain. The warm wind was blowing in from the sea. 'The river! the river! the river! the river!'

'There isn't even a stream here. Can't you wait?' said Kichijiro. But without even waiting for my answer he ran down the slope.

When his appearance was lost from sight behind a crag, the surroundings suddenly became deadly silent except for the dry sound of insects fluttering in the grass. A lizard crawled uneasily over a stone and then fled away speedily. Its furtive face as it stared at me reminded me of the Kichijiro who had just vanished from sight. Had he really gone in search of water for me? Or had he gone to betray me, to tell someone that I was here?

Grasping my staff and moving on, I found that the dryness in my throat was even more unbearable, and now I realized only too clearly that the wretch had deliberately made me eat the dried fish. I recalled the words of the Gospel how Christ had said, 'I thirst'; and one of the soldiers put a sponge full of vinegar on hyssop and held it to his mouth. I closed my eyes. In the distance a hoarse call echoed as though someone was looking for me. 'Father! Father!' Kichijiro ran dragging his feet in the old slovenly way and carrying a pitcher of water. 'Are you running away?', he asked as he looked sorrowfully down at me.

I snatched the pitcher of water that he offered me, and placing it to my lips drank greedily and shamelessly. The water poured down through my hands wetting my knees.

'Father, you were running away. Don't you trust me?'

'I don't want to hurt your feelings,' I said. 'We're both tired. Please go away. Leave me alone!'

'Alone? Where would you go? It's dangerous. I know a village of hidden Christians. There is a church there and a father.'

'A father?' Unconsciously I raised my voice. I couldn't believe that there might be a priest other than myself on the island. I looked at Kichijiro with growing suspicion.

'Yes, father. And not a Japanese. I've heard so.'

'Impossible!'

'Father, you don't trust me.' He stood there tearing at the grass and snivelling in his weak voice. 'No one trusts me.'

'And yet you know how to look after yourself. Mokichi and Ichizo have sunk to the bottom of the sea like stones and yet. . . . .'

'Mokichi was strong—like a strong shoot. But a weak

shoot like me will never grow no matter what you do.'
He seemed to feel that I had dealt him a severe rebuke,
because with a look like a whipped dog he glanced
backwards. Yet I had not said these words with the
intention of rebuking him; I was only giving expression
to a sad reflection that was rising in my mind. Kichijiro
was right in saying that all men are not saints and
heroes. How many of our Christians, if only they had
been born in another age from this persecution would
never have been confronted with the problem of apostasy
or martyrdom but would have lived blessed lives of
faith until the very hour of death.

'I have nowhere to go. I'm just wandering around the
mountains,' complained Kichijiro.

A feeling of pity surged up within my breast. I bade
him kneel down and in obedience to my command he
tremblingly bent his knees down to the earth. 'Do you
feel like confessing for Mokichi and Ichizo?' I asked.

Men are born in two categories: the strong and the
weak, the saints and the commonplace, the heroes and
those who respect them. In time of persecution the
strong are burnt in the flames and drowned in the sea;
but the weak, like Kichijiro, lead a vagabond life in the
mountains. As for you (I now spoke to myself) which
category do you belong to? Were it not for the consciousness of your priesthood and your pride, perhaps you like
Kichijiro would trample on the *fumie*.

'Our Lord is crowned with thorns. Our Lord is crucified.' With all the simplicity of a child imitating its mother Kichijiro repeated my words one by one while a lizard once again crawled over and around the white surface of the rock. In the woods resounded the voice of the cicada; the scent of the grass was wafted over the white rock.

Then coming along the road we had traversed I heard the sound of footsteps. Men, looking in our direction and hastening their steps, made their way through the bushes.

'Father, forgive me!' Still kneeling on the bare ground Kichijiro cried out in a voice choked with tears. 'I am weak. I am not a strong person like Mokichi and Ichizo.'

Already the men were seizing me and dragging me to my feet. One of them, with a gesture of contempt, threw into the face of Kichijiro still kneeling a number of tiny silver coins.

Without a word they pushed me in front of them. Stumbling and reeling I was driven along the dry road. Once I looked back, but already the tiny face of my betrayer was far in the distance. That face with its fearful eyes like a spider. . . . .

Chapter 5

THE world outside was flooded with sunlight; but the interior of the village seemed strangely dark. While he was being dragged here children and adults alike, dressed in rags, had kept staring at him with glimmering eyes like animals from between the thatch-roofed huts.

Perhaps they were Christians, he reflected; and he made an effort to force a smile to his lips. But it was all an illusion: there was no response. Once a naked child tottered up to where he was; but its mother, a woman with dishevelled hair, rushed forward, tumbling over herself in haste, and clasping the child in her arms hurried back again. To calm his anguished trembling that night the priest thought earnestly about a man who had been dragged from the Garden of Gethsemane to the palace of Caiphas.

Once outside the village his eyes were suddenly dazzled by the glare of the sun. He felt overcome with giddiness. The fellow behind, constantly muttering something, kept pushing him on. Forcing a smile the priest asked if he might be permitted to rest for a moment, but the other, hard-faced and grim, shook his head in refusal. The fields beneath the glaring sun were heavy with the smell of manure; the sky-larks chattered with pleasure in the sky; great trees, the names of which he did not know, cast a pleasant shadow on the road; and the leaves gave forth a fresh sound as they rustled in the breeze. The road through the fields gradually narrowed, and when they reached the far side they found a hollow stretching into the mountain. Here there was a tiny hut made of twigs. Its black shadow fell on the slimy earth. Here four or five men and women clad in peasant clothing, their hands bound, were sitting together on the grass. They seemed to be talking among themselves, but when they recognized the priest they opened their mouths in amazement. Having brought the priest to the group, the guards seemed to think their work was done and began to exchange chatter and banter, laughing all the time. They didn't even seem preoccupied lest the priest might escape. As the priest sat down on the ground, the men and women bowed their heads respectfully.

For some time he remained silent. A fly attempted to lick the perspiration which was flowing down his forehead and then it kept buzzing persistently around his face. As he turned his ears to the dull sound of its wings and felt the warm rays of the sun on his back, a glow of well-being gradually began to penetrate his whole body.

At last he had been captured—this was indeed difficult to stomach; but on the other hand he had never expected to find such nonchalance here, and he began to ask himself if it might not all be an illusion. For some indefinable reason the word 'sabbath—day of rest' rose to his mind. The guards were talking and laughing among themselves as if nothing were afoot. The bright sun fell cheerfully on the bushes and the hut in the little hollow. And so this was the day of his capture, the day he had looked forward to with mingled fear and anxiety. Could it really be a day of such peace and calm? Yet somehow or other he also felt an inexpressible dissatisfaction—a kind of disillusion that he was not privileged to be a tragic hero like so many martyrs and like Christ himself.

'Father!' It was one of the men, with a decaying eye, who spoke moving his manacled wrists. 'Father, what happened?'

At this, all the others raised their heads and with faces filled with curiosity waited for the priest's answer. They were like a bunch of ignorant beasts, he thought, quite unaware of the fate that awaited them. When he explained that he had been captured in the mountains they seemed not to understand what he said, and the man putting his hand to his ear asked the same question again. Finally they seemed to get the meaning. 'Ah!' A sigh, devoid of either assent or emotion, rose from among them.

'Doesn't he speak well!' exclaimed one of the women

like a child, marvelling at the priest's command of Japanese. 'He's really clever, isn't he?'

The guards only kept laughing at all this, making no attempt to scold the men and women nor to forbid them to speak. Indeed the one-eyed man with some degree of familiarity began to speak to one of the guards who answered him with a pleasant smile.

'What are those men doing?', whispered the priest to one of the women. And she answered that they were waiting for the arrival of the government officials who were supposed to come to the village. 'Anyhow, father,' she went on, 'we are Christians. Those men are not Christians. They are gentiles.' Obviously she saw deep meaning in this distinction.

'Won't you eat something, father?' she continued; and with her manacled wrists she succeeded in taking from her bosom a couple of small cucumbers; then nibbling at one herself she gave the other to the priest. When he bit it, his mouth was filled with its green stench. Since coming to this country, he reflected, he had caused nothing but hardship to these poor Christians; and he nibbled at the cucumber with his front teeth. He had received from them the little hut in which he had dwelt; they had given him the clothing he now wore; he had eaten their food. Now it was his turn to give something. But what could he give? The only thing he had to offer was his life and his death.

'Your name?', he asked.

'Monica.' Her answer was somewhat bashful, as though her Christian name was the only ornament she possessed in the whole world. What missionary had given the name of Augustine's mother to this woman whose body was reeking with the stench of fish?

'And this man?' He made a gesture towards the one-eyed man still talking to the guards.

'You mean Mozaemon? His name is Juan.'

'What father baptized you?'

'It was not a father; it was a brother: Brother Ishida. You must know him, father.'

The priest shook his head. The only person he knew in this country was Garrpe.

'You don't know him?' The woman spoke with astonishment as she scrutinized the priest's face, 'Why, he was killed at Unzen.'

'But are you all at ease?' Now at last he expressed the doubt that had been in his heart. 'Don't you realize that we are all going to die in the same way?'

The woman lowered her eyes and stared intently at the bushes at her feet. Once again a fly, enticed by the smell of humanity, buzzed around his neck.

'I don't know,' she said. 'Brother Ishida used to say that when we go to Heaven we will find there everlasting peace and happiness. There we will not have to pay taxes every year, nor worry about hunger and illness. There will be no hard labor there. We have nothing but troubles in the world, so we have to work hard. Father, isn't it true that there is no such anguish in Heaven?'

He felt like shouting out: 'Heaven is not the sort of place you think it is!' But he restrained himself. These peasants had learned their catechism like children; they dreamt of a Heaven in which there was no bitter taxation and no oppression. Who was he to put a cruel end to their happy dream?

'Yes,' he said blinking his eyes, 'there nothing can be stolen from us; we can be deprived of nothing.'

But now, yet another question rose to his lips: 'Do you know a father by the name of Ferreira?'

The woman shook her head. Was the very name of Ferreira a word that was not even to be mentioned by the Christians?, he asked himself.

Suddenly from the cliff above a loud voice rang out. Looking up the priest saw a smiling little plump samurai somewhat advanced in years, followed by two peasants. When he saw the old man's smile he realized that this was the samurai who had conducted the investigation at Tomogi.

'Hot, isn't it?' The samurai, waving his fan, came slowly down the cliff as he spoke. 'From now on it gets really hot. The open fields become unbearable.'

Monica, Juan and the other men and women put their manacled wrists on their knees and bowed politely. Out of the side of his eye the old man saw the priest bow his head along with the others, but he ignored him and walked straight on. As he passed there was a dry swish of his cloak. His clothes gave forth a sweet perfume.

'We've had no evening showers these days. The road is all dusty. It's a nuisance for old people like us to come so far.' He sat down in the middle of the prisoners, cooling his head and neck with his white fan. 'Don't keep on causing trouble to an old man like me,' he said.

The light of the sun made his laughing face look so flat that the priest recalled the statues of the Buddha he had seen in Macao. These had never aroused within him an emotion similar to that called forth by the face of Christ. Only the flies kept buzzing around. At one time they would graze the necks of the Christians, then they would fly in the direction of the old man, and then back again.

'It wasn't from hatred that we arrested you. You must see our reasons. Why should we arrest you when you pay your taxes and work hard? We know better than anyone that the peasants are the backbone of the country.'

Mingled with the whirling of the flies' wings was the swish of the old man's fan. From afar the clucking of the chickens was carried by the fresh warm wind to the place where they were. Is this the famous cross-examination, thought the priest, his eyes cast down like the others. All those Christians and missionaries who had been tortured and punished—had they heard the gentle voice of persuasion prior to their suffering? Had they too heard the buzzing of flies in a sleepy atmosphere like this? He had thought to be overcome with fear and trembling but, strange to say, no terror rose up within his heart. He had no acute realization of the proximity of torture and death. He felt like a man who, on a rainy day, thinks of a sunlit mountain far away.

'I'll give you time to think it over. Afterwards, give me a reasonable answer,' said the old man, bringing the conversation to an abrupt end as the forced smile faded from his lips. Now there appeared on his face instead that avaricious pride the priest had seen so often on the faces of the merchants at Macao. 'Off with you!' he said.

The guards stood up among the bushes and urged on their captives. The priest went to stand up with the others, but the old man twisting his face up like a monkey and for the first time revealing hatred and rancour in his flashing eyes shouted out. 'You,' he cried, drawing up his tiny figure to its full stature and putting one hand on his sword, 'stay here.'

With a faint smile, the priest sat down again among the bushes. The little old fellow straightened up and, bent back like a rooster, he strutted along, obviously showing the prisoners his determination not to be beaten by a foreigner. A monkey, the priest reflected. He needn't stand there with his hand on his sword. I'm not going to run away.

He watched the group as, all manacled, they climbed the height and disappeared from sight into the distant plateau. 'Hoc passionis tempore piis adauge gratiam.' The prayer rose up to his dry lips bitterly. 'Lord,' he murmured, 'do not increase their suffering. Already it is too heavy for them. Until today they have been able to bear it. Can you give even more trials to people already crushed with the burdens of taxation, officialdom and cruelty?'

The old man put a cup to his lips and wet his throat much as a chicken would sip water. 'I have met quite a number of fathers,' he said. 'I have cross-examined them sometimes. . . . .' He moistened his lips and spoke now with a servile voice which was in striking contrast with his previous attitude. 'You understand Japanese?'

A few wisps of cloud hung in the sky. The hollow began to darken a little. In the shrubs round about the stifling humming of insects began to make itself heard for the first time.

'Peasants are fools,' he said. 'It all depends on you whether or not they are to be set free.'

The priest did not quite understand what he was getting at, but the expression on the other's face made it clear that the cunning old rascal was setting some trap for him.

'Peasants cannot think for themselves. Even if they talk the thing over they will come to no conclusion. But if you say a single word. . . . .'

'What are you trying to say?' asked the priest.

'Apostatize! Apostatize!' The old man laughed and waved his fan as he spoke.

'And supposing I refuse?' The priest replied quietly, laughing all the time. 'Then you'll kill me, I suppose.'

'No, no,' said the old man. 'We won't do that. If we did that the peasants would become even more stubborn. We made that mistake in Omura and Nagasaki. The Christians there are a stubborn crowd.'

The old man heaved a deep sigh as he spoke, but it was immediately clear to the priest that the whole thing was a comedy. He even began to feel a secret joy in teasing this old fellow who looked like a monkey.

'Now if you are really a father at heart, you ought to feel pity for the Christians. Isn't that so?'

Unconsciously the priest felt his mouth drop. What a simpleton this old fellow was. Did he think to win something with this childish logic? What he had forgotten, however, was that if this official was as simple as a child, he was equally simple in flaring up in anger when defeated in argument.

'What about it?', said the old man.

'Punish me alone,' said the priest, shrugging his shoulders and laughing.

An angry color rose up to the forehead of the old man. From the far distant clouds a faint dull roar of thunder rumbled.

'It is because of you that they must suffer,' concluded the old man.

They pushed him into the little hut. Through those

brushwood walls standing on the naked soil the white rays of sunlight penetrated like pieces of thread. Outside he could hear the muffled voices of the chattering guards. Where had they brought the Christians? They had simply vanished from sight and that was all. Sitting on the ground and clasping his knees he thought about Monica and her one-eyed companion. Then he thought about the village of Tomogi, about Omatsu and Ichizo and Mokichi. And his heart grew heavy. If only, if only he had a moment for reflection he might at least have given those poor Christians a brief blessing. But he hadn't even thought of it. This was proof that he hadn't had a moment's respite. At least he should have asked them what date it was, what day of the month it was. But he had forgotten that too. Since coming to this country he seemed to have lost all sense of time—of months and days; so that now he could no longer reckon how many days had passed since Easter or what saint's feast was celebrated today.

Since he had no rosary he began to recite the Paters and Aves on the five fingers of his hand; but just as the water dribbles back down from the mouth of the man whose lips are locked by sickness, the prayer remained empty and hollow on his lips. Rather was he drawn by the voices of the guards outside the hut. What was so funny that they should keep raising their voices and laughing heartily? His thoughts turned to the fire-lit garden and the servants; the figures of those men holding black flaming torches and utterly indifferent to the fate of one man. These guards, too, were men; they were indifferent to the fate of others. This was the feeling that their laughing and talking stirred up in his heart. Sin, he reflected, is not what it is usually thought to be; it is not to steal and tell lies. Sin is for one man to walk brutally over the life of another and to be quite oblivious of the wounds he has left behind. And then for the first time a real prayer rose up in his heart.

Suddenly a ray of bright light broke upon his closed eyelids. Someone was opening the door of the hut, quietly and stealthily, so as to make no noise. Next, tiny and menacing eyes were peering in at him. When the priest looked up the intruder quickly tried to withdraw.

'He's quiet, isn't he?' Someone else was now speaking to the guard who had looked in; and now the door opened. A flood of light rushed into the room and there appeared the figure of a man, not the old samurai but another, without a sword.

'Señor, gracia,' he said.

So he was speaking Portuguese. The pronunciation was strange and halting, but it was certainly Portuguese.

'Señor.'

'Palazera â Dios nuestro Señor.'

The sudden inrush of blinding light had made the priest somewhat dizzy. He listened to the words—yes, there were mistakes here and there; but there was no doubt about the meaning.

'Don't be surprised,' went on the other in Portuguese. 'In Nagasaki and Hirado there are a number of interpreters like myself. But I see that you, father, have quite a grasp of our language. Could you guess where I learnt my Portuguese?'

Without waiting for an answer, the man went on talking; and as he spoke he kept moving his fan just like the old samurai had done. 'Thanks to you Portuguese fathers seminaries were built in Arima and Amakusa and Omura. But this doesn't mean that I'm an apostate. I was baptized all right; but from the beginning I had no wish to be a Christian nor a brother. I'm only the son of a court samurai; nothing but learning could make me great in the world.'

The fellow was earnestly stressing the fact that he was not a Christian. The priest sat in the dark with expressionless face, listening to him as he prattled on.

'Why don't you say something?' exclaimed the man, getting angry now. 'The fathers always ridiculed us. I knew Father Cabral—he had nothing but contempt for everything Japanese. He despised our houses; he despised our language; he despised our food and our customs—and yet he lived in Japan. Even those of us who graduated from the seminary he did not allow to become priests.'

As he talked, recalling incidents from the past, his voice became increasingly shrill and violent. Yet the priest, sitting there with his hands clasping his knees,

knew that the fellow's anger was not altogether un-
justified. He had heard something about Cabral from
Valignano in Macao; he remembered how Valignano had
spoken sadly of the Christians and priests who had left
the Church because of this man's attitude towards Japan.

'I'm not like Cabral,' he said finally.

'Really?' The fellow spoke with a laugh. 'I'm not so
sure.'

'Why?'

In the darkness the priest could not make out what
kind of expression the fellow wore. But he somehow
guessed that this low laughing voice issued from a face
filled with hatred and resentment. Accustomed as he
was to hearing the Christians' confessions with closed
eyes, he could make such conjectures confidently. But,
he thought as he looked toward the other, what this
fellow is fighting against is not Father Cabral but the
fact that he once received baptism.

'Won't you come outside, father? I don't think we
need now fear that you will run away.'

'You never know,' said the priest with the shadow of
a smile, 'I'm not a saint. I'm scared of death.'

'Father, sometimes courage only causes trouble for
other people. We call that blind courage. And many of
the priests, fanatically filled with this blind courage, forget that they are only causing trouble to the Japanese.'

'Is that all the missionaries have done? Have they only
caused trouble?'

'If you force on people things that they don't want, they are inclined to say: "Thanks for nothing!" And Christian doctrine is something like that here. We have our own religion; we don't want a new, foreign one. I myself learned Christian doctrine in the seminary, but I tell you I don't think it ought to be introduced into this country.'

'Your and my way of thinking are different,' said the priest quietly dropping his voice. 'If they were the same I would not have crossed the sea from far away to come to this country.'

This was his first controversy with a Japanese. Since the time of Xavier had many fathers engaged in such an exchange with the Buddhists? Valignano had warned him not to underrate the intelligence of the Japanese. They were well-versed in the art of controversy, he had said.

'Well, then, let me ask a question.' Opening and closing his fan as he spoke, he came to the attack. 'The Christians say that their Deus is the source of love and mercy, the source of goodness and virtue, whereas the buddhas are all men and cannot possess these qualities. Is this your stand also, father?'

'A buddha cannot escape death any more than we can. He is something different from the Creator.'

'Only a father who is ignorant of Buddhist teaching could say such a thing. In fact, you cannot say that the buddhas are no more than men. There are three kinds of buddhas—*hossin, goshin* and *oka*. The *oka* buddha shows eight aspects for delivering human beings and giving them benefits; but the *hossin* has neither beginning nor end, and he is unchangeable. It is written in the sutras that the buddha is everlasting and never changes. It is only a Christian who could regard the buddhas as mere human beings. We don't think that way at all.'

The fellow kept pouring out his answers as though he had learnt them all by rote. Undoubtedly he had examined many missionaries in the past and had kept reflecting on the best way of beating them down. Obviously he had ended up by using big words that he himself did not understand.

'But you hold that everything exists naturally, that the world has neither beginning nor end,' said the priest, seizing on the other's weak point and taking the offensive.

'Yes, that is our position.'

'But an object without life must either be moved from outside by something else, or from within. How were the buddhas born? Moreover, I understand that these buddhas have merciful hearts—but antecedent to all this, how was the world made? Our Deus is the source of his own existence; he created man; he gave existence to all things.'

'Then the Christian God created evil men. Is that what you are saying? Is evil also the work of your Deus?' The interpreter laughed softly as he spoke, enjoying his victory.

'No, no,' cried the priest shaking his head. 'God created everything for good. And for this good he bestowed on man the power of thought; but we men sometimes use this power of discrimination in the wrong way. This is evil.'

The interpreter clicked his tongue in contempt. But the priest had scarcely expected him to be convinced by his explanation. This kind of dialogue soon ceased to be dialogue, becoming a play of words in which one tried vigorously to down one's opponent.

'Stop this sophistry,' shouted the interpreter. 'You may satisfy peasants with their wives and children in this way; but you can't beguile me. But now let me put you one more question. If it is true that God is really loving and merciful, how do you explain the fact that he gives so many trials and sufferings of all kinds to man on his way to Heaven?'

'Sufferings of every kind? I think you are missing the point. If only man faithfully observes the commandments of our Deus he should be able to live in peace. If we have the desire to eat something, we can satisfy it. God does not order us to die of hunger. All we are asked to do is to honor God our Creator, and that is enough. Or again, when we cannot cast away the desires of the flesh, God does not order us to avoid all contact with women; rather does he tell us to have one wife and do his divine will.'

As he finished speaking, he felt that his answer had been well framed. In the darkness of the hut he could clearly feel that the interpreter was lost for words and reduced to silence.

'Enough! We can't go on for ever with this useless banter,' said the other angrily, now passing into Japanese. 'I didn't come here for this nonsense.'

Far in the distance a cock was crowing. From the slightly open door a single ray of light penetrated the darkness of the room, and in it a myriad of dust particles were dancing. The priest looked at them intently.

The interpreter breathed a deep sigh. 'If you don't apostatize,' he said, 'the peasants will be suspended in the pit.'

The priest could not quite understand the meaning of what he was saying.

'Yes, five peasants will be suspended upside down in the pit for several days.'

'Suspended in the pit?'

'Yes, father, unless you apostatize.'

The priest was silent. Were these words serious? or were they a threat? He peered into the darkness, his eyes gleaming.

'Father, have you ever heard of Inoue? He's the magistrate. Sometime you will meet him face to face for investigation.'

'I-NO-U-E'—only with these syllables did the interpreter's Portuguese seem to come to life. They hit into the priest's ears and his whole body instantly shook and trembled.

'The fathers who apostatized after Inoue's cross-examination are: Fathers Porro, Pedro, Cassola and Father Ferreira.'

'Father Ferreira?'

'Yes, do you know him?'

'No, I don't know him,' cried the priest excitedly shaking his head. 'He belongs to a different congregation; I've never heard his name; I've never met him. . . . . Is this father alive now?'

'He's alive alright. In fact he has taken a Japanese name, and he lives in a mansion in Nagasaki together with his wife. He is in good repute now.'

Suddenly there arose before the priest's eyes the streets of a Nagasaki he had never seen. For some reason he could not understand, this city of his imagination was filled with labyrinthine roads, and the golden sun was glittering on the windows of the tiny houses. And there, walking along the street, wearing clothes just like those of this interpreter, was Ferreira. No, this could not be. Such a fancy was ludicrous.

'I don't believe you,' he said.

But with a scornful laugh the interpreter went out.

The door closed again behind him; the white ray of sunlight was suddenly extinguished; once again, just as before, the voices of the guards resounded against the walls of the hut.

'A selfish rascal if ever there was one,' the interpreter was saying. 'But anyhow he'll end up by apostatizing.'

This was obviously a reference to himself, the priest thought; and clasping his knees he silently ruminated on the four names the interpreter had trotted out as if having learnt them by rote. Fathers Porro and Pedro he did not know. He felt sure that at Macao he had heard the name of Father Cassola. This missionary was Portuguese but, unlike himself, he had come not from Macao but from the Spanish controlled Manila and he had secretly entered Japan. After his arrival there had been no news of him, and the Society of Jesus had taken it for granted that he had met with a glorious martyrdom. But behind these three figures was the face of Ferreira— Ferreira for whom he had been searching since his arrival in Japan. If the words of the interpreter were not simply a threat, this Ferreira too, as the rumor had said, had betrayed the Church at the hands of the magistrate Inoue.

If even Ferreira had apostatized, would he have the strength to endure the sufferings now in store for him? A terrible anguish rose up in his breast. Violently he shook his head trying to control the ugly imaginings and the words that rose up to his throat like nausea. But the more he tried to crush this picture the more vividly it came before his eyes, eluding the control of his will. 'Exaudi nos, Pater omnipotens, et mittere digneris Sanctum qui custodiat, foveat, protegat, visitet, atque defendat omnes habitantes. . . . .' Repeating the prayer again and again he tried wildly to distract his attention; but the prayer could not tranquillize his agonized heart. 'Lord, why are you silent? Why are you always silent.....?'

Evening came. The door opened. One of the guards put some pumpkin in a wooden bowl, placed it in front of him and went out without saying a word. Raising the thing to his lips he was struck by its sweaty smell. It seemed to have been cooked two or three days previously, but in his present mood he would have been glad to eat leather to fill his empty stomach. Before he had finished gulping it down the flies were circling around his hands. I'm just like a dog, he reflected as he licked his fingers. There had been a time when the missionaries had frequently been invited to meals at the houses of feudal lords and samurai. This was the time when the Portuguese ships had come regularly to the harbors of Hirado and Yokoseura and Fukuda, laden with merchandise; and this was a time, too, according to Valignano, when the missionaries were never in want of bread and wine. They had sat at clean tables, said their grace and leisurely eaten their repast. And here he was, forgetting even to pray, and pouncing upon this food for dogs. His prayer was not one of thanksgiving to God; it was a prayer of petition for help; it was even an excuse for voicing his complaint and resentment. It was disgraceful for a priest to feel like this. Well he knew that his life was supposed to be devoted to the praise of God not to the expression of resentment. Yet in this day of trial, when he felt himself like Job in his leprosy, how difficult it was to raise his voice in praise to God!

Again the door grated. The same guard appeared. 'Father, we're going now,' he said.

'Going? Where?'

'To the wharf.'

As he stood up he felt giddy from the pangs of his empty stomach. Outside the hut it was already dusk, and the trees hung their branches languidly as though they had been exhausted by the heat of the day. Mosquitoes swarmed around their faces; the croaking frogs could be heard in the distance.

Three guards stood around him, but none of them seemed to worry lest he might try to escape. They talked to one another in loud voices, sometimes breaking out into laughter. One of them separated himself from the others and began to relieve himself in the bushes. If I wished, thought the priest, I could now break away from the other two and make a getaway. But while this thought was passing through his mind, one of the guards suddenly turned to him and said: 'Father, that hut was a gloomy place.'

Yes, he was a good fellow, this guard. And suddenly the priest felt somehow impressed by the fellow's pleasant, laughing face. If he escaped it was these peasants who would suffer the consequences. Forcing a weak smile he nodded to his companion.

They passed along the road by which they had come in the morning. The priest's hollow eyes were fascinated by the huge trees rising up from the middle of fields loud with the croaking of frogs. He remembered having seen these trees before. In them enormous ravens were now flapping their wings and screeching with raucous voice. What a sombre chorus it was—the croak of frogs and the caw of ravens!

As they entered the village, the white smoke rising from the scattered houses drove away the swarms of mosquitoes. A man wearing a loincloth stood clasping a child in his arms. Seeing the priest he opened his mouth like an idiot and burst out laughing. The women with their eyes sadly lowered watched the four men as they marched past.

Through the village they went, and then out again into the paddy fields. The road went downhill until at last a dry breath of salty wind blew into the sunken flesh of the priest's cheeks. Below was a harbor—if, indeed, it could be called a harbor, for it was no more than a landing-place of black pebbles heaped together with two forlorn little boats pulled up on the beach. While the guards were pushing poles under the boats, the priest picked up the peach-colored shells that were lying in the sand and played with them in his hands. They were the only beautiful things he had seen in this long, long day. Putting one to his ear he listened to the faint, muffled roar that issued forth from its deepest center. Then quite suddenly a dark shudder shook his whole being and in his hand he crushed that shell with its muffled roar.

'Get on board!' came the order.

The water in the bottom of the boat was white with dust; it was cold to his swollen feet. His feet drenched, both hands clutching the side of the ship, he closed his eyes and sighed. As the boat slowly moved away from land, his sunken eyes rested on the mountains over which he had wandered until this morning. In the evening mist the dark blue mountain rising up from the sea looked like the swelling breast of a woman. Looking down again to the shore he caught sight of a man, a beggar he seemed, running wildly along. As he ran he was shouting something; then his feet would sink in the sand and he would fall down. Yes, it was the man who had betrayed him. Falling down and then getting up, then falling again, Kichijiro was shouting something in a loud voice. Now it sounded like hissing; now it sounded like weeping; but what he was saying the priest could not make out. Yet he had no inclination to hate the fellow, no feeling of resentment. After all, sooner or later he was bound to be captured, and a feeling of resignation already filled his breast. At last Kichijiro seemed to realize that he would never catch up. And so he stood, erect like a pole, at the water's edge. As the boat moved away, his motionless figure grew smaller and smaller in the evening mist.

As night came, the boat entered an inlet. Opening his sleepy, half-closed eyes he saw that the guards disembarked and were replaced by other men. Their conversation was interspersed with a dialect that seemed rich in consonants; but in his utter exhaustion the priest did not feel like making the effort to understand what they were saying. The only thing he noticed was that the words Nagasaki and Omura were used frequently, and he felt vaguely that it was in this direction that he was being brought. When he had been in the hut, he had had the strength to pray for the one-eyed man and for the woman who had given him the cucumber; but now he had no longer strength to pray even for himself—much less to speak to others. Where he was being brought, what was going to be done to him—even this did not matter. Closing his eyes he again fell asleep. Sometimes he would open his eyes, and always he could hear the monotonous sound of the oars in the water. One of the men was rowing; the other two crouched in the boat with dark, sullen faces. 'Lord, may Thy will be done,' he murmured as though in his sleep. But even though his halting words seemed to resemble those of so many saints who had entrusted their all to the providence of God, he felt that his were different. What is happening to you?, he asked himself. Are you beginning to lose your faith?, said the voice from the depths of his being. Yet this voice filled him with disgust.

'Where are you going?' he called in a husky voice to the three new guards, as he opened his eyes again. But the others remained stiffly silent as if to threaten him. 'Where are you going?' he called again in a loud voice.

'Yokose-no-Ura' answered one of the men in a low voice that somehow seemed filled with shame.

He had frequently heard the name of Yokose-no-Ura from Valignano. It was a port which had been opened with the permission of the local lord by Frois and Almeida; and the Portuguese ships which until then had called at Hirado began to make use of this port alone. A great Jesuit church had been built on the hill overlooking the harbor and on it the fathers had erected a huge crucifix—so big indeed that the missionaries could clearly see it from their ships when, after many days and nights of long travel, they finally reached Japan. The Japanese residents also on Easter Sunday would walk in procession to the top of the hill, singing hymns and carrying lighted candles in their hands. Even the feudal lords themselves would come here; and some of them eventually received baptism.

From the boat the priest strained his eyes for any trace of a village or its harbor that might be Yokose-no-Ura, but sea and land alike were painted in the same thick black nor was any light to be seen. There was absolutely no trace of village or house. Yet the thought was constantly in his mind that somewhere here, as in Tomogi and Goto, there might still be Christians in

146

hiding. If so, did they know that here in a little boat, crouching with fear and trembling like a wild dog, was a priest?

'Where is Yokose-no-Ura?', he asked one of the guards.

'There's nothing left of it,' came the answer.

The village had been burnt to the ground; and its inhabitants had been completely dispersed. The sea and the land were silent as death; only the dull sound of the waves lapping against the boat broke the silence of the night. Why have you abandoned us so completely?, he prayed in a weak voice. Even the village was constructed for you; and have you abandoned it in its ashes? Even when the people are cast out of their homes have you not given them courage? Have you just remained silent like the darkness that surrounds me? Why? At least tell me why. We are not strong men like Job who was afflicted with leprosy as a trial. There is a limit to our endurance. Give us no more suffering.

So he prayed. But the sea remained cold, and the darkness maintained its stubborn silence. All that could be heard was the monotonous dull sound of the oars again and again.

Will I turn out a failure?, he asked himself. He felt that unless grace gave him courage and strength he could endure no more.

The sound of the oars ceased. One of the men faced the sea and yelled: 'Is anyone there?'

The oars had stopped; but from somewhere beyond the sound of other oars could be heard.

'It might be someone night-fishing. Leave him alone.' This time it was the old man who spoke in a whisper, the one who had been silent until now.

The noise of the oars from beyond stopped, and a weak voice could be heard trying to answer. The priest had a feeling that he had heard this voice somewhere before, but he could not recall where.

Now it was morning. They had reached Omura. As the milky mist was gradually blown away by the wind, his tired eyes fell upon the white wall of a castle surrounded by a grove at the side of the bay. It was still in process of construction, and the scaffolding of logs was all around it. A flock of crows flew crossways over the grove. At the back of the castle was a cluster of houses of thatch and straw. This was his first view of a Japanese town. As the light grew brighter, he noticed for the first time that the three guards who had been his companions in the boat had great thick bludgeons at their feet. Probably they had received orders to throw him mercilessly into the sea should he show any signs of trying to escape.

At the wharf was a jostling crowd of spectators, headed by some samurai wearing great big swords by the sleeves of their garments. The samurai would yell at the spectators who would alternately stand up and sit down on the hill on the beach waiting patiently for the arrival of the boat. When the priest disembarked there was a great cry from amongst the people; and as he was escorted by the samurai through their midst, his eyes met those of a number of men and women staring at him with looks of pain and anguish. He was silent; they too were silent. But as he passed in front of them he raised his hand and lightly gave them a blessing. Immediately, alarm and consternation showed itself on their faces and they lowered their eyes. Some even turned away their faces. If things were normal, he should have been able to place the bread of the body of Christ in those mouths now tightly shut. But here he had neither chalice nor wine nor altar with which to celebrate Mass.

When he was set up on the bare-backed horse with his wrists tightly bound a howl of derision arose from the crowd. Although Omura was dignified with the name of town, with its thatch-roofed houses it looked little different from the villages he had seen until now. The bare-footed women with flowing hair and skirts stood arranging shells and firewood and vegetables on the road. From amongst the people on the road strolling minstrels in *hakama*, and black-clothed bonzes would look up at him and laugh scornfully. Sometimes stones from the hands of children skimmed past his face as he was led along the long and narrow road. If Valignano was right, this Omura was the district upon which the missionaries had expended their greatest effort. It had

had many churches and a seminary; the peasants and even the samurai 'listened to our talks with great enthusiasm'—as Frois had put it in one of his letters. Even the feudal lords had become ardent Christians and he had heard that they were practically converted in a body. But now, when the children threw stones and the bonzes shouting in derision covered him with ugly spittle, there was no samurai amongst the officials who made any attempt to check them.

The road skirted the sea and then headed straight for Nagasaki. When they passed a village called Suzuda, he noticed a farmhouse filled with flowers the names of which he did not know. The samurai at one time stopped their horses and ordered one of the men to bring some water which they then offered to the priest. But it simply dribbled down from his mouth on to his hollow chest.

'Look! Isn't he big?' The women, pulling their children by the sleeves, pointed at him with derision.

When the sluggish procession got under way again, he looked back. The sad thought occurred to him that he might never again see blooming white flowers like those he had just looked at. As they rode along, the samurai would pull off their plumed hats and wipe the sweat from their brows; then fixing their hair they would sit up astride their horses.

Now the road became white and winding and the priest noticed the figure of a man like a beggar leaning on his staff and following after them. It was Kichijiro.

Just as he had stood on the shore open-mouthed watching the boat move away, so now with kimono thrown open he slouched along. Seeing that the priest had noticed him, he got all excited and tried to hide in the shelter of a tree. The priest was perplexed. Why did this fellow who betrayed him come following after him in this way? And now it occurred to him that the man who had been in the other ship that morning might have been Kichijiro.

Jostled up and down upon the horse, his sunken eyes sometimes fell vaguely upon the sea. Today it was shimmering black and threatening.

After they got away from Suzuda, the number of people on the roads began slowly to increase. Merchants leading cattle that had burdens on their backs; travellers with big, umbrella-like straw hats and wearing straw coats. When these saw the procession they would stand by the roadside gaping in astonishment at the strange thing they had run into. Sometimes farmers would throw away their hoe and come running to stare at the funny sight. Previously the priest had always been keenly interested in the Japanese—in their appearance, in their clothing and so on; but now he could arouse no interest within himself, such was his utter exhaustion. He simply closed his eyes and thought of the Stations of the Cross, one by one, now being prayed at some monastery; and he kept moving his dry tongue as he tried to mutter the words of the prayers. This was a prayer well known to all seminarians and Christians, a meditation calling to mind the details of the Passion of Christ. When this man had gone out through the gate of the Temple up the sloping path to Golgotha bearing his cross, struggling for every step and reeling as he walked, the swelling mob, all agog with curiosity, had followed after him. 'Women of Jerusalem, weep not for me but for yourselves and for your children. For the day will come. . . . .' These words came up in his mind. Many centuries ago, that man tasted with his dried and swollen tongue all the suffering that I now endure, he reflected. And this sense of suffering shared softly eased his mind and heart more than the sweetest water.

'Pange lingua. . . . .' He felt the tears streaming down his cheeks. 'Bella premunt hostilia, da robur fer auxilium.' No matter what happens never will I apostatize, he said to himself.

In the afternoon they reached a town called Isahaya. Here stood a mansion surrounded by a moat and an earthen wall, while clustered around it were houses of straw and thatch. When they came in front of one of the houses, some men wearing swords bowed respectfully to the procession of samurai and brought along two big dishes of rice. While the samurai ate, the priest was taken down from his horse for the first time and strapped to a tree like a dog. Nearby, beggars with tousled hair sat squatting and staring at him like beasts with glimmering eyes. He had no longer the energy to give them a smile.

Someone put a few grains of rice in a broken dish in front of him. Casually he raised his eyes to the donor. It was Kichijiro.

There he was squatting now in the middle of the beggars. Sometimes he would turn his eyes as though he wanted to look at the priest, but when their eyes met he would turn his face away in haste. The priest looked at that face with serenity. When he had seen this fellow at the shore, he had been too tired even to hate him; but now he was simply incapable of showing any generosity. Seething with anger he reflected on the scene in the plain when the dried fish he had been forced to eat caused in his throat that terrible thirst. 'Go, what thou dost do quickly.' Even Christ had cast these words of anger at the Judas who betrayed him. For a long time the priest had thought that these words were a contradiction in the love of Christ; but now when he saw the trembling face of this fellow as he squatted on the ground, sometimes raising his eyes like a whipped dog, a black and cruel emotion rose from the very depths of his being. 'Go,' he whispered in his heart, 'what thou dost do quickly.'

The samurai had finished eating their rice and were already astride their horses. The priest was put up on his; and the procession began its slow march again. The bonzes raised their voices in derision; the children threw stones. The men with their beasts of burden and the travellers in their Japanese clothes looked up at the samurai and stared at the priest. All was just the same as before. He looked back—and there he was, Kichijiro, separated somewhat from the others, leaning on his staff and following after. What thou dost do quickly, muttered the priest in his heart. What thou dost do quickly.

Chapter 6

THE sky grew dark; clouds moved slowly over the mountain tops and down over the fields. This was the open plain of Chizukano. Here and there clusters of shrubs seemed to be crawling over the earth; but everywhere else only the black-brown ground stretched out endlessly. The samurai were engaged in earnest discussion; and when they had finished they gave the order for the priest to be taken down from his horse. The long period of sitting on horseback with hands tightly bound had taken its toll; and when he stood up on the ground, a searing pain shot through his thighs. So he crouched down to the ground.

One of the samurai was smoking tobacco with a long pipe. This was the first time since coming to Japan that the priest had seen tobacco. The samurai took two or three pulls, belched out the smoke and then passed on the pipe to his companion. Meanwhile the officials looked on enviously.

For a long time, now standing, now sitting on a rock, they all stood looking toward the south. Some of them relieved themselves in the shadow of the rock. The northern sky was still clear in spots, but toward the south heavy, evening clouds were already gathering. Sometimes the priest would look back over the road along which they had come, but there was no sign of Kichijiro—he must have been delayed on the way. Probably he had got tired of crawling after them and had dropped away.

'They're here! They're here!' yelled the guards, pointing toward the south; and from that direction there slowly approached a band of samurai and their attendants, similar to the ones here waiting. Immediately the samurai with the pipe jumped astride his horse and galloped with all speed toward the oncoming crowd. Still on horseback he greeted the newcomers with a bow which was solemnly answered. Now the priest knew that he was going to be handed over to a new escort.

When the exchange of greetings had come to an end and the band that had escorted him from Omura turned their horses and vanished off along the road to the north where the sun's rays still fell gently, the priest was surrounded by the group that had come for him from Nagasaki. Once again he was put up on the bare-backed horse.

The prison was on the slope of a hill, surrounded by trees. Only just built, it looked like a kind of storehouse; inside, it was slightly raised from the ground. Light entered through a little barred window and a small grating, fixed with a sliding wooden door through which a plate could barely be passed. Here food was pushed in to him once each day. After arriving, he had been brought out twice for investigation, and this gave him a chance to see what the place looked like outside—a bamboo fence faced threateningly inwards, while further outside were the thatch-roofed houses in which dwelt the guards.

When he was thrown in here there were no other prisoners except himself. All day long he sat silently and pensively in the darkness listening to the voices of the guards; it was not unlike his previous stay in that hut on the island. Sometimes the guards would talk to him, anxious as they were to while away the time; and so he learnt that he was just outside Nagasaki, but he could not find out what his position was in relation to the center of the city. Only during the day he could hear far in the distance the loud cries of working men, the sound of trees being hewn down, of nails being driven in; and this made him guess that this region was being newly developed. When night fell, he could hear the song of the turtle-dove amidst the trees.

In spite of everything his prison life was filled with a strange tranquillity and peace. The tension and anguish of those days of wandering through the mountains now seemed like a dream from a past life. He could not guess what the next day might bring, but he felt almost no fear. He got some strong Japanese paper and string from the guards, and with this he made a rosary with which almost all day long he prayed, biting at the sacred words.

At night as he lay in bed with his eyes closed listening to the song of the turtle-dove in the trees, behind his closed eyelids he would pass through every scene in the life of Christ. From childhood the face of Christ had been for him the fulfillment of his every dream and ideal. The face of Christ as he preached to the crowd the Sermon on the Mount. The face of Christ as he passed over the Lake of Galilee at dusk. Even in its moments of terrible torture this face had never lost its beauty. Those soft, clear eyes which pierced to the very core of a man's being were now fixed upon him. The face that could do no wrong, utter no word of insult. When the vision of this face came before him, fear and trembling seemed to vanish like the tiny ripples that are quietly sucked up by the sand of the sea-shore.

This was the first time since coming to Japan that he had been able to pass day after day in peaceful tranquillity. He began to wonder if the continuation of this unbroken peace was a proof that his death was not far away. So gently did these quiet days flow through his heart.

But on the ninth day he was suddenly dragged out of his prison. Accustomed to a cell with no ray of light, the brightness of the sun seared his hollow eyes cutting them like a sword. The cry of the cicada was cascading from the trees like a waterfall, while behind the guards' hut was a resplendent view of bright red flowers. Now he felt more keenly than ever what a vagabond he was, his hair and beard grown long, the flesh hanging loose around his bones, his arms thin like needles. He wondered if he was being brought out for cross-examination, but he was led straight to the guards' room and put into a cell. Why he was brought here he did not know.

Only the next day did he discover the reason. Suddenly the silence was broken by the angry barking voices of the guards, and he could hear the confused scuffling of several men and women being dragged out from the prison gate into the courtyard. Until the previous day these prisoners had been enclosed in a pitch-black prison like his own.

'If you carry on this way, you'll be punished.' The guards shouted raising angry voices; and the prisoners resisted with equal anger.

'Stop this rampaging. Stop!' And so the angry dispute between guards and prisoners continued for some time. Then all became quiet again. When evening came, suddenly from out the prison came the sound of voices raised in prayer: 'Our Father who art in Heaven, hallowed be Thy name Thy Kingdom come, Thy will be done on earth as it is in Heaven. Give us this day our daily bread, and forgive us our trespasses as we forgive those who trespass against us; and lead us not into temptation but deliver us from evil. Amen.'

In the mist of the evening their voices rose up like a fountain and then died away. 'Lead us not into temptation.' In those praying voices was there not a note of pathos? a plaintive tone? Blinking his sunken eyes the priest moved his lips in unison with that prayer. 'Yet you never break the silence,' he said. 'You should not be silent for ever.'

The next day the priest asked the guards if he might visit the prisoners, who were being forced to work in the fields under heavy guard. This being granted he went out to where five or six men and women were lifelessly moving hoes. As they looked up at him with astonishment, he remembered who they were. He also remembered the tattered peasant clothing. But it was their faces—those faces that they turned up at him. Was it from the constant deprivation of light in the prison cell that the men looked like this, with their long beards and long hair, while the women's faces were deadly white.

'Oh!' cried one of the women, 'it's father. I would never have recognized him.'

It was the woman who on that day had given him the cucumber taken from her bosom. And beside her, looking like a beggar, was the one-eyed fellow showing his decaying yellow teeth and laughing with a touch of nostalgia.

From this day on he got permission from the guards; and every morning and evening, twice each day, he went into the Christians' prison. The guards knew that the prisoners would repay their generosity by creating no disturbance at this time. Having no bread and wine, the priest could not offer Mass; but at least he could recite with them the Credo, Pater Noster and Ave Maria; and he had a chance to hear their confessions.

'Put not your trust in princes: in the children of men, in whom there is no salvation. His spirit shall go forth, and he shall return into his earth: in that day all their thoughts shall perish. Blessed is he who hath the God of Jacob for his helper, whose hope is in the Lord his God: who made heaven and earth, the sea, and all things that are in them.'

As the priest uttered these words of the psalmist, not one of the prisoners so much as coughed, but all strained their ears in fervent attention. Even the guards were listening. This was a text of Scripture he had read time and again; but it had never come to his lips with such a wealth of meaning both for himself and for the Christians. Each word seemed to sink into his heart with new significance and new richness.

'Blessed are the dead who die in the Lord. From henceforth now. . . . .'

'You will not meet with greater suffering than this,' said the priest in a voice filled with earnest fervor. 'The Lord will not abandon you for ever. He it is who washes our wounds; his is the hand that wipes away our blood. The Lord will not be silent for ever.'

When evening came, he administered the sacrament of penance to the Christians; but since he had no confessional, he put his ear to the hole through which the food was passed and the penitent whispered his sins in a low voice. And so he heard the confession. While this was going on, the others huddled together in a corner, trying as far as possible not to make things difficult for the penitent. Here in the prison, for the first time since the days of Tomogi, he was able to exercise his faculties as a priest; and the realization of this made him pray secretly that such a life might continue for ever.

After hearing the confessions, he got the paper he had received from the officials, made himself a quill from a chicken's wing which had fallen in the courtyard, and began to write down all his reminiscences since coming to Japan. He did not know, of course, if what he wrote would ever reach Portugal; but there was the possibility that some Christian might hand it to a Chinese in Naga-.saki. And with this faint hope he pushed his quill over the pages.

At night, as he sat in the dark listening to the sound of the turtle-dove in the trees, he felt the face of Christ looking intently at him. The clear blue eyes were gentle with compassion; the features were tranquil; it was a face filled with trust. 'Lord, you will not cast us away any longer,' he whispered, his eyes fixed upon that face. And then the answer seemed to come to his ears: 'I will not abandon you.' Bowing his head he strained his ears for the sound of that voice again; but the only thing he could hear was the singing of the turtle-dove. The darkness was thick and black. Yet the priest felt that for one instant his heart had been purified.

One day he heard the sound of the bolt; and a guard put in his head at the door. 'Change your clothes,' he shouted, as he threw some heavy garments on the floor. 'Look! You have red clothes, and underwear of *jittoku* and cotton. Take them all. They're yours.' The guard went on to explain that *jittoku* was the material worn by Buddhist monks.

'Thanks very much,' answered the priest, a smile on his sunken face, 'but please take them away. I don't want them.'

'You won't take them? You won't take them?' The guard shook his head like a child and looked longingly at the garment. 'But they are a gift from the officials at the magistrate's office.'

Comparing his own hemp clothing with these completely new garments, he asked himself why the officials had presented him with the clothing of a bonze. Was it a gesture of pity toward a prisoner? or was it one more trap to ensnare him? He could not make out which it might be. But anyhow, with this clothing, he reflected that from now his connection with the magistrate's office had begun.

'Quickly! Quickly!' urged the guard. 'The officials will soon be here.'

He had not thought that his cross-examination would come so quickly. In his imagination every day he had dramatically pictured the scene as being like the meeting of Pilate and Christ—the crowd howling, Pilate perplexed, Christ standing silent. But here the only sound was the cry of the cicada inviting him to sleep. The prison of the Christians was rapt in its usual afternoon silence.

Getting hot water from the guard he washed himself and then slowly put on the cotton clothes, passing his arms slowly through the sleeves. The cloth was not pleasing to the touch, and at the same time he felt with a shudder of humiliation that by wearing this clothing he was making a pact with the magistrate's office.

In the courtyard a number of chairs were arranged in a single row; and one by one they cast a dark shadow on the ground. Forced to squat on the right of the gate with his hands on his knees, he waited and waited. Unaccustomed to this posture as he was, he perspired profusely at the pain in his knees; but he did not want the officials to see his agony. Reflecting earnestly on how Christ must have looked at the time of the scourging he endeavoured to distract his mind from the pain in his knees.

After a time came the sound of a retinue and of horses' hooves, and the guards all together squatted down bowing their heads low. Into the courtyard with haughty step came a number of samurai, fans in hand. Talking together they passed by without so much as a glance in the direction of Rodrigues and then languidly sat down on the chairs. The guards, still bowed down, brought them cups and they slowly sipped the hot water.

After a brief interval, the samurai on the extreme right called to the guards; and the priest, flinching from the pain in his aching knees, was dragged before the five chairs.

From the tree behind, a cicada continued to sing. Perspiration flowed down his back, and he was acutely conscious of a great number of eyes fixed on him from behind; for the Christians from their prison were undoubtedly listening intently to every question and answer that passed between him and his interlocutors. Now he understood why Inoue and the officials had deliberately chosen this place of questioning: they wanted to show him cornered and defeated to the peasants. 'Gloria Patri et Filio et Spiritui Sancto'—he closed his sunken eyes and forced a smile to his face, but he himself realized that his countenance was only hardening like a mask.

'The Governor of Chikugo is anxious about your perplexity,' said the samurai on the extreme right earnestly in Portuguese. 'If you are in difficulties, please say so.'

The priest bowed his head in silence. Then raising it his eyes met those of the old man who was sitting in the middle chair of the five. A kind smile playing on his lips, the old man watched the priest with the curiosity of a child who has been given a new toy. Then a statement was read:

'Native country: Portugal. Name: Rodrigues. Said to have come from Macao to Japan. Is that correct?'

The samurai on the extreme right said in a voice charged with emotion: 'Father, we are deeply moved by the strength of your determination in coming here from thousands of miles away through all kinds of hardships. Undoubtedly you have suffered deeply.'

There was a gentle tone in his words, and this very gentleness pierced the priest's heart, giving him pain.

'Precisely because we know this, our duty of investigation is painful for us.'

At the solicitous words of the official his strained emotion seemed to yield. 'Were it not for the barriers of country and politics, could we not clasp hands and talk?'—such was the sentiment that suddenly filled his heart. Yet he immediately felt that it was dangerous to give way to such sentimentality.

'Father, we are not disputing about the right and wrong of your doctrine. In Spain and Portugal and such countries it may be true. The reason we have outlawed Christianity in Japan is that, after deep and earnest consideration, we find its teaching of no value for the Japan of today.'

The interpreter immediately came to the heart of the discussion. The old man in front with the big ears kept looking down on the priest sympathetically.

'According to our way of thinking, truth is universal,' said the priest, at last returning the smile of the old man. 'A moment ago you officials expressed sympathy for the suffering I have passed through. One of you spoke words of warm consolation for my travelling thousands of miles of sea over such a long period to come to your country. If we did not believe that truth is universal, why should so many missionaries endure these hardships? It is precisely because truth is common to all countries and all times that we call it truth. If a true doctrine were not true alike in Portugal and Japan we could not call it "true".'

Here and there the interpreter was stuck for words; yet with a face expressionless like a puppet he conveyed the meaning to the other four.

Only the old man straight in front of him kept nodding his head as though in complete agreement with what the priest was saying; and while nodding he slowly began to pass his left hand over his right, as though rubbing them together.

'All the fathers keep saying the same thing. And yet. . .' The interpreter slowly translated the words of yet another samurai. 'A tree which flourishes in one kind of soil may wither if the soil is changed. As for the tree of Christianity, in a foreign country its leaves may grow thick and the buds may be rich, while in Japan the leaves wither and no bud appears. Father, have you never thought of the difference in the soil, the difference in the water?'

'The leaves should not wither; the buds should appear,' said the priest raising his voice. 'Do you think I know nothing? In Europe, to say nothing of Macao where I resided for some time, people are familiar with the work of the missionaries; and it is well known that when many landowners gave permission for evangelization the number of Christians reached three hundred thousand.'

The old man constantly kept nodding, all the time rubbing his hands together. While the other officials with tense expression were listening to the words of the interpreter, only the old man seemed completely on the side of the priest.

'If the leaves do not grow and the flowers do not blossom, that is only when no fertilizer is applied.'

The voice of the cicada was no longer heard; but the afternoon sun became even more severe. The officials were silent as though at a loss what to say. The priest, sensing that the Christians in prison behind him were straining their ears to hear what was being said, felt that he was winning in the controversy. A pleasant sensation rose slowly within his breast.

'Why did you begin this process of persuasion?' The priest lowering his eyes spoke quietly. 'No matter what I say you will not change your minds. And I also have no intention of altering my way of thinking.'

Even as he spoke he felt a sudden onrush of emotion. The more conscious he became of being watched by the Christians from behind the more he went on making himself a hero. 'No matter what I say I will be punished,' he exclaimed.

The interpreter translated the words mechanically to the others. The rays of the sun made that flat face seem even more flat. Now for the first time the old man's hands stopped moving, and shaking his head he looked at the priest as though he were soothing a naughty child. 'We will not punish the fathers without reason,' he said.

'That is not the idea of Inoue. If you were Inoue you would punish me instantly.'

At these words the officials laughed heartily as though they had been told a joke.

'What are you laughing at?'

'Father, this is Inoue, the Governor of Chikugo. He is here in front of you.'

Stupefied he gazed at the old man who, naive as a child, returned his glance still rubbing his hands. How could he have recognized one who so utterly betrayed all his expectations? The man whom Valignano had called a devil, who had made the missionaries apostatize one by one—until now he had envisaged the face of this man as pale and crafty. But here before his very eyes sat this understanding, seemingly good, meek man.

Whispering a word or two to the samurai beside him Inoue, the Governor of Chikugo, stood up from his chair with some difficulty. The other officials followed after him, one by one, and going out through the door by which they had entered disappeared from sight. The cicada cried; the afternoon light flashed; the deserted chairs cast an even blacker shadow on the ground.

Then without reason a violent emotion arose within the priest's breast and tears welled up in his eyes. It was like the emotion one feels after accomplishing something great. The prison had been silent; but now quite suddenly someone began to sing:

> We're on our way, we're on our way,
> We're on our way to the temple of Paradise,
> To the temple of Paradise. . . .
> To the great Temple. . . . .

The song continued long after the guard had let him back to the bare floor of his room. At least he had not confused the Christians; he had done nothing to disturb their faith; his conduct had not been base and cowardly. Such were his thoughts.

The rays of the moon fell through the prison bars, forming on the wall a shadow that reminded the priest of the man of Galilee. The eyes were lowered, but they looked toward him. On this shadow face the priest put contours: he drew in the eyes and the mouth. Today he had done well, he reflected; and he glowed with pride like a child.

From the courtyard came the sound of clappers. The guards were making their round of the prison. Every night they did this.

The third day. The guards chose three men from among the Christians and had them dig three holes in the middle of the courtyard. From his prison window the priest could see in the brilliant rays of the sun the figure of the one-eyed man (wasn't Juan his name?) wielding his spade with the others, shovelling mud into a basket and carrying it away. Because of the intense heat, he wore only a loincloth, and the perspiration on his back glistened like steel.

Why were they digging holes, he asked one of the guards; and he was told that they were making a privy. The Christians were then deep down in the hole they had dug unsuspectingly throwing up mud.

In the process of digging, one man fell sick from sunstroke. The guards yelled at him and struck him; but he crouched down, unable to move. Juan and the other Christians took him up in their arms and brought him into the prison.

After some time one of the guards came to call the priest. The condition of the sick man had undergone a sudden change, and the Christians kept asking for the priest. Running to the prison in haste, he found Juan and Monica and the others standing around the sick man who lay in the dark, ashen like a stone.

'Won't you take something to drink?' asked Monica, holding to his lips some water in a broken cup. But the water only dribbled down from his mouth on to his throat.

'Your suffering is terrible. Can you keep going?', she asked.

When night came, the sick man began to struggle for

breath. It had been impossible to perform such labor with a weakened body, sustained only by a little millet. The priest knelt by his side and prepared to administer the sacrament of the sick; but when he made the sign of the cross the sick man heaved his breast. This was the end. The guards gave orders to the Christians to burn the body; but they all protested that such a course of action was contrary to Christian teaching—with Christians burial in the earth was the customary tradition. And so the next day the man was buried in the copse at the rear of the prison.

'Hisagoro is now happy,' murmured one of the Christians enviously. 'His suffering is over. He has entered eternal rest.'

The other men and women listened vacantly to these words.

Now it is afternoon. The heavy hot air begins to stir. And then the rain begins to fall. It makes a monotonous and melancholy sound as it patters on the wooden roof of the prison and on the grove where they have buried the dead man. Clasping his knees, the priest continues to ask himself how long the authorities intend to let him lead a life like this. Not that everything is going perfectly in this prison life, but provided no stir is created the guards tacitly agree to the prayers of the Christians; they allow the priest to visit them and to write his letters. He wonders why they permit all this. It seems so strange.

Through the bars of his window he caught sight of a man wearing a cape who was being angrily upbraided by the guards. The cape prevented him from seeing who it was; but obviously it was not one of the crowd in the prison. The person seemed to be pleading for something; but the guards shook their heads and drove him away without listening to what he was saying.

'If you carry on like this, you'll be beaten,' shouted one of the guards brandishing a big stick; and the fellow scuttled away in the direction of the gate like a wild dog.

But the next moment he was back again in the courtyard, standing there in the rain, staring intently in front of him.

When night came, the priest looked out through the bars of his cell, and there he was still, the man in the cape, standing obstinately without moving, drenched by the rain. No guard came out of the hut. They seemed to have given up the attempt to chase him away.

When the man looked toward the priest, their eyes met. It was Kichijiro. For a moment a spasm of fear crossed that face and Kichijiro retreated backwards a few steps.

'Father!' His voice was like the whining of a dog. 'Father! Listen to me!'

The priest withdrew his face from the window and tried to block his ears against the sound of that voice. How could he ever forget the dried fish, the burning thirst in his throat. Even if he tried to forgive the fellow, he could not drive from his memory the hatred and anger that lurked there.

'Father! father!' The entreating voice continued like that of a child pleading with its mother.

'Won't you listen to me, father! I've kept deceiving you. Since you rebuked me I began to hate you and all the Christians. Yes, it is true that I trod on the holy image. Mokichi and Ichizo were strong. I can't be strong like them.'

The guards, unable to bear it any longer, came out with sticks; and Kichijiro fled away, screaming as he ran.

'But I have my cause to plead! One who has trod on the sacred image has his say too. Do you think I trampled on it willingly? My feet ached with the pain. God asks me to imitate the strong, even though he made me weak. Isn't this unreasonable?'

Sometimes there would be a lull; then angry voices and the pleading cry and tears.

'Father, what can I do, a weak person like me? I didn't betray you for money. I was threatened by the officials.'

'Get out of here quickly,' shouted the guards, putting their heads out of the lodge. 'Don't presume on our kindness.'

'Father, listen to me. I have done something for which I can never make amends. And you officials! I am a Christian. Put me in prison.'

The priest closed his eyes and began to recite the

Credo. He felt a sense of joy in being able to abandon this whimpering fellow in the rain. Even though Christ prayed, Judas had hanged himself in the field of blood—and had Christ prayed for Judas? There was nothing about that in the Scriptures; and even if there was, he could not put himself into such a frame of mind as to be able to do likewise. In any case, to what extent could the fellow be trusted? He was looking for pardon; but this perhaps was no more than a passing moment of excitement.

Bit by bit, the voice of Kichijiro quietened and then died out. Looking through the bars, he saw the guards pushing the fellow roughly in the back, dragging him to the prison.

With night the rain ceased. A ball of rice and some salted fish were pushed in to him. The fish was already rotten and inedible. As always he could hear the voices of the Christians raised in prayer. Receiving permission from the guards, he went to visit them in prison; and there was Kichijiro pushed into a corner all by himself, separated from the others. The Christians refused to be associated with him.

'Be careful of this fellow,' they whispered to the priest in a low voice. 'The officials often make use of apostates; perhaps they want to trap us.'

It was true that the magistrate sometimes put fallen Christians in with the others in order to foment trouble and urge them to renounce their faith. It could be that

Kichijiro had again received money to do precisely this. But anyhow it was impossible for the priest to trust Kichijiro any more.

'Father, father!' Seeing that the priest had come to the prison, Kichijiro was again pleading in the darkness. 'Let me confess my sins and repent!'

The priest had no right to refuse the sacrament of penance to anyone. If a person asked for the sacrament, it was not for him to concede or refuse according to his own feelings. He raised his hand in blessing, uttered dutifully the prescribed prayer and put his ear close to the other. As the foul breath was wafted into his face, there in the darkness the vision of the yellow teeth and the crafty look floated before his eyes.

'Listen to me, father,' Kichijiro whimpered in a voice that the other Christians could hear. 'I am an apostate; but if I had died ten years ago I might have gone to paradise as a good Christian, not despised as an apostate. Merely because I live in a time of persecution. . . . I am sorry.'

'But do you still believe?', asked the priest, doing his best to put up with the foul stench of the other's breath. 'I will give you absolution, but I cannot trust you. I cannot understand why you have come here.'

Heaving a deep sigh and searching for words of explanation, Kichijiro shifted and shuffled. The stench of his filth and sweat was wafted toward the priest. Could it be possible that Christ loved and searched after this dirtiest of men? In evil there remained that strength and beauty of evil; but this Kichijiro was not even worthy to be called evil. He was thin and dirty like the tattered rags he wore. Suppressing his disgust, the priest recited the final words of absolution, and then, following the established custom, he whispered, 'Go in peace.' With all possible speed getting away from the stench of that mouth and that body, he returned to where the Christians were.

No, no. Our Lord had searched out the ragged and the dirty. Thus he reflected as he lay in bed. Among the people who appeared in the pages of the Scripture, those whom Christ had searched after in love were the woman of Capharnaum with the issue of blood, the woman taken in adultery whom men had wanted to stone— people with no attraction, no beauty. Anyone could be attracted by the beautiful and the charming. But could such attraction be called love? True love was to accept humanity when wasted like rags and tatters. Theoretically the priest knew all this; but still he could not forgive Kichijiro. Once again near his face came the face of Christ, wet with tears. When the gentle eyes looked straight into his, the priest was filled with shame.

The *fumie* had begun. The Christians stood herded together in a line like asses cast out from the city. This time they were confronted not by the same officials as the other day, but by a younger group of subordinates who sat on stools, arms folded. The guards, holding poles, kept watch. Today, too, the cicada sang with bracing voice; the sky was clear and blue; the air was bright and refreshing. It would not be long, however, until the oppressive heat would come again. The only one not dragged out into the courtyard was the priest himself; and he, pressing to the bars a face on which the flesh hung limply, stared at the *fumie* spectacle which was now to begin.

'The sooner you get through with it, the sooner you'll get out of here,' roared one of the officials. 'I'm not telling you to trample with sincerity and conviction. This is only a formality. Just putting your foot on the thing won't hurt your convictions.'

The officials kept insisting to the Christians that to trample on the *fumie* was no more than a formality. All you had to do was to put your foot on it. If you did that, nobody cared what you believed. In accordance with orders from the magistrate, you were asked to put your foot lightly on the *fumie*; and then you would immediately be released.

The four men and women listened to the harangue with expressionless faces. As for the priest, his face pressed to the bars, he could not make out what the fellows were getting at. And the four bloated Christian faces, with protruding cheek-bones ghastly and pallid from deprivation of sunshine—they were like puppets with no will of their own.

What was to come had come. This he well understood; but he could not feel convinced that his own fate and that of the Christians would soon be sealed. The officials were talking to the Christians as though asking a favor. The peasants were shaking their heads; and then the officials with worried faces all drew back some distance.

Next the guards placed on the ground between the peasants and the stools on which the officials were now sitting a *fumie* wrapped in a cloth. Then they returned to their places.

Going down the list, one of the officials called out the names: 'Ikitsukijima, Kubo-no-ura, Tobei.' The four Christians sat there vacantly. Getting excited, a guard struck with his stick the fellow on the extreme left, but he did not stir. Two or three times he was pushed in the back; he fell forward and crouched to the ground, but he made no effort to move from the place where he had fallen.

'Kubo-no-ura, Chokichi.'

The one eyed fellow shook his head two or three times. What a child he looked!

'Kubo-no-ura, Haru.'

The woman who had given the priest the cucumber bent her back and hung her head. In this position she was pushed on by the guard, but she did not so much as raise her eyes.

Finally the old man, Mataichi, was called. But he, too, clung to the earth where he stood.

But now the officials raised no angry voices and uttered no reproach. One would think that they had been expecting this from the beginning, the way they remained seated on their stools whispering to one another in low voices. Then suddenly they arose and withdrew to the guards' hut.

The sun stood directly over the prison; and its rays beat down upon the four Christians left behind. Their squatting figures threw black shadows on the ground, while the cicada again began to sing as though disrupting the glistening air. The guards and the Christians even began to talk and joke with one another as though the previous relationship of cross-examining and cross-examined had vanished. But then from the hut one of the officials called out that all could return to the prison except the one-eyed man, Chokichi.

Relaxing his hands from the bars they had been clutching, the priest sat down on the floor. What would happen next he did not know. But, at any rate, today had passed peacefully, and this thought filled him with a deep sense of relief. If today passed by well, that was enough: tomorrow would look after itself. If tomorrow he were alive. . . .

'Isn't it a pity to throw it away?', one voice was saying. And the other answered: 'Yes, it's an awful pity.' What precisely the conversation was all about he could not make out; but at any rate the wind blew toward him an easy-going conversation between the guard and the one-eyed fellow. A fly jumped down from the bars and began to buzz around the priest's head—the sound of its wings was almost soporific.

Suddenly someone ran across the courtyard. Then the swish of a sharp sound. Then a thud. Already, as the priest clutched the bars, the official was sheathing his sharp, glittering sword: the execution was over. the dead body of the one-eyed man lay prostrate on the ground. Grabbing it by the feet, one of the guards began to drag it slowly toward the hole the Christians had dug. The black blood flowing from it lay all around like the sash of a garment.

Suddenly, from out the prison came the high-pitched scream of a woman, her voice going on and on as though she was singing a hymn. Then it faded out, and the air around became deadly calm. Only the hands of the priest as they clutched the bars trembled as though cramped and paralyzed.

'Look to it,' shouted another official, facing the prison and with his back to the priest 'This is what happens when you make light of life. It's a tiring business; but the sooner you go through with it, the sooner you get out of here. I'm not telling you to trample out of conviction. If you just go through with the formality, it won't hurt your beliefs.'

Shouting in a loud voice, a guard next brought out Kichijiro. Wearing only a loincloth and trembling from head to foot, he came before the officials, bowing again and again. Then raising his thin, wasted foot he placed it on the *fumie*.

'Quickly! Get out!' shouted one of the officials, pointing to the gate; and Kichijiro, tumbling over himself in haste, disappeared from sight. Not once did he look back toward the hut where the priest was. But for the priest, what the fellow did was no longer of any importance.

The white rays of the sun beat down dazzlingly on the open courtyard. Beneath its merciless rays there lay on the ground the black dye which was the blood from the body of the one-eyed man.

Just as before, the cicada kept on singing their song, dry and hoarse. There was not a breath of wind. Just as before, a fly kept buzzing around the priest's face. In the world outside there was no change. A man had died; but there was no change.

'So it has come to this. . . .' He shivered as he clutched the bars. 'So it has come to this. . . .'

Yet his perplexity did not come from the event that had happened so suddenly. What he could not understand was the stillness of the courtyard, the voice of the cicada, the whirling wings of the flies. A man had died. Yet the outside world went on as if nothing had happened. Could anything be more crazy? Was this martyrdom? Why are you silent? Here this one-eyed man has died—and for you. You ought to know. Why does this stillness continue? This noon-day stillness. The sound of the flies—this crazy thing, this cruel business. And you avert your face as though indifferent. This . . . this I cannot bear.

Kyrie Eleison! Lord, have mercy! His trembling lips moved a while in prayer, but the words faded from his lips. Lord, do not abandon me any more! Do not abandon me in this mysterious way. Is this prayer? For a long time I have believed that prayer is uttered to praise and glorify you; but when I speak to you it seems as though I only blaspheme. On the day of my death, too, will the world go relentlessly on its way, indifferent just as now? After I am murdered, will the cicada sing and the flies whirl their wings inducing sleep? Do I want to be as heroic as that? And yet, am I looking for the true, hidden martyrdom or just for a glorious death? Is it that I want to be honored, to be prayed to, to be called a saint?

Clasping his knees, he sat on the floor looking straight in front of him. 'It was almost noon. Until the third hour darkness covered the whole earth.' When that man had died on the cross, from within the temple had issued three bugle calls, one long, one short, and then one long again. Preparations for the ceremony of the Pasch had begun. In blue, flowing robes the high priest had ascended the stairway of the temple and, standing before the altar on which lay the sacrificial victim, had blown the trumpet. At that time, the sky had darkened and behind the clouds the sun had faded. 'Darkness fell. The veil of the temple was rent in twain from the top

even to the bottom.' This was the image of martyrdom
he had long entertained; but the martyrdom of these
peasants, enacted before his very eyes—how wretched
it was, miserable like the huts they lived in, like the
rags in which they were clothed.

Chapter 7

FIVE days later, in the evening, he had his second meeting with Inoue, the Lord of Chikugo. The day had been deadly still; but now the leaves of the trees began to stir gently sending forth a fresh whisper in the evening breeze. And so he found himself face to face with Inoue. Apart from the interpreter, the magistrate had no companion. When the priest entered with his guard, the other, fondling a large bowl in his hands, was slowly sipping hot water.

'I'm afraid I have neglected you,' said Inoue, still holding the bowl in both hands while his great eyes stared curiously at the priest. 'I had business in Hirado.'

The magistrate ordered the interpreter to bring hot water to the priest; and all the time a smile played around his lips. Then he slowly began to speak about his journey to Hirado. 'You should go to Hirado if you get a chance, father.' He seemed to talk as if the priest were a free man. 'There is a castle of the Matsuura's on a mountain facing a tranquil inlet.'

'Yes, I have heard from the missionaries in Hirado that it is a beautiful town.'

'I would not say beautiful; I'd rather say interesting.' Inoue shook his head as he spoke. 'When I see that town I think of a story I heard long ago. It is about Takenobu Matsuura of Hirado who had four concubines who constantly quarrelled out of jealousy. Takenobu, unable to bear it any longer, ended up by expelling all four from his castle. But perhaps this is not a suitable story for the ears of a celibate priest.'

'This Matsuura must have been a very wise man.' Since Inoue had become so frank, the priest also felt relaxed as he spoke.

'Do you really mean that? If you do, I feel happy. Hirado, and indeed our whole Japan, is just like Matsuura.' Twisting the bowl around in his hand, the Lord of Chikugo went on: 'Spain, Portugal, Holland, England and such-like women keep whispering jealous tales of slander into the ear of the man called Japan.'

As he listened to the interpreter's translation, the priest began to realize what Inoue was getting at. How often he had heard at Goa and Macao how the Protestant countries like England and Holland, and the Catholic countries like Spain and Portugal had come to Japan and, jealous of one another's progress, had spoken calumnies about one another to the Japanese. And the missionaries, too, out of rivalry had at one time strictly forbidden their Japanese converts to consort with the English and the Dutch.

'Father, if you think that Matsuura was wise, you

surely realize that Japan's outlawing of Christianity is not unreasonable and foolish.'

As he spoke, the laugh never faded from those fat, full-blooded cheeks and the magistrate stared intently at the priest's face. For a Japanese, the eyes seemed strangely brown while the side-locks (were they perhaps dyed?) showed no trace of white.

'Our Church teaches monogamy. . . .' The priest deliberately chose a bantering turn of phrase. 'If a man has a lawful wife, I wonder if it is a wise thing to let himself be burdened with concubines. What if Japan were to choose one lawful wife from among these four?'

'And by this lawful wife you mean Portugal?'

No, no! I mean our Church.'

As the interpreter unemotionally passed on this reply, Inoue's face fell; and raising his voice he laughed. Considering his age, it was a high-pitched laugh; but there was no emotion in the eyes he now turned on the priest. His eyes were not laughing.

'Father, don't you think it is better for this man called Japan to stop thinking about women from foreign countries and to be united with a woman born in the same country, a woman who has sympathy for his way of thinking.'

The priest knew well what Inoue meant by the foreign woman; but since the other was carrying on the argument in this apparently frivolous way, he felt that he too must continue along the same lines. 'In the Church,' he said, 'the nationality of the woman is not important. What matters is her fidelity to her husband.'

'I see. And yet if love of husband and wife were based only on emotion no one would have to suffer from what we call the persistent love of an ugly woman.' The magistrate nodded his head as though satisfied with his own way of speaking. 'There are some men in the world who get upset by the persistent affection of an ugly woman.'

'You look upon missionary work as the forcing of love upon someone?'

'Yes, that's what it is—from our standpoint. And if you don't like the expression, let's put it this way. We call a woman who cannot bear children barren; and we think that such a woman has not the capacity to be a wife.'

'If our doctrine makes no progress here in Japan, this is not the fault of the Church. It is the fault of those who tear the Japanese Christians from the Church like a husband from his wife.'

The interpreter, searching for words, was momentarily silent. This was the time when the evening prayer ought to come floating from the Christians' prison; but today there was no sound. Suddenly the priest thought of the death sentence of five days before: a stillness that seemed to resemble this moment, but in reality so different. It was the time when the body of the one-eyed man lay prostrate on the ground in the flashing sun and the guard unemotionally seizing one leg had dragged it off to the hole in the ground, leaving a trail of blood just like a great line that had been traced over the earth with a brush. Was it possible, reflected the priest, that the order for this execution had been given by the benevolent old man who sat before him?

'Father,' said the Lord of Chikugo, 'you and the other missionaries do not seem to know Japan.'

'And you, honorable magistrate,' answered the priest, 'you do not seem to know Christianity.'

At this they both laughed. 'And yet,' said Inoue, 'thirty years ago, when I was a retainer of Gamo, I asked for the guidance of the fathers.'

'And then?'

'My reasons for opposing Christianity are different from those of the people at large. I have never thought of Christianity as an evil religion.'

The interpreter listened to these words with astonishment on his face; and while he stammered and searched for words, the old man kept looking at the bowl in his hands with its little remaining hot water, all the time laughing.

'Father, I want you to think over two things this old man has told you. One is that the persistent affection of an ugly woman is an intolerable burden for a man; the other, that a barren woman should not become a wife.'

As the magistrate stood up to go, the interpreter bowed his head down to the ground, his hands joined in front of him. The guard, all flustered, set out the sandals into which the Lord of Chikugo slowly put his feet; and without so much as a backward glance he vanished into the darkness of the courtyard. At the door of the hut was a swarm of mosquitoes; outside could be heard the neighing of a horse.

Now it was night. Softly the rain began to fall making a sound like the pattering of pebbles in the trees at the back of the hut. Resting his head on the hard floor and listening to the sound of the rain, the priest thought of a man who had been put on trial like himself. It was on the morning of April 7th that this emaciated man had been driven down the slope at Jerusalem. The rays of the dawn stretched out beyond the Dead Sea bathing the mountain range in golden white, the brook Cedron babbled on, ever giving forth its fresh sound. No one gave him any chance to rest. After the scribes and the elders had pronounced sentence of death, it was necessary to get the approval of Pilate, the Roman Governor. In his camp outside the town, not too far from the temple, Pilate had heard the news and now he should be waiting.

From childhood the priest had memorized every detail of that decisive morning of April 7th. This emaciated man was his perfect ideal. His eyes, like those of every victim, were filled with sorrowful resignation as he looked reproachfully at the crowd that ridiculed and spat at him. And in this crowd stood Judas. Why had Judas followed after? Was he incited by lust for revenge—

to watch the final destruction of the man he had sold? Anyhow, whatever about that, this case was just like his own. He had been sold by Kichijiro as Christ had been sold by Judas; and like Christ he was now being judged by the powerful ones of this world. Yes, his fate and that of Christ were quite alike; and at this thought on that rainy night a tingling sensation of joy welled up within his breast. This was the joy of the Christian who relishes the truth that he is united to the Son of God.

On the other hand, he had tasted none of the physical suffering that Christ had known; and this thought made him uneasy. At the palace of Pilate, that man had been bound to a pillar two feet high to be scourged with a whip tipped with metal; and nails had been driven into his hands. But since his confinement in this prison, to his astonishment neither the officials nor the guards had so much as struck him. Whether or not this was the plan of Inoue or not, he did not know; but he felt that it was not impossible that from now on, day after day might pass without any physical molestation.

What was the reason for this? How often he had heard of countless missionaries captured in this country, and how they had been subjected to indescribable tortures and torments. There was Navarro who at Shimabara was roasted alive with fire; there were Carvalho and Gabriel who were immersed again and again in the boiling sulphur water at Unzen; there were those missionaries deprived of food in the prison of Omura until they died of starvation. Yet here he was in prison, permitted to pray, permitted to talk to the Christians, eating food which, though not precisely plentiful, was at least served up three times a day; and the officials and the magistrate, when they visited him, far from showing themselves severe, contented themselves with formalities and then went away. What could they possibly be aiming at?

The priest reflected on the days in the hut of Tomogi Mountain with Garrpe, and how they had talked about torture and whether they could endure it, if once it came their way. Of course the only thing was to pray for God's grace; but at that time he had felt in his heart that he could fight until death. In his wanderings through the mountains, too, he had entertained the strong conviction that, once captured, he would be subjected to physical torture. And he had felt (was it a sign of his tense emotion?) that whatever torment came his way, he could clench his teeth and bear it.

But now his resolution had somehow weakened. Rising from the floor and shaking his head, he asked himself if his courage had begun to crumble. And was it because of the life he was now leading? Then suddenly, from the depths of his heart, someone spoke to him: 'It is because your life here is so pleasant.'

Since coming to Japan, it was practically only in this prison that he had had the chance to live the life of a priest. In Tomogi he had lain in hiding; after this he had

had contact with none of the peasants except Kichijiro. It was only since coming here that he had a chance to live with the people and to spend a great part of the day in prayer and meditation without suffering the pangs of hunger.

Like sand flowing through an hour glass, each day here passed quietly by. His feelings, formerly tense and taut like iron, now gradually relaxed. He began to feel that the torture and physical suffering he had believed inevitable might not fall to his lot after all. The officials and the guards were generous; the chubby-faced magistrate carried on his pleasant conversation about Hirado. Now that he had once tasted the tepid waters of peace and security, would he have the resolution again to wander through those mountains and conceal himself in a hut?

And then for the first time it came to him that the Japanese officials and their magitsrate were making no move because, like a spider watching its prey caught in the web, they were waiting for his spirit to weaken. Bitterly he recalled the forced laugh of the Lord of Chikugo, and how the old man rubbed his hands together. Now he could see clearly why the magistrate had made such a gesture.

And in the background of all this fancy was the fact that from that time until yesterday the daily two meals had been increased to three. The good-natured guards, ignorant of what was involved, would show their gums as they laughed and said: 'Won't you eat up? Why, this is the wish of the magistrate. Not too many prisoners are treated like this.'

The priest, looking into the wooden bowl with its hard rice and dry fish, would shake his head and beg them to give it to the Christians. Already the flies were buzzing over the rice. When evening came, the guards brought two straw mats. Yes, the priest began slowly to realize what this change in treatment imported. It might simply mean that the day of his torture was at hand. His relaxed physique would be all the more weak in its resistance to pain. The officials were using this underhand means of slowly sapping his vitality, then suddenly the torture would come. Undoubtedly this was their plan.

The pit. . . . .

The word he had heard from the interpreter on that day of his capture on the island now rose up in his memory. If Ferreira had apostatized, this was because, like himself, he had been well treated at first; and then, when he was weakened in body and spirit, quite suddenly this torture had been inflicted upon him. Otherwise it was unthinkable that such a great man would so suddenly renounce his faith. Yes, what diabolical means they devised!

'The Japanese are the most intelligent people we have met so far.' Reflecting on the words of Xavier he laughed cynically.

He had refused the proffered food; he had not used the straw mats at night; no doubt this had reached the ears of the officials and the magistrate through the guards; yet no word of censure had been uttered. It was impossible for him to know whether or not they realized that their plans had been thwarted.

One morning, ten days after the visit of the Lord of Chikugo, he was awakened by a disturbance in the courtyard. Putting his face to the barred window he saw the three Christians urged along by a samurai being brought away from the prison. In the mist of the morning, the guards dragged them along, their wrists chained together. The last of the three was the woman who had given him the cucumber.

'Father,' they shouted up to him as they passed his prison, 'we are going to forced labor.'

Pushing his hands through the bars, the priest blessed them one by one with the sign of the cross. His fingers barely touched the forehead of Monica as she, with a touch of sadness and smiling like a child, raised her face.

That whole day was quiet and still. Toward noon the temperature gradually rose, and the fierce rays of the sun pierced mercilessly through the bars of the prison. He asked the guards who brought the food when the three Christians would come back and received the answer that they would return by evening, if the work was finished. By order of the Lord of Chikugo, a number of temples were being built at Nagasaki so that the demand for workers was well-nigh limitless.

'Tonight is Urabon, father. I suppose you know what Urabon is?'

The guards explained that at Urabon the people of Nagasaki hung lanterns at the eaves of their houses and lit candles in them. The priest answered that in the West there was the feast of Hallowe'en in which the people did something similar.

Far in the distance he could hear the chanting voices of children, and straining his ears, the words were carried to him:

'O lantern, bye-bye-bye,

If you throw a stone at it, your hand withers away

O lantern, bye-bye-bye

If you throw a stone at it, your hand withers away.'

Somehow there was a plaintive note in the children's broken song.

It was evening. On the crape myrtle a cicada had settled and was singing. Even that voice faded away in the calm of the evening—but the three Christians had not returned. As he ate his supper beneath the oil lamp, he could hear the faint voices of the children in the distance. At dead of night the rays of the moon flowed brightly through the bars, wakening him from sleep. The festival was over; the darkness was thick and deep; but whether or not the Christians had returned he did not know.

The next morning he was wakened by the guards and told to put on his clothes and come out immediately.

'What is all this about?' he asked.

In answer to his question as to where they were going, the guards replied that they themselves did not know. This early hour of the morning had been chosen, however, to avoid the crowds of curious onlookers who would certainly gather to stare at the foreign Christian priest.

Three samurai were waiting for him. They, too, gave the simple explanation that this was the wish of the magistrate and then, placing themselves in front and behind with their captive in the middle, they started off in silence along the morning road.

In the morning mist the merchants' houses of straw and thatch with their doors shut looked just like melancholy old men. On both sides of the roads stretched rice paddies; timber was piled up everywhere. The fresh fragrance of the wood, mingled with the smell of the mist, was wafted to their nostrils. The roads of Nagasaki were still in course of construction. In the shade of the new constructions, beggars and outcasts lay sleeping with straw mats thrown over them.

'So this is your first time in Nagasaki.' It was one of the samurai who spoke with a laugh. 'Lots of hills, aren't there?'

Indeed there were lots of hills. On some of them were clustered little thatched huts. A cock announced the dawn of day; below the eaves faded lanterns lay strewn on the ground like remnants of the feast of the previous night. Just below the hill was the sea all around the long peninsula. Filled with reeds it stretched out into the distance like a milk-white lake. As the mist gave way to a clear sky, there appeared in the background a number of low hills.

Near the sea was a pine grove where a number of baskets were placed; while four or five bare-footed samurai squatted eating something. As their mouths moved, their eyes, blazing with curiosity, were fixed upon the priest.

Within the grove a white curtain was stretched out and a number of stools were placed there. One of the samurai pointed to a stool and told the priest to sit down. To the priest, who had been waiting for a cross-examination, his gesture came as something of a surprise.

The gray sand stretched out, gently continuing on to the inlet, while the overcast sky gave a brown appearance to the lazy sea. The monotonous sound of the waves biting at the shore reminded the priest of the death of Mokichi and Ichizo. On that day, too, the misty rain had fallen ceaselessly on the sea, and on that rainy day the sea-gulls had flown in near the stakes. The sea was silent as if exhausted; and God, too, continued to be silent. To this problem that kept flitting across his mind he had as yet no answer.

'Father!'

A voice sounded from behind. Looking back he saw a man with long hair flowing down his neck smiling as he played with a fan. He was stout and square-faced.

'Ah!' It was the voice rather than the face that told the

priest that this was the interpreter with whom he had conversed in the hut on the island.

'Do you remember? How many days have passed since our last meeting? But what a pleasure to see you again! The prison you are now in is newly built. It's not so bad to live in. Before it was set up, the Christian missionaries were almost always confined in the prison of Suzuda in Omura. On rainy days the water leaked in; on windy days the breeze broke in; the prisoners really had a tough time there.'

'Will the magistrate come soon?' To stop the other's babbling the priest changed the subject, but his companion clapped his fan against the palm of his hand and went on: 'Oh no. The Lord of Chikugo will not come. But what do you think of him? What do you think of the magistrate?'

'He treated me kindly. I got food three times a day; I was even provided with covering for my bed. I'm beginning to think that because of this kind of life my body has betrayed my heart. I suppose that's what you are waiting for.'

The interpreter absent-mindedly turned his eyes away. 'As a matter of fact,' he said, 'there is a plan from the magistrate's office to have you meet someone who will soon arrive here. He is Portuguese like yourself. You'll have a lot to talk about, I suppose.'

The priest looked intently at the yellow eyes of the interpreter, from whose face the smile was quickly fading. The name of Ferreira rose up in his mind. So this was it! These fellows had at last brought along Ferreira as a means to make him apostatize. For a long time he had felt almost no hatred for Ferreira, nothing but the pity that a superior person feels for the wretched. But now that the moment for confronting him seemed to have arrived, a terrible uneasiness overtook him, and his heart pounded with confusion. Why this should be, he himself did not know.

'Do you know who this person is?', asked the interpreter.

'Yes, I know.'

'I see.'

The interpreter, a faint smile playing around his lips, waved his fan as he looked intently at the gray shore. And there, far in the distance, appeared the tiny figures of a group of men moving toward them.

'He's in that group.'

The priest did not want to show his agitation, but unconsciously he rose from the stool on which he was sitting. Bit by bit the group drew near the pine grove and now he was able to distinguish individuals one from another. Two samurai, acting as guards, were walking in front. Behind them followed three prisoners bound to one another by chains. Then Monica, reeling and stumbling. And behind the three the priest saw the figure of his companion Garrpe.

'Aha!' shouted the interpreter with an air of triumph. 'Is that what you expected, father?'

The priest's eyes followed Garrpe, taking in every detail. Probably Garrpe did not know who awaited him in this grove. Like himself he was wearing peasant clothing; like himself from the knees down his white legs protruded awkwardly; stretching out his legs as best he could and breathing deeply, he walked behind the others.

It was no surprise to the priest to find that his old friend had been captured. From the time of their landing at the shore of Tomogi, they had both been convinced that the day of their apprehension would come. What the priest wanted to know was where Garrpe was taken and what were his thoughts now in captivity.

'I would like to talk to Garrpe,' he said.

'You would, would you? But the day is long. It's still morning. No need to hurry.'

As if to tantalize the priest, the interpreter deliberately yawned and began to cool his face with his fan.

'By the way, father, when I spoke to you on the island there was something I forgot to ask. Tell me. This mercy that the Christians talk about—what is it?'

'You're like a cat that teases a little animal,' murmured the priest, looking at the other with his sunken eyes. 'This is a despicable delight you take in talking to me. Tell me, where was Garrpe captured, and how?'

'Without reason we are not allowed to reveal to prisoners the business of the magistrate's office.'

But now, suddenly the procession had stopped on the gray sand. The officials were unloading a pile of straw mats from the animal at the rear.

'Ah!' The interpreter looked at the scene with a smile of delight. 'Do you know what they are going to use those mats for?'

The officials began to roll the mats around the bodies of the prisoners, only Garrpe being left free. Soon, with only their heads protruding from the matting they looked just like basket worms.

'Now they'll be put on boats and rowed out into the shoals. In this inlet the water is so deep you can't see the bottom.'

The sluggish waters made the same monotonous sound as they gnawed at the shore. Clouds covered the leaden sky which hung down low over the earth and sea.

'Look! One of the officials is talking to Father Garrpe.' The interpreter seemed to be singing, such was his glee. 'What is he saying? Probably he is saying something like this: "If you are a father possessed of true Christian mercy, you ought to have pity for these three unfortunates wrapped around with straw coats. You shouldn't stand by idle and see them killed."'

Now the priest understood only too well what the interpreter was getting at; and anger shook his whole body like a gust of wind. Were he not a priest, he would wring the fellow's neck.

'And the magistrate. He says that if Father Garrpe

apostatizes—well, in a word, all three lives will be spared. In any case, these three have already apostatized. Yesterday, at the magistrate's office they trampled on the *fumie*.'

'They trampled . . . and yet this cruelty . . . even now.' The priest stammered as he spoke, but words did not come.

'The people we want to apostatize are not these small fry. In the islands off the coast there are still lots and lots of peasants who are secretly faithful to Christianity. It is to get them that we want the fathers to apostatize.'

'Vitam praesta puram, iter para tutum.' The priest tried to recite the *Ave Maris Stella* but instead of the words of the prayer there arose vividly in his mind the picture of the cicada singing in the crape myrtle, the trail of red-black blood on the ground of the courtyard beneath the blazing sun. He had come to this country to lay down his life for other men, but instead of that the Japanese were laying down their lives one by one for him. What was he to do? According to the doctrine he had learnt until now, it was possible to pass judgment on certain actions distinguishing right from wrong and good from evil. If Garrpe shook his head in refusal, these three Christians would sink like stones in the bay. If he gave in to the sollicitations of the officials, this would mean the betrayal of his whole life. What was he to do?

'What answer will this Garrpe give? I have been told

that in Christianity the first thing is mercy and that God is Mercy itself. . . Oh! Look at the boat.'

Suddenly two of the Christians, all wrapped up as they were, stumbled forward as if to run away. But from behind, the officials pushed them, sending them flying forward so that they fell prostrate in the sand. Only Monica, looking like a basket worm, remained staring at the sluggish sea. In the priest's heart there arose the taste of that cucumber she had taken from her breast for him, and her laughing voice.

'Apostatize! Apostatize!' He shouted out the words in his heart to Garrpe who was listening to the officials, his back turned toward the priest.

'Apostatize! You must apostatize.' Feeling the perspiration trickle down his forehead he closed his eyes and then, cowardly though it might be, turned away from the scene that would meet his eyes.

You are silent. Even in this moment are you silent? When he opened his eyes the three basket worms, goaded on by the officials, were already facing the boat.

I would apostatize. I would apostatize. The words rose up even to his throat, but clenching his teeth he tried to stop himself from uttering the words aloud. Now two officials with lances followed the prisoners and, rolling up their kimonos to the waist, clambered into the boat which, rocked by the waves, began to leave the shore. There is still time! Do not impute all this to Garrpe and to me. This responsibility you yourself must bear. But now Garrpe had rushed forward and, raising both arms, had plunged from the shore into the sea. Sending up clouds of spray he was approaching the boat and, as he swam, he was shouting something.

'Lord, hear our prayer. . .'

In that voice there was no tone of censure, nothing of anger, and it would fade out as the black head sank down between the waves. 'Lord, hear our prayer. . .!' Leaning over the side of the boat, the officials showed their white teeth as they laughed. One of them, passing his lance from one hand to the other, mocked Garrpe as he tried to get near the boat. But now the head was lost in the sea and the voice was still. But then, all at once, it appeared again like a piece of black dust, buffeted about by the waves. The voice was feebler than before, but again and again it kept shouting something.

Now an official set up one of the Christians at the side of the ship and pushed him vigorously with the tip of his lance. Just like a puppet the figure of straw fell into the sea and disappeared from sight. Then with dramatic speed the next went under. Finally Monica was swallowed up by the sea. Only the head of Garrpe, like a piece of wood from a shipwrecked boat, floated for some time on the water until the waves from the boat covered it over.

'This is a horrible business. No matter how many times one sees it, it's horrible,' said the interpreter getting up from his stool. Then suddenly reeling on the priest with hatred in his eyes he said: 'Father, have you thought of the suffering you have inflicted on so many peasants just because of your dream, just because you want to impose your selfish dream upon Japan. Look! Blood is flowing again. The blood of those ignorant people is flowing again.'

Then, as if to spit out the words, 'At least Garrpe was clean. But you . . . you . . . you are the most weak-willed. You don't deserve the name of "father".'

'O lantern, bye-bye-bye
If you throw a stone at it, your hand withers away
O lantern, bye-bye-bye
If you throw a stone at it, your hand withers away.'

The *bon* festival was over; but still far in the distance the children chanted their song. In the houses of Nagasaki they were now giving the beggars and outcasts all kinds of vegetables to comfort the spirits of the dead. The crape myrtle showed no change; the cicada continued its daily song; but gradually these voices were losing their power.

'How is he?' It was one of the officials who spoke in the course of his daily round.

'No change. He just sits staring at the wall all day long.' Answering in a low voice, the guard pointed to the room in which the priest was confined.

The official looked through the barred window at the priest sitting on the floor in the rays of the sun, his back to the window. All day long, facing the wall, he watched the dark sea and the little black head of Garrpe floating on its surface. Now the three Christians, all rolled up, sank like pebbles.

When he shook his head, the vision would disappear; but when he closed his eyes it would come stubbornly up again behind his eye-lids.

'You're weak-willed,' the interpreter had said, rising from his stool. 'You're not worthy to be called "father".'

He had not been able to save the Christians; nor like Garrpe had he been able to sink beneath the waves in pursuit of them. His pity for them had been overwhelming; but pity was not action. It was not love. Pity, like passion, was no more than a kind of instinct. Long ago he had learnt this, sitting on the hard benches of the seminary; but it had only been bookish knowledge at that time.

'Look! Look! For you blood is flowing; the blood of peasants is flowing out over the ground.'

Then in the garden of the sun-drenched prison the trail of blood went on and on. The interpreter had said that it was the selfish dream of the missionaries that trailed out this line of blood. The Lord of Chikugo had compared this selfish dream to the excessive love of an ugly woman. The persistent love of an ugly woman was an insupportable burden for a man, he had said.

'And yet'—before his eyes floated the laughing face of the interpreter and the rich, fleshy face of the Lord of

Chikugo, one superimposed upon the other—'you came to this country to lay down your life for them. But in fact they are laying down their lives for you.'

The contemptuous laughing voice opened the priest's wounds, piercing them like a needle. He shook his head weakly. No, it was not for him that the peasants had been dying for so long. They had chosen death for themselves—because they had faith; but this answer had no longer power to heal his wounds.

And so the days passed by, one by one. In the crape myrtle, the lifeless voice of the cicada went on as ever.

'How is he?' It was one of the officials who spoke in the course of his daily round.

'No change. He sits staring at the wall all day long.' The guard pointed to the room as he answered in a low voice.

'I got instructions from the magistrate to come and see how things are going. Everything is proceeding according to the Lord of Chikugo's plan.' The official removed his face from the bars and a smile of satisfaction played about his lips, like that of a doctor inspecting the progress of a patient.

Now the *obon* is over. The streets of Nagasaki are quiet. At the end of the month a thanksgiving day is held, and the village heads from Nagasaki and Urakami contribute chests of early ripened rice to the magistrate's office. On August 1st every official and representative of each town has to present himself in white ceremonial robes to the magistrate.

Slowly the full moon comes. In the grove behind the prison the owl and the turtle-dove answer each other, singing in the night. Above the grove the moon, completely round, is bathed in an eerie red color as it comes out from the dark clouds and then is hidden again. The old men whisper ominously that this coming year may bring something untoward.

It is August 13th. In the houses of Nagasaki, people make fish salads and cook sweet potatoes and beans. On that day the officials working at the magistrate's office offer fish and cakes to the magistrate who in turn gives the officials sake, soup and dumpling.

That night the guards drank sake until it was late. The raucous voices and the clinking of the cups were brought constantly to his ears. The priest squatted on the ground, his hunched shoulders bathed in the silver moon-light that pierced the bars of his prison. His wasted form was reflected on the wall; sometimes he gave a start as a cockroach chirruped in the trees. Closing his sunken eyes, he relished the thick darkness that enveloped him. On this night when all those whom he knew were fast asleep, a thrust of poignant pain passed through his breast; and he thought of yet another night. Yes, crouching on the ashen earth of a Gethsemane that had imbibed all the heat of the day, alone and separated from his sleeping disciples, a man had said: 'My soul is sorrowful even unto death.' And his sweat had become like drops of blood. This was the face that was now before his eyes. Hundreds and hundreds of times it had appeared in his dreams; but why was it that only now did the suffering, perspiring face seem so far away? Yet tonight he focused all his attention on the emaciated expression on those cheeks.

On that night had that man, too, felt the silence of God? Had he, too, shuddered with fear? The priest did not want to think so. Yet this thought suddenly arose within his breast, and he tried not to hear the voice that told him so, and he wildly shook his head two or three times. The rainy sea into which Mokichi and Ichizo had sunk, fastened to stakes! The sea on which the black head of Garrpe, chasing after the little boat, had struggled wildly and then floated like a piece of drifting wood! The sea into which those bodies wrapped in straw matting had dropped straight down! This sea stretched out endlessly, sadly; and all this time, over the sea, God simply maintained his unrelenting silence. 'Eloi, Eloi, lama sabacthani!' With the memory of the leaden sea, these words suddenly burst into his consciousness. 'Eloi, Eloi, lama sabacthani!' It is three o'clock on that Friday; and from the cross this voice rings out to a sky covered with darkness. The priest had always thought that these words were that man's prayer, not that they issued from terror at the silence of God.

Did God really exist? If not, how ludicrous was half of his life spent traversing the limitless seas to come and plant the tiny seed in this barren island! How ludicrous the life of the one-eyed man executed while the cicada sang in the full light of day! How ludicrous was the life of Garrpe, swimming in pursuit of the Christians in that little boat! Facing the wall, the priest laughed aloud.

'Father, what's the joke?' The raucous voices of the drunken guards had ceased; and one passing by the door asked the question.

And yet when morning came and the strong rays of the sun once more pierced through the bars, the priest regained some of his spirit and recovered from the loneliness of the previous night. Stretching out both feet and resting his head against the wall he whispered words from the psalms in a sorrowful voice: 'My heart is steadfast, O God, my heart is steadfast! I will sing and make melody! Awake my soul! Awake, O harp and lyre! I will awake the dawn ' In childhood these words had always risen in his mind when he watched the wind blow over the blue sky and through the trees; but that was a time when God was not as now an object of fear and perplexity but one who was near to the earth, giving harmony and living joy.

Sometimes the officials and the guards would look at him through the bars, eyes alight with curiosity; but the priest no longer gave them so much as a glance. Sometimes he did not even touch the food offered to him three times each day.

Now it was September. One afternoon, when the air was already tinged with a certain freshness, he was suddenly paid a visit by the interpreter.

'Today I want you to meet someone.' The interpreter spoke in his usual jesting manner, playing with his fan. 'No, no. Not the magistrate, not the officials. A person I think you want to meet.'

The priest remained silent, his lifeless eyes fixed on the other. He had a clear recollection of the words the interpreter had cast at him on another occasion, but strangely enough he could not hate the fellow nor even be angry with him. He felt too weary even to hate.

'I hear you don't eat much.' The interpreter spoke with his usual thin smile. 'It would be better not to brood so much.'

With these words he cocked his head on one side, then went out, then came in again, going out and coming in several times.

'What's keeping that palanquin,' he said. 'It's time it was here.'

But by now the priest had no interest in whom he was going to meet. His listless eyes simply fixed themselves on the relentless figure of the interpreter, who kept running out and in.

But now the voices of the palanquin-carriers could be

heard at the entrance. Next they were engaged in conversation with the interpreter.

'Father, let's go.'

Without a word the priest stood up, and slowly and sluggishly made his way out. The blinding rays of the sun cut his eyes, bloodshot and yellow with exhaustion. Two carriers, wearing only loincloths, stood there with the palanquin on their shoulders and stared intently at him. 'He is heavy! He's big and fat,' they grumbled as the priest clambered in.

They had closed down the blind to avoid the idle curiosity of passers-by, so that he could see nothing of what was going on outside. Only all sorts of sounds and noises came to his ears. The shrieking of children; the bells of the bonzes; the noise of construction. Here and there the evening sun piercing through the blind struck his face. But not only was there noise; there were also smells of all kinds wafted to where he sat. The smell of trees and of mud; the smell of hens, of cows and of horses. Closing his eyes for a moment, the priest drew deep down into his bosom the life of these people who surrounded him. Then suddenly there rose up within him a longing to talk to others, to be like other people, to hear the words of other men, to plunge into the daily life of men. Yes, he had had enough of this—of this hiding in that charcoal hut, of the roaming through the mountains in terror of his pursuers, of the sight of Christians massacred daily before his very eyes. He no longer had the strength to put up with all this. And yet. . . 'With thy whole heart, with thy whole soul, with thy whole mind, with thy whole strength. . ' He had become a priest in order to aim at one thing, and one thing alone.

The sounds alone told him that now they had entered the town. Before it had been the clucking of hens and the mooing of cattle, but now it was the restless shuffling of feet that pierced the blind to where he was sitting—shrill voices buying and selling, the wheels of carts and voices raised in altercation.

Where he was going, and whom he would meet—these things were not important to him now. No matter who it was, the same old questions would be put, the same cross-examination of his work would go on. The questioning was all a formality. Like Herod when he faced Christ, these people put questions without any interest in the answer. Besides, why had the Lord of Chikugo refused to kill him alone and, without acquitting him, left him alive? But anyhow, to go into all this business was only troublesome and disturbing.

'We're here!'

Wiping away the sweat with his hand, the interpreter stopped the palanquin and raised the blind. Getting out, the priest's eyes were suddenly struck by the evening sun, and he saw before him the guard who had looked after him in prison. Probably they had brought along this man for fear that he might break loose and try to escape during the journey.

214

Above a flight of stairs stood a two-storied gate, behind which was a small temple bathed in the light of the evening sun and with brown mountains and cliffs stretching out behind. In the dull and dim temple two or three cocks strutted arrogantly around. A young bonze came out; looking up at the priest with eyes that flashed hostility he disappeared from sight without so much as a word of greeting—even to the interpreter.

'The bonzes don't like you priests,' said the interpreter, a note of delight in his voice as he squatted down on the floor and looked out at the garden. 'Sitting alone all day long looking at the wall and brooding is poison for you,' he went on. 'Stop this nonsense; it doesn't help anybody to cause useless trouble.'

But the priest, as usual, was paying no attention to his teasing. What distracted him just now was that in this temple compound with its smell of incense and Japanese food, somehow his nostrils suddenly picked on an alien smell in the midst of it all. It was the smell of meat. It was meat—from which he had been forced to abstain for so long that he had become sensitive to the slightest smell of it.

Then far away he heard the sound of footsteps. Someone was approaching along the lengthy corridor.

'Who are you going to meet? Have you guessed yet?'

This time the priest's face stiffened; and for the first time he nodded. He felt his knees tremble involuntarily. Yes, he had known that some day he must meet this man; but never had he thought that it would be in a place like this.

'Well, it's time for you to meet him.' The interpreter spoke in high delight, watching the trembling figure of the priest. 'This is the magistrate's order.'

'Inoue?'

'Yes. And the other person, he would like to meet you too.'

Following on the heels of an old monk walked Ferreira in a black kimono, his eyes cast down. The stocky little monk self-confidently puffing out his chest emphasized the servility of the tall Ferreira who, with lowered eyes, looked just like a big animal which, with a rope around its neck, is trailed reluctantly along.

The old monk came to a halt, and Ferreira without a word glanced at the priest and then sat down in a corner of the floor lightened by the setting sun. For some time there was a deathly silence.

'Father!' At last Rodrigues spoke in a trembling voice. 'Father!'

Raising his bowed head a little, Ferreira glanced at the priest. For an instant there flashed into his eyes a servile smile and momentary shame; but then wide-eyed he looked down at the other deliberately and challengingly.

But Rodrigues, conscious of his priesthood, was at a loss for words. His heart was too full to speak; anything he said would be like a lie; nor did he wish to incite even

216

more the condescending curiosity of the bonze and the interpreter who were gazing steadily at him. Nostalgia, anger, sadness, hatred—all kinds of conflicting emotions simmered within his breast. Why do you put on such a face?, he cried out in his heart. I did not come here to condemn you. I am not here as your judge. I am no better than you. He tried to force a smile to his lips; but instead of a smile a white tear fell from his eye and flowed slowly down his cheek.

'Father, so long since we have met. . .' At last the trembling voice of Rodrigues broke the silence. Even as he spoke he was aware how foolish and silly the words sounded; but nothing else would come to his lips.

And yet Ferreira remained silent, the challenging smile still lingering on his lips. The priest understood very well how the weak and servile smile could give place to this challenging expression. And it was precisely because he understood, that he felt he would like to collapse on the spot like a withered tree.

'Please . . . say . . . something.' Rodrigues was almost panting as he spoke. 'If you have pity for me . . . please . . . say . . . something.'

Suddenly he knew what he himself wanted to say; and strange words seemed to rise in his throat. You have shaved off your beard, was what he wanted to say. But he himself could not understand why such strange sentiments should come into his mind. Only that in the old days the Ferreira whom he and Garrpe had known had had such a well-groomed beard. It was something that had given to his whole appearance an air of kindness combined with gravity. But now the chin and upper lip were smooth and clean shaven. The priest felt his eyes drawn to this part of Ferreira's face. Somehow it reflected a terrible sensuality.

'What can I say to you on such an occasion?', said Ferreira.

'You're deceiving yourself.'

'Deceiving myself? How can I explain the part of me that is not all self-deception?'

The interpreter was now getting up on his knees to make sure that he missed nothing of the Portuguese. Two or three chickens jumped up from the ground on to the veranda and fluttered their wings.

'Have you been living here for long?'

'About a year, I suppose.'

'What is this place?'

'It is a temple called Saishoji.'

Hearing the word 'Saishoji' from the lips of Ferreira, the old monk who had been staring in front of him like a Buddha in stone turned his face toward them.

'I also am in a prison somewhere in Nagasaki. Where precisely it is I do not know myself.'

'I know it. It is in the outskirts of the city.'

'What are you doing all day, Ferreira?'

A flash of pain crossed Ferreira's face as he put his hand on the well-shaven chin.

'The honorable Sawano spends his day writing.' This time it was the interpreter who broke in, speaking in Ferreira's stead.

'At the magistrate's order I am translating a book on astronomy.' Ferreira spoke out the words rapidly as if he wanted to shut the mouth of the interpreter. 'Yes, that's what I'm doing. And I am of some use. I am of some use to the people of this country. The Japanese already have knowledge and learning of all kinds, but in the line of astronomy and medicine a Westerner like myself can still help them. Of course in this country there is an outstanding knowledge of medicine learnt from China; but it is by no means useless to add to it our knowledge of surgery. The same is true of astronomy. For that reason I have asked the Dutch commander to be kind enough to lend us lenses and telescopes. So I am not useless in this country. I can perform some service. I can!'

The priest stared at this Ferreira who kept persistently talking on and on. He could not understand why the man had suddenly become so eloquent. And yet he somehow felt he could understand the other's psychology in the constant emphasizing that he was of some use to this country. Ferreira was not only talking to him. The interpreter and the bonze were there too; and Ferreira wanted them to hear. Besides, he kept prattling to justify his existence in his own eyes: 'I am useful to this country!'

The priest blinked his eyes sorrowfully as he looked

at Ferreira. Yes, to be useful to others, to help others, this was the one wish and the only dream of one who had dedicated himself to the priesthood. The solitude of the priestly life was only when one was useless to others. The priest realized that even now, after his apostasy, Ferreira had not been able to escape from the old psychological orientation that had motivated him. Ferreira seemed to be relying on his old dream of helping others like a crazy woman who offers her breast to a baby.

'Are you happy?', murmured Rodrigues.

'Who?'

'You!'

A flame again flashed into the challenging eyes of Ferreira. 'There are all kinds of subjective factors in the concept of happiness,' he said.

That's not what you used to say—were the words that rose to the priest's lips, only to be suppressed. After all, he was not here to censure Ferreira for his apostasy and betrayal of his disciples. He had no desire to irritate that deep wound that lay beneath the surface of the other's mind and which he tried to conceal.

'That's so. He is helping us Japanese. He even has a Japanese name: Sawano Chuan.' It was the interpreter who spoke from his position between the two, leering into both faces. 'And he's writing another book,' he went on. 'It's a book to refute the teaching of Deus and to show the errors of Christianity. *Gengiroku* it is called.'

This time Ferreira had not been quick enough to stop the mouth of the interpreter. For an instant he turned his gaze to the fluttering chickens, trying to look as if he had not heard what the other had said.

'The magistrate has read his manuscript,' went on the interpreter. 'He praises it. He says it is well done. You should have a look at it yourself: you have plenty of time in prison.'

Now the priest saw clearly why Ferreira had spoken so rapidly and hastily about his translation of astronomy. Ferreira—the man who, at the bidding of the Lord of Chikugo, had to sit at his desk every day. Ferreira—who was writing that this Christianity to which he had devoted his life was false. The priest felt he could almost see the bent back of Ferreira as he plied his quill.

'Cruel!' said Rodrigues.

'What is cruel?'

'Cruel! Worse than any torture! I can't think of anything more dastardly.'

Suddenly, as Ferreira tried to turn his face away, the priest saw a white tear glistening in his eye. The black Japanese kimono! The chestnut hair bound back in Japanese style! The name: Sawano Chuan! And yet this man is still alive! Lord, you are still silent. You still maintain your deep silence in a life like this!

'Sawano Chuan, we did not bring this father here today just for a lengthy discussion.' It was the interpreter who now spoke and, turning toward the old bonze who, like a stone Buddha, was squatting on the floor bright with the rays of the western sun, 'Come!' he said. 'The bonze is busy too. Get your work done quickly.'

Now Ferreira seemed to lose his former fighting spirit. On his eyelash the white tear still glistened, but the priest felt that the man's stature had suddenly shrunk so that he looked quite small.

'I've been told to get you to apostatize,' said Ferreira in a tired voice. 'Look at this!' And he pointed quietly to behind his ear where there was a scar. It was a brown scar like that left after a burn.

'It's called the pit. You've probably heard about it. They bind you in such a way that you can move neither hands nor feet; and then they hang you upside down in a pit.'

The interpreter extended both hands in a gesture of dread, as though he himself shuddered at the very thought of it. He said: 'These little openings are made behind the ears so that you won't die immediately. The blood trickles out drop by drop. It's a torture invented by the Magistrate Inoue.'

Before the priest's mind there floated the picture of Inoue: the big ears, the rich complexion, the fleshy face. There before him was that face as it had appeared when Inoue slowly played with the bowl, turning it in his hands while sipping the hot water. This was the face upon which had played the smile of assent when the priest argued in his own defence. When yet another man was being tortured, it was said that Herod had sat down to dine at a table decorated with flowers.

'Think it over,' went on the interpreter. 'You're the only Christian priest left in this country. Now you're captured and there's no one left to teach the peasants and spread your doctrine. Aren't you useless?' But now the interpreter's eyes narrowed and his voice quite suddenly assumed a kind and gentle tone: 'You heard what Chuan said. He's translating books of astronomy and medicine; he's helping the sick; he's working for other people. Think of this too: as the old bonze keeps reminding Chuan, the path of mercy means simply that you abandon self. Nobody should worry about getting others into his religious sect. To help others is the way of the Buddha and the teaching of Christianity—in this point the two religions are the same. What matters is whether or not you walk the path of truth. Sawano is writing this in his *Gengiroku*.'

When he had finished speaking, the interpreter looked toward Ferreira for support.

The full light of the evening sun flowed down upon the thin back of the aging Ferreira clad in Japanese-garments. Staring at that thin back, the priest sought in vain for the Ferreira who had won his respect at the seminary in Lisbon long ago. Yet now, strange to say, no sentiments of contempt filled his mind. He simply felt his breast swell with the pity one feels for a living being that has lost its life and its spirit.

'For twenty years. . .' Lowering his eyes Ferreira whispered weakly. 'For twenty years I have labored in this country. I know it better than you.'

'During those twenty years as Superior you did marvellous work,' said the priest, raising his voice in an attempt to encourage the other. 'I read with great respect the letters you sent to the headquarters of the Society.'

'Well, before your eyes stands the figure of an old missionary defeated by missionary work.'

'No one can be defeated by missionary work. When you and I are dead yet another missionary will board a junk at Macao and secretly come ashore somewhere in this country.'

'He will certainly be captured.' This time it was the interpreter who quickly interrupted. 'And whenever one is captured it is Japanese blood that will flow. How many times have I told you that it is the Japanese who have to die for your selfish dream. It is time to leave us in peace.'

'For twenty years I labored in the mission.' With emotionless voice Ferreira repeated the same words. 'The one thing I know is that our religion does not take root in this country.'

'It is not that it does not take root,' cried Rodrigues in a loud voice, shaking his head. 'It's that the roots are torn up.'

At the loud cry of the priest, Ferreira did not so much as raise his head. Eyes lowered he answered like a puppet without emotion: 'This country is a swamp. In time you will come to see that for yourself. This country is a more terrible swamp than you can imagine. Whenever you plant a sapling in this swamp the roots begin to rot; the leaves grow yellow and wither. And we have planted the sapling of Christianity in this swamp.'

'There was a time when the sapling grew and sent forth leaves.'

'When?' For the first time Ferreira gazed directly at the priest, while around the sunken cheeks played the faint smile of one who pities a youngster with no knowledge of the world.

'When you first came to this country churches were built everywhere, faith was fragrant like the fresh flowers of the morning, and many Japanese vied with one another to receive baptism like the Jews who gathered at the Jordan.'

'And supposing the God whom those Japanese believed in was not the God of Christian teaching...' Ferreira murmured these words slowly, the smile of pity still lingering on his lips.

Feeling an incomprehensible anger rising up from the depth of his heart, the priest unconsciously clenched his fists. 'Be reasonable,' he told himself desperately. 'Don't be deceived by this sophistry. The defeated man uses any self-deception whatsoever to defend himself.'

'You are denying the undeniable,' he said aloud.

'Not at all. What the Japanese of that time believed

225

in was not our God. It was their own gods. For a long time we failed to realize this and firmly believed that they had become Christians.' Ferreira sat down on the floor with a gesture of tiredness. The bottom of his kimono fell open exposing dirty bare legs, thin like poles. 'I am saying this neither to defend myself nor to convince you. I suppose that no one will believe what I am saying. Not only you but the missionaries in Goa and Macao and all the European priests will refuse to believe me. And yet, after twenty years of labor here I knew the Japanese. I saw that little by little, almost imperceptibly, the roots of the sapling we had planted decayed.'

'Saint Francis Xavier. . .' Rodrigues, unable to contain himself any longer, interrupted the other with a gesture. 'Saint Francis Xavier, when he was in Japan, did not have that idea.'

'Even that saint,' Ferreira nodded, 'failed to notice this. But his very word "Deus" the Japanese freely changed into "Dainichi" (The Great Sun). To the Japanese who adored the sun the pronunciation of "Deus" and "Dainichi" was almost the same. Have you not read the letter in which Xavier speaks of that mistake?'

'If Xavier had had a good interpreter such a strange and trifling error would never have arisen.'

'By no means. You don't understand what I'm saying.' For the first time nervous irritation appeared around his temples as Ferreira answered. 'You understand nothing. And the crowd that comes for sight-seeing to this country from the monasteries of Goa and Macao calling themselves apostles—they understand nothing either. From the beginning those same Japanese who confused "Deus" and "Dainichi" twisted and changed our God and began to create something different. Even when the confusion of vocabulary disappeared the twisting and changing secretly continued. Even in the glorious missionary period you mentioned the Japanese did not believe in the Christian God but in their own distortion.'

'They twisted and changed our God and made something different!' The priest slowly bit the words with his teeth. 'Isn't even that our Deus?'

'No! In the minds of the Japanese the Christian God was completely changed.'

'What are you saying?' At the priest's loud cry the chicken that had been quietly nibbling food on the bare floor fluttered off into a corner.

'What I say is simple. You and those like you are only looking at the externals of missionary work. You're not considering the kernel. It is true, as you say, that in my twenty years of labor in Kyoto, in Kyushu, in Chugoku, in Sendai and the rest churches were built; in Arima and Azuchi seminaries were established; and the Japanese vied with one another to become Christians. You have just said that there were 200,000 Christians, but even that figure is conservative. There was a time when we had 400,000.'

'That is something to be proud of.'

'Proud? Yes, if the Japanese had come to believe in the God we taught. But in the churches we built throughout this country the Japanese were not praying to the Christian God. They twisted God to their own way of thinking in a way we can never imagine. If you call that God. . . ' Ferreira lowered his eyes and moved his lips as though something had occurred to him. 'No. That is not God. It is like a butterfly caught in a spider's web. At first it is certainly a butterfly, but the next day only the externals, the wings and the trunk, are those of a butterfly; it has lost its true reality and has become a skeleton. In Japan our God is just like that butterfly caught in the spider's web: only the exterior form of God remains, but it has already become a skeleton.'

'Nothing of the sort! I don't want to listen to your nonsensical talk. I have not been in Japan as long as you, but with these very eyes I have seen the martyrs.' The priest covered his face with his hands and his voice penetrated through his fingers. 'With my own eyes. I have seen them die, burning with faith.' The memory of the rain-drenched sea with the two black stakes floating on its surface arose painfully before his mind's eye. Nor could he forget the one-eyed man killed in plain daylight; while indelibly imprinted on his mind was the picture of the woman who had given him a cucumber: she had been trussed into a basket and drowned in the sea. If these people had not died for their faith what a blasphemy to man! Ferreira is lying.

'They did not believe in the Christian God.' Ferreira spoke clearly and with self-confidence, deliberately emphasizing every word. 'The Japanese till this day have never had the concept of God; and they never will.'

These words descended on the priest's heart like the weight of a huge, immovable rock and with something of that power that had been there when as a child he first heard about the existence of God.

'The Japanese are not able to think of God completely divorced from man; the Japanese cannot think of an existence that transcends the human.'

'Christianity and the Church are truths that transcend all countries and territories. If not, what meaning is there in our missionary work?'

'The Japanese imagine a beautiful, exalted man—and this they call God. They call by the name of God something which has the same kind of existence as man. But that is not the Church's God.'

'Is that the only thing you have learnt from your twenty years in this country?'

'Only that.' Ferreira nodded in a lonely way. 'And so the mission lost its meaning for me. The sapling I brought quickly decayed to its roots in this swamp. For a long time I neither knew nor noticed this.'

At the last words of Ferreira the priest was overcome with an uncontrollable sense of bitter resignation. The evening light began to lose its power; the shadows little by little stole over the floor. Far in the distance the priest could hear the monotonous sound of the wooden drum and the voice of the bonzes chanting the sad sutras. 'You,' the priest whispered facing Ferreira, 'you are not the Ferreira I knew.'

'True. I am not Ferreira. I am a man who has received from the magistrate the name of Sawano Chuan,' answered Ferreira lowering his eyes. 'And not only the name. I have received the wife and children of the executed man.'

It is the hour of the boar. Once again in the palanquin, escorted by officials and guards, he is on the road. It is now dead of night; no need to worry about casual passers-by peering into the palanquin. The officials had given the priest permission to raise the blind. If he wanted he could have escaped, but he no longer felt like doing so. The road was terribly narrow and twisted; and though the guards told him that they were already within the town, there were still clusters of farmhouses that looked like huts; but when they passed beyond them they found here and there the long fences of temples and groves of trees: Nagasaki had not yet taken on the shape of a city. The moon rose up beyond the dark trees and together with the palanquin seemed to move ever toward the west.

'You feel better now?' The official who rode along beside him spoke kindly.

Arriving at the prison the priest uttered a word of

gratitude to the guards and the officials, and then went inside. He heard the dull sound of the bolt being shot. It had been a long time since he had been here, and now at last he was back. It seemed such an age since he had heard the intermittent singing of the turtle-dove in the grove. In comparison with his ten days in prison this one day had been long and painful.

That he had at last met Ferreira was scarcely a reason for surprise. And the changed features and manner of the old man—now he came to think of it, this was something he had expected since coming to this country. The emaciated figure of Ferreira as he came tottering along that corridor from afar was not so terrifying. Now it did not matter. It did not matter. But to what extent was all he had said true?

The priest sat staring at the blank wall while the rays of the moon pierced through the bars bathing his back with light. Hadn't Ferreira talked in this way just to defend his own wrong and weakness? Yes, that was it. Of course it was so. One part of him kept insisting on this; but then quite suddenly a gust of fear would seize him and he would wonder if what Ferreira said were not perhaps true. Ferreira had said that this Japan was a bottomless swamp. The sapling decayed at its roots and withered. Christianity was like this sapling: quite unperceived it had withered and died.

'It's not because of any prohibition nor because of persecution that Christianity has perished. There's something in this country that completely stifles the growth of Christianity.' The words of Ferreira, uttered slowly syllable by syllable, pierced the priest's ears. 'The Christianity they believe in is like the skeleton of a butterfly caught in a spider's web: it contains only the external form; the blood and the flesh are gone.' So Ferreira had gone on with blazing eyes. And somehow in his words there was a certain sincerity unlike the self-deception of a defeated man.

Now the footsteps of the guards could be heard in the distance. When they faded out, the only sound was the hoarse rasping of insects in the blackness of the night.

'It cannot be true. No, no. It is impossible.' Rodrigues did not have enough missionary experience to refute Ferreira; but to accept the other's word .was to lose everything for which he had come to this country. Banging his head against the wall he kept murmuring monotonously: 'It cannot be so. It is impossible.'

Yes, it is impossible, impossible. How could anyone sacrifice himself for a false faith? With his own eyes he had seen those peasants, poverty-stricken martyrs. If they had not had a true belief in salvation, how could they sink like stones in the mist-covered sea? On any account they were strong Christians. Even if their belief was simple and crude, it breathed a conviction that had been implanted in Japan not by these officials nor by Buddhism, but by the Christian Church.

The priest recalled Ferreira's sadness. In the course of

their conversation Ferreira had said not one word about the poor Japanese martyrs. Of course he had deliberately avoided this issue; he had tried to avoid any thought of people who were stronger than himself, people who had heroically endured torture and the pit. Ferreira was trying to increase, even by one, the number of weaklings like himself—to share with others his cowardice and loneliness.

In the darkness he asked himself if now Ferreira was sleeping. No, he could not be asleep. The old man, in some part of the same city, was sitting in the darkness like himself, his eyes open, staring in front of him, biting at the depths of his solitude. And this loneliness was much colder, much more terrible than that which he endured in this prison cell. In order to pile weakness upon weakness he was trying to drag others along the path that he himself had walked. Lord, will you not save him? Turning to Judas you said, 'What thou dost, do quickly.' Will you number this man, too, among the abandoned sheep?

And so, comparing his own loneliness and sadness with that of Ferreira, he felt for the first time some self-respect and satisfaction—and he was able quietly to laugh. Then, lying down on the hard, bare floor, he waited for the onrush of sleep.

Chapter 8

THE next day the interpreter visited him again. 'Well, have you thought it over?' he said. This time he did not talk like a cat that plays with its prey; his expression was somehow stern. 'Sawano has told you. Give up this stubbornness! We're not telling you to trample in all sincerity. Won't you just go through with the formality of trampling? Just the formality! Then everything will be alright.'

The priest remained silent, his eyes fixed on a point on the wall. It was not that the other's eloquence irritated him; it simply passed through his ears without conveying any meaning.

'Come now! Don't cause more trouble. I'm asking you in all sincerity. It's not pleasant for me either.'

'Why don't you hang me in the pit?'

'The magistrate keeps saying that it's better to make you see reason and accept our teaching.'

Clasping his knees with his hands, the priest shook his head like a child. The interpreter heaved a deep sigh and for some time remained silent. A fly buzzed around with whirling wings.

'I see . . . well, it can't be helped then.'

The dull sound of the bolt shot into place fell on the priest's ears; and with that dull sound he knew that all reasonable discussion had come to an end.

To what extent he would be able to endure the torture he could not tell. Yet somehow it no longer held for his exhausted body the terror it had aroused when he wandered through the mountains. He was numbed with pain now. He felt that it would be better for death to come as soon as possible if it was the only way to escape from this painful day-after-day suspense. Even life with anguish about God and about faith was a melancholy prospect. Secretly he prayed in his heart that the fatigue of mind and body would quickly bring him death. Behind his eyelids like a hallucination floated the head of Garrpe sinking down into the sea. How he envied his companion! Yes, how he envied Garrpe freed from anguish such as this!

The next day, as he had expected, no breakfast was brought to him. Toward noon the door was opened; and a big fellow he had never yet seen, naked to the waste, showed his hollow face inside. He bound both of the priest's hands behind his back so tightly that when he moved his body even a little, the rope would bite into his wrists and an involuntary cry of pain would escape from his clenched teeth. While binding his hands, the fellow kept muttering insults which the priest could not well understand. 'At last the time has come,' he thought within himself; but strange to say, this emotion was accompanied by a freshness and a sense of elation such as he had never before experienced.

He was dragged outside. In the courtyard bathed in sunlight were three officials, four guards, and the interpreter—all standing in line and staring at him. The priest looked at them, especially at the interpreter; and a smile of triumph passed over his face. No matter what the circumstances, no man can completely escape from vanity, he reflected; and then he joyfully recalled that until this moment he had not even noticed this fact.

The big fellow grabbed the priest lightly in his arms and set him astride the bare back of a horse. Rather than a horse, it looked like a thin and starved donkey. It tottered forward and behind it marched the officials, the guards and the interpreter.

Already the road was jammed with Japanese waiting for the line to pass by; and from his position astride the horse the priest smiled down at them. Old people, mouths agape with astonishment; children nibbling at cucumbers; women who would first laugh, stare at him like idiots and then suddenly retreat in terror when their eyes met his. On each of these faces the light threw a different shadow. Then behind his ear came flying something like a brown clump—it was a piece of horse manure that someone had pitched at him.

He made up his mind that he would not let the smile leave his lips. Here he was riding through the streets of Nagasaki on a donkey. Another man had entered Jerusalem—likewise riding a donkey. And it was that man who had taught him that the most noble expression on the face of man is the glad acceptance of injury and insult. He would preserve such an expression until the end. This was the face of a Christian among the infidel.

A group of Buddhist monks, openly displaying feelings of hostility toward him, gathered under the shade of a huge tree and then, coming up and thronging around the donkey on which he was seated, brandished sticks as if to threaten and intimidate him. The priest looked at the faces that surrounded him, wondering if he might find some secret believer; but it was in vain. There was no face that was not stamped with hostility or hatred or curiosity. And there in the midst of them he caught sight of one who looked just like a dog that begs for pity. Unconsciously the priest stiffened. It was Kichijiro.

Clad in tatters, Kichijiro stood in the front rank waiting. When his eyes met those of the priest, he cowered and quickly tried to conceal himself in the crowd. But the priest from his position on the tottering donkey knew just how far the fellow had followed after him. Amongst all these infidels this was the only man he knew.

('Alright! Alright! I am not angry now. Our Lord is not angry.') The priest nodded toward Kichijiro as if to give him the consolation given to the penitent after confession.

According to the records, it is said that on this day the crowd escorted the priest from Hakata to Katsuyama and then passed on through Goto. When missionaries were captured, on the day before their punishment it was customary for the magistrate to have them dragged around Nagasaki in this way as show-pieces. The place through which the procession went was always the old market-place of Nagasaki where houses are close together and people throng in crowds. On the day after their being dragged around, it was customary for them to be brought to the place of execution.

In the time of Omura Sumitada when the port of Nagasaki was first opened, Goto-machi was the territory where the immigrants from the Goto Islands lived, and from here the bay of Nagasaki could be seen glittering in the afternoon sun. The crowds that came jostling after the procession pushed one another aside just as they did at a festival, trying to get a view of the queer foreign barbarian bound astride a bare-backed horse. When the priest would try to straighten his tortured body, the cry of derision was raised with even greater glee.

At first he had tried to force a smile; but now his face had hardened and it was no longer possible. The only thing he could do was to close his eyes and try not to see the faces that jibed at him, the faces with those protruding teeth. He wondered if that man had smiled gently when the multitude surrounded Pilate's mansion with shrieks and howls of anger. Even that man was incapable of such a thing, he reflected. 'Hoc passionis tempore. . .' The words of the prayer fell from his lips like pebbles and as he continued they came only with great difficulty. He was distracted by the tormenting pain of the rope which bit into his wrists whenever he moved his body, but what grieved him most was his inability to love these people as Christ had loved them.

'Well, father. How is it? Does no one come to help you?' It was the interpreter who, coming up beside him, quite suddenly shouted up. 'To your right and left are there nothing but voices of derision? And to think that you came to this country for them; and yet not a single one feels that he needs you. You're a useless fellow—useless.'

'And yet. . .' For the first time the priest shouted in a loud voice, as from the horse's back he glared at the interpreter with blood-shot eyes. 'And yet in that crowd there may be some who are praying in the silence of their hearts.'

'Now I'm going to tell you something. Alright? Long ago, here in Nagasaki there were eleven churches and two hundred thousand Christians. And where is it all now? Where are they hiding now? There are people in this crowd who were once Christians; but now they ridicule you with all their might and main to prove to those around that they are not Christians.'

'Insult me as much as you like. You only give me more courage.'

'Tonight. . .' The interpreter laughed as he slapped the belly of the horse with the palm of his hand. 'Alright? Tonight, you will apostatize. Inoue said so very clearly. Until now, when Inoue has said that one of the fathers will apostatize he has never been wrong. He was right in the case of Sawano. . . he will be right in your case, too.'

The interpreter rubbed his hands in a gesture of supreme confidence and then withdrew from his position beside the priest.

'In the case of Sawano. . .' It was these last words that remained in the priest's ears. From the bare back of the horse he trembled and strove to drive the words from his mind.

Beyond the bay an enormous column of clouds, glistened gold-edged in the afternoon light. For some reason he could not understand, these clouds looked like some gigantic castle in the sky in their great billowing whiteness. Many times before he had seen columns of white cloud; but never before had they stirred such emotion in his breast. He began to understand the beauty of the hymn of the Christians which he had heard when first he came to Japan: 'We're on our way. We're on our way. We're on our way to the temple of Paradise. . . Far away is the temple of Paradise.' His only solace and support was in the thought of that other man who had also tasted fear and trembling. And then there was joy in the thought that he was not alone. In this very sea those two Japanese peasants, bound to stakes, had endured the same suffering for a whole day before passing on to the far temple of Paradise. Suddenly his breast was filled with a wild joy in the thought that he was united with these two Japanese, united with Garrpe, united with that man nailed to the cross. And that man's face pursued him like a living, vivid image. The suffering Christ! The patient Christ! From the depths of his heart he prayed that his own face might draw near to that face.

Raising their whips, the officials drove the crowd aside and the people scattered like flies—meekly, without resistance, terror in their eyes; and making way for the procession they watched it depart.

At last the afternoon was over. The evening sun fell glistening on the red roof of a temple at the left of the road. Just beyond the town a mountain seemed to be floating in the sky. Now again stones and pieces of manure came flying through the air striking the priest on the cheek.

Walking beside the horse, the interpreter kept up the same line of argument. 'Come now! I'm not urging you to something bad. Apostatize! Just say one word. Please! If you do this, your horse will never bring you back to prison.'

'Where are you bringing me now?'

'To the magistrate's office. I don't want to make you

suffer. Please! I'm not saying anything wrong. Just say the word: "I apostatize."'"

Biting his lip, the priest sat silently on the horse. The blood from his cheek flowed down on to his chin. The interpreter looked at him, and with one hand on the belly of the horse kept on walking, a sad expression on his face.

Bending down, the priest made his way into the room in the thick darkness. Suddenly he was halted by a foul stench. It was the smell of urine. The floor was completely covered with it; and for a moment he stood still, trying to keep himself from vomiting. After some time, through the darkness he was at last able to distinguish the walls from the floor; and with his fingers against the wall groping his way around the room, he suddenly hit against another wall. Stretching out his arms he realized that the tips of his fingers could touch both walls at the same time. This gave him some idea of the size of the room he was in.

He strained his ears, but could hear no voice. It was impossible to know what part of the magistrate's building he was in. But the deathly silence assured him that there was no one anywhere near. The walls were made of wood, and as he touched the upper part his fingers discovered a large, deep crack. At first he thought that this was one of the cracks between the boards, but somehow he also had the feeling that it could not be so. As he kept on feeling it with his hands, he gradually realized that it was the letter 'L'. The next letter was 'Λ'. Like a blind man his fingers felt their way around the ensuing letters and found 'Laudate Eum'. Beyond this his fingers felt nothing more. Probably some missionary, cast into this prison, had cut out these words in Latin for the benefit of the next person who might be here. While in this place, this missionary had not apostatized; he had been burning with faith. And here, all alone in the dark, the priest was filled with emotion to the point of tears at the thought of what had happened. He felt that to the end he himself was being protected in some way.

He did not know what time of night it was. In the long journey through the streets to the magistrate's office, the interpreter and the officials whom he did not know had kept repeating the same questions. Where had he come from; what society did he belong to; how many missionaries were in Macao. But they had not urged him to renounce his faith. Even the interpreter seemed to change his tune completely; for with expressionless face he had simply performed his duty of translating the words of the officials. When this absurd examination was finished, they had brought him back to his cell.

'Laudate Eum'. Leaning his head against the wall, the priest followed his usual custom of thinking about that man whom he loved. Just as a young man might envisage the face of his intimate friend who is far away, the priest from long ago had the habit of imagining the face of

Christ in his moments of solitude. And yet since he had been captured—especially during the nights of imprisonment in that copse when he had listened to the rustling of the leaves—a different sensation filled his breast when the face of that man rose behind his closed eye-lids. Now in the darkness, that face seemed close beside him. At first it was silent, but pierced him with a glance that was filled with sorrow. And then it seemed to speak to him: 'When you suffer, I suffer with you. To the end I am close to you.'

While thinking of this face, the priest thought also of Garrpe. Soon he would be with Garrpe again. In his dreams at night he had sometimes seen that black head chasing after the boat and sinking in the sea; and then he was intolerably ashamed to think about himself who had abandoned the Christians. So intolerable was the thought that sometimes he would try not to think about Garrpe at all.

Far in the distance he heard a voice. It was like that of a couple of dogs yelping and fighting. He strained his ears, but the sound had already ceased and then for a long time it continued. Unconsciously the priest laughed to himself in a low voice. He had realized that it was the sound of someone snoring. One of the guards was sound asleep, drunk with sake.

For some time the snoring continued intermittently. Now it was high, now low like the sound of a badly played flute. Here he was in this dark cell overwhelmed with the emotion of a man who faces death, while another man snored in this carefree way—the thought struck him as utterly ludicrous. Why is human life so full of grotesque irony, he muttered quietly to himself.

The interpreter had confidently asserted that tonight he would apostatize. (If only he knew my true feelings. . .) As these thoughts crossed his mind, the priest withdrew his head from against the wall and laughed gently. Before his eyes there floated the untroubled face of that guard snoring in his deep sleep. If he's snoring like that, he doesn't fear that I'll try to escape, he reflected. Yet he no longer had the slightest intention of trying to escape; but just to give himself some distraction he pushed the door with both hands; but the bolt was shot from outside and he could not move it.

Theoretically, he knew that death was near; but, strangely enough, emotion did not seem to keep pace with reason.

Yes, death was drawing near. When the snoring ceased, the tremendous stillness of the night surrounded the priest. It was not that the stillness of the night was completely without sound. Just as the darkness floats over the trees, the awfulness of death suddenly descended upon him, filling him with terror. Wringing his hands he yelled in a loud voice. And then the terror receded like the tide. But once again, like the tide, it came surging on. He tried earnestly to pray to Our Lord; and intermittently there came into his mind the words: 'his sweat became like drops of blood'. As he saw the emaciated face of that man, there was no consolation in the thought that he, too, had tasted this same terror in the face of death. Wiping his brow with his hand, the priest got up and began to walk around his narrow cell to give himself some distraction. He could not stay still; he had to move.

At last, far in the distance, he heard a voice. Even if this was the executioner come to put him to the torture, this was better than the cold darkness that was cutting him more deeply than any sword. The priest put his ear to the door to get something of what the voice was saying.

Someone seemed to be upbraiding someone else. There was a voice of derision mingled with a voice of entreaty. The wrangling would stop far away; then again it seemed to come near to where he was. As the priest listened to the voices, his thoughts suddenly turned in a completely different direction. The reason why darkness is terrifying for us, he reflected, is that there remains in us the instinctive fear the primitive man had when there was as yet no light. Such was the crazy thought that came into his mind.

'Didn't I tell you to go away immediately?' A man was scolding someone.

Then the fellow who had been scolded would cry out in a tearful voice. 'I'm a Christian,' he was shouting. 'Let me meet the father.'

The voice was somehow familiar. Yes, it was the voice

of Kichijiro. 'Let me meet the father! Let me meet the father!'

'Keep quiet! If you keep shouting like that, I'll thrash you.'

'Thrash me! Thrash me!' The voice was mingled all the time with that of another.

'Who is he?' said yet another voice.

'He seems to be crazy. He's like a beggar; but since yesterday he keeps saying that he's a Christian.'

Then suddenly the voice of Kichijiro echoed out loudly: 'Father, forgive me! I've come to make my confession and receive absolution. Forgive me!'

'What are you talking about?' Then there was a sound like that of a falling tree as Kichijiro was struck by the gaoler.

'Father, forgive me!'

The priest closed his eyes and silently uttered the words of absolution. A bitter taste lay on his tongue.

'I was born weak. One who is weak at heart cannot die a martyr. What am I to do? Ah, why was I born into the world at all?' The voice broke off like the fading of the breeze, and then it could be heard far in the distance. Suddenly before the priest's eyes there floated the vision of Kichijiro as he had been when he returned to Goto— the popular man among his fellow Christians. If there had been no persecution, this fellow would undoubtedly have lived out his life as a happy, good-humored Christian man. 'Why was I born into the world! Why?. . . .

Why. . .?' The priest thrust his fingers into his ears to shut out that voice that was like the whining of a dog.

Yes, he had whispered the words of absolution for Kichijiro; but this prayer had not come from the depths of his heart. He had simply recited the words out of a sense of priestly duty. That was why they still lay heavy on his tongue like the residue of some bitter food. His resentment against Kichijiro, it was true, had now vanished; but yet deep down in his memory was still engraved the memory of his betrayal—the smell of the dried fish that this fellow had made him eat, the burning thirst that had followed. Even though he no longer entertained emotions of hatred and anger, he could not erase from his memory the feeling of contempt. Again he bit at those words of warning that Christ had addressed to Judas.

These were words that from of old he had never understood when he read the Bible. And not only these words, but the whole role of Judas in that man's life was something he had never been able to grasp. Why had that man included among his disciples the man who would eventually betray him? Even though he knew the real intention of Judas, why had he made as if he knew nothing for such a long time? Wasn't Judas no more than a puppet made use of for that man's crucifixion?

And yet. . . and yet. . . if that man was love itself, why had he rejected Judas in the end? Judas had hanged himself at the field of blood; had he been cast aside to sink down into eternal darkness?

Even as a seminarian and a priest, such doubts had arisen in his mind like dirty bubbles that rise to the surface of water in a swamp. And in such moments he tried to think of these bubbles as things that soiled the purity of his faith. But now they came upon him with a persistence that was irresistible.

Shaking his head, he heaved a sigh. The Last Judgment would come. It was not given to man to understand all the mysteries of the Scriptures. Yet he wanted to know; he wanted to find out. 'Tonight you will certainly apostatize,' the interpreter had said confidently. How like the words that man had addressed to Peter: 'Tonight, before the cock crows you will deny me thrice.' The dawn was still far away; it was not time for the cock to crow.

Ah! That snoring again! It was like the sound of a windmill turned around in the breeze. The priest sat down on the floor soaked with urine, and like an idiot he laughed. What a queer thing man was! Here was the stupid groaning snore, now high, now low, of some ignorant fellow who felt no fear of death. There, fast asleep like a pig, opening his big mouth he could snore just like that. He felt that he could see the guard's face with his own eyes. It was a fat face, heavy with sake and bloated, health itself—but for the victims the face was terribly cruel. Moreover this guard did not possess any aristocratic cruelty; rather was it the cruelty of a low-class fellow toward beasts and animals weaker than himself. He had seen such fellows in the countryside in Portugal, and he knew them well. This fellow had not the slightest idea of the suffering that would be inflicted on others because of his conduct. It was this kind of fellow who had killed that man whose face was the best and the most beautiful that ever one could dream of.

Yes, and that on this, the most important night of his whole life, he should be disturbed by such a vile and discordant noise—this realization suddenly filled him with rage. He felt that his life was simply being trifled with; and when the groaning ceased for a moment, he began to beat on the wall. But the guards, like those disciples who in Gethsemane slept in utter indifference to the torment of that man, did not get up. Again he began to beat wildly on the wall. Then there came the noise of the door being opened, and from the distance the sound of feet hastening rapidly toward the place where he was.

'Father, what is wrong? What is wrong?' It was the interpreter who spoke; and his voice was that of the cat playing with its prey. 'It's terrible, terrible! Isn't it better for you not to be so stubborn? If you simply say, "I apostatize," all will be well. Then you will be able to let your strained mind relax and be at ease.'

'It's only that snoring,' answered the priest through the darkness.

Suddenly the interpreter became silent as if in astonishment. 'You think that is snoring. . . that is. . . Sawano, did you hear what he said? He thought that sound was snoring!'

The priest had not known that Ferreira was standing beside the interpreter. 'Sawano, tell him what it is!'

The priest heard the voice of Ferreira, that voice he had heard every day long ago—it was low and pitiful. 'That's not snoring. That is the moaning of Christians hanging in the pit.'

Ferreira stood there motionless, his head hanging down like an old animal. The interpreter, true to type, put his head down to the barely opened door and for a long time peered in at the scene. Waiting and waiting, he heard no sound, and uneasily whispered in a hoarse voice: 'I suppose you're not dead. Oh no! no! It's not lawful for a Christian to put an end to that life given him by God. Sawano! The rest is up to you.' With these words he turned around and disappeared from sight, his footsteps echoing in the darkness.

When the footsteps had completely died out, Ferreira, silent, his head hanging down, made no movement. His body seemed to be floating in air like a ghost; it looked thin like a piece of paper, small like that of a child. One would think that it was impossible even to clasp his hand.

'Eh!' he said putting his face in at the door. 'Eh! Can you hear me?'

There was no answer and Ferreira repeated the same

words. 'Somewhere on that wall,' he went on, 'you should be able to find the lettering that I engraved there. 'Laudate Eum.' Unless they have been cut away, the letters are on the right-hand wall . . . Yes, in the middle. . . Won't you touch them with your fingers?'

But from inside the cell there came not the faintest sound. Only the pitch darkness where the priest lay huddled up in the cell and through which it seemed impossible to penetrate.

'I was here just like you.' Ferreira uttered the words distinctly, separating the syllables one from another. 'I was imprisoned here, and that night was darker and colder than any night in my life.'

The priest leaned his head heavily against the wooden wall and listened vaguely to the old man's words. Even without the old man's saying so, he knew that that night had been blacker than any before. Indeed, he knew it only too well. The problem was not this; the problem was that he must not be defeated by Ferreira's temptings—the tempting of a Ferreira who had been shut up in the darkness just like himself and was now enticing him to follow the same path.

'I, too, heard those voices. I heard the groaning of men hanging in the pit.' And even as Ferreira finished speaking, the voices like snoring, now high, now low, were carried to their ears. But now the priest was aware of the truth. It was not snoring. It was the gasping and groaning of helpless men hanging in the pit.

While he had been squatting here in the darkness, someone had been groaning, as the blood dripped from his nose and mouth. He had not even adverted to this; he had uttered no prayer; he had laughed. The very thought bewildered him completely. He had thought the sound of that voice ludicrous, and he had laughed aloud. He had believed in his pride that he alone in this night was sharing in the suffering of that man. But here just beside him were people who were sharing in that suffering much more than he. Why this craziness, murmured a voice that was not his own. And you call yourself a priest! A priest who takes upon himself the sufferings of others! 'Lord, until this moment have you been mocking me?', he cried aloud.

'Laudate Eum! I engraved those letters on the wall,' Ferreira repeated. 'Can't you find them? Look again!'

'I know!' The priest, carried away by anger, shouted louder than ever before. 'Keep quiet!' he said. 'You have no right to speak like this.'

'I have no right? That is certain. I have no right. Listening to those groans all night I was no longer able to give praise to the Lord. I did not apostatize because I was suspended in the pit. For three days, I who stand before you was hung in a pit of foul excrement, but I did not say a single word that might betray my God.' Ferreira raised a voice that was like a growl as he shouted: 'The reason I apostatized... are you ready? Listen! I was put in here and heard the voices of those people for whom God did nothing. God did not do a single thing. I prayed with all my strength; but God did nothing.'

'Be quiet!'

'Alright. Pray! But those Christians are partaking of a terrible suffering such as you cannot even understand. From yesterday—in the future—now at this very moment. Why must they suffer like this? And while this goes on, you do nothing for them. And God—he does nothing either.'

The priest shook his head wildly, putting both fingers into his ears. But the voice of Ferreira together with the groaning of the Christians broke mercilessly in. Stop! Stop! Lord, it is now that you should break the silence. You must not remain silent. Prove that you are justice, that you are goodness, that you are love. You must say something to show the world that you are the august one.

A great shadow passed over his soul like that of the wings of a bird flying over the mast of a ship. The wings of the bird now brought to his mind the memory of the various ways in which the Christians had died. At that time, too, God had been silent. When the misty rain floated over the sea, he was silent. When the one-eyed man had been killed beneath the blazing rays of the sun, he had said nothing. But at that time, the priest had been able to stand it; or, rather than stand it, he had been able to thrust the terrible doubt far from the threshold of his mind. But now it was different. Why is God continually silent while those groaning voices go on?

'Now they are in that courtyard.' (It was the sorrowful voice of Ferreira that whispered to him.) 'Three unfortunate Christians are hanging. They have been hanging there since you came here.'

The old man was telling no lie. As he strained his ears the groaning that had seemed to be that of a single voice suddenly revealed itself as a double one—one groaning was high (it never became low): the high voice and the low voice were mingled with one another, coming from different persons.

'When I spent that night here five people were suspended in the pit. Five voices were carried to my ears on the wind. The official said: "If you apostatize, those people will immediately be taken out of the pit, their bonds will be loosed, and we will put medicine on their wounds." I answered: "Why do these people not apostatize?" And the official laughed as he answered me: "They have already apostatized many times. But as long as you don't apostatize these peasants cannot be saved."'

'And you. . .' The priest spoke through his tears. 'You should have prayed. . . .'

'I did pray. I kept on praying. But prayer did nothing to alleviate their suffering. Behind their ears a small incision has been made; the blood drips slowly through this incision and through the nose and mouth. I know it well, because I have experienced that same suffering in my own body. Prayer does nothing to alleviate suffering.'

The priest remembered how at Saishoji when first he met Ferreira he had noticed a scar like a burn on his temples. He even remembered the brown color of the wound, and now the whole scene rose up behind his eyelids. To chase away the imagination he kept banging his head against the wall. 'In return for these earthly sufferings, those people will receive a reward of eternal joy,' he said.

'Don't deceive yourself!' said Ferreira. 'Don't disguise your own weakness with those beautiful words.'

'My weakness?' The priest shook his head; yet he had no self-confidence. 'What do you mean? It's because I believe in the salvation of these people. . .'

'You make yourself more important than them. You are preoccupied with your own salvation. If you say that you will apostatize, those people will be taken out of the pit. They will be saved from suffering. And you refuse to do so. It's because you dread to betray the Church. You dread to be the dregs of the Church, like me.' Until now Ferreira's words had burst out as a single breath of anger, but now his voice gradually weakened as he said: 'Yet I was the same as you. On that cold, black night I, too, was as you are now. And yet is your way of acting love? A priest ought to live in imitation of Christ. If Christ were here. . .'

For a moment Ferreira remained silent; then he suddenly broke out in a strong voice: 'Certainly Christ would have apostatized for them.'

Night gradually gave place to dawn. The cell that until now had been no more than a lump of black darkness began to glimmer in a tiny flicker of whitish light.

'Christ would certainly have apostatized to help men.'

'No, no!' said the priest, covering his face with his hands and wrenching his voice through his fingers. 'No, no!'

'For love Christ would have apostatized. Even if it meant giving up everything he had.'

'Stop tormenting me! Go away, away!' shouted the priest wildly. But now the bolt was shot and the door opened—and the white light of the morning flooded into the room.

'You are now going to perform the most painful act of love that has ever been performed,' said Ferreira, taking the priest gently by the shoulder.

Swaying as he walked, the priest dragged his feet along the corridor. Step by step he made his way forward, as if his legs were bound by heavy leaden chains—and Ferreira guided him along. In the gentle light of the morning, the corridor seemed endless; but there at the end stood the interpreter and two guards, looking just like three black dolls.

'Sawano, is it over? Shall we get out the *fumie*?' As he spoke the interpreter put on the ground the box he was carrying and, opening it, he took out a large wooden plaque.

'Now you are going to perform the most painful act of

love that has ever been performed.' Ferreira repeated his former words gently. 'Your brethren in the Church will judge you as they have judged me. But there is something more important than the Church, more important than missionary work: what you are now about to do.'

The *fumie* is now at his feet.

A simple copper medal is fixed on to a grey plank of dirty wood on which the grains run like little waves. Before him is the ugly face of Christ, crowned with thorns and the thin, outstretched arms. Eyes dimmed and confused the priest silently looks down at the face which he now meets for the first time since coming to this country.

'Ah,' says Ferreira. 'Courage!'

'Lord, since long, long ago, innumerable times I have thought of your face. Especially since coming to this country have I done so tens of times. When I was in hiding in the mountains of Tomogi; when I crossed over in the little ship; when I wandered in the mountains; when I lay in prison at night. . . Whenever I prayed your face appeared before me; when I was alone I thought of your face imparting a blessing; when I was captured your face as it appeared when you carried your cross gave me life. This face is deeply ingrained in my soul— the most beautiful, the most precious thing in the world has been living in my heart. And now with this foot I am going to trample on it.'

The first rays of the dawn appear. The light shines on his long neck stretched out like a chicken and upon the bony shoulders. The priest grasps the *fumie* with both hands bringing it close to his eyes. He would like to press to his own face that face trampled on by so many feet. With saddened glance he stares intently at the man in the center of the *fumie*, worn down and hollow with the constant trampling. A tear is about to fall from his eye. 'Ah,' he says trembling, 'the pain!'

'It is only a formality. What do formalities matter?' The interpreter urges him on excitedly. 'Only go through with the exterior form of trampling.'

The priest raises his foot. In it he feels a dull, heavy pain. This is no mere formality. He will now trample on what he has considered the most beautiful thing in his life, on what he has believed most pure, on what is filled with the ideals and the dreams of man. How his foot aches! And then the Christ in bronze speaks to the priest: 'Trample! Trample! I more than anyone know of the pain in your foot. Trample! It was to be trampled on by men that I was born into this world. It was to share men's pain that I carried my cross.'

The priest placed his foot on the *fumie*. Dawn broke. And far in the distance the cock crew.

Chapter 9

THERE was little rain that summer. In the calm of the evening Nagasaki was sultry like a steam bath. When dusk came, the reflected light from the bay made one feel the heat even more terribly. Ox-drawn carts moved into the city from outside with their loads of straw sacks, and the wheels glittered as they sent up clouds of white dust. Wherever one went, the air was heavy with the stench of fertilizer.

Now it is the middle of summer. The lanterns are hanging from the eaves of the houses as well as from those of the big trading houses where they bear images of flowers, birds and insects. Though not yet evening the playful children are gathered together singing their song:

O lantern, bye-bye-bye
If you throw a stone at it, your hand withers away,
O lantern, bye-bye-bye
If you throw a stone at it, your hand withers away.

Leaning against the window he sang the song to himself. He did not understand the meaning of what the children were chanting, but it somehow held a sad and plaintive note. Whether this stemmed from the song itself or from the heart of the person who sang he could not tell.

In the house opposite, a woman with long tresses flowing down her back was arranging peaches and jujubes and beans on a shelf. This was the shelf for the spirits of the dead, and it was one of the ceremonies that the Japanese performed to console the spirits who were supposed to return to their homes on the fifteenth day. To him it was no longer a rare sight. He had a vague remembrance of looking it up in the Dutch dictionary given him by Ferreira, and the translation he found there was 'hetsterffest'.

The children played, forming a row and staring at him as he leant against the window. 'Apostate Paul! Apostate Paul!' they kept shouting. Some of them even threw stones in through the window.

'Naughty children!' It was the woman with long hair who spoke, turning to scold the children and chasing them away. With a sad smile he watched them run away. He thought of the Feast of All Souls in Lisbon, reflecting on its resemblance to the *bon* festival—that feast when the windows of the houses in Lisbon displayed lighted candles.

His house was in Sotouramachi on one of the many narrow slopes of Nagasaki. Without permission from the magistrate's office, he could not go out. His only consolation was to lean against the window and watch the people going to and fro. In the morning, women with boxes of vegetables on their heads would pass by to the town from Omura and Isahaya. At noon, men wearing only a loincloth, singing in loud voices and leading lean horses with burdens on their backs, would pass by. In the evening, bonzes ringing their bells would pass down the slope. He would stare at this scenery of Japan, drinking in every detail as though later he were to describe it all in detail to someone back at home in his own country. But then the thought would rise in his mind that never again would he see his native land, and a bitter smile of resignation would pass over his sunken cheeks.

On such occasions, feelings of desperation would rise up in his breast as he reflected on the whole thing. Whether the missionaries in Macao and Goa had heard about his apostasy he did not know. But from the Dutch merchants who were allowed to enter the country at Dejima he gathered that news had probably reached them. This meant that he had been expelled from the mission.

And not only was he expelled from the mission, he was deprived of all his rights as a priest, and perhaps he was regarded as a renegade by the missionaries. 'What matter about all this. It is not they who judge my heart but only Our Lord,' he would murmur shaking his head and biting his lips.

Yet there were times during the night when this vision would suddenly rise up before his eyes and the harrowing thought would sear through his soul. Then, all unconsciously, he would cry out and jump up from his bed: the Inquisition, just like the Last Judgment in the *Apocalypse,* was pursuing him vividly and realistically.

'What do you understand? You Superiors in Macao, you in Europe!' He wanted to stand face to face with them in the darkness and speak in his own defence. 'You live a carefree life in tranquillity and security, in a place where there is no storm and no torture—it is there that you carry on your apostolate. There you are esteemed as great ministers of God. You send out soldiers into the raging turmoil of the battlefield. But generals who warm themselves by the fire in a tent should not reproach the soldiers that are taken prisoner. . .' (But no, this is only my self-justification. I'm deceiving myself.) The priest shook his head weakly. (Why even now am I attempting this ugly self-defence?)

I fell. But, Lord, you alone know that I did not renounce my faith. The clergy will ask themselves why I fell. Was it because the torture of the pit was unendurable? Yes. I could not endure the moaning of those peasants suspended in the pit. As Ferreira spoke to me his tempting words, I thought that if I apostatized those miserable peasants would be saved. Yes, that was it. And yet, in the last analysis, I wonder if all this talk about love is not, after all, just an excuse to justify my own weakness.

I acknowledge this. I am not concealing my weakness. I wonder if there is any difference between Kichijiro and myself. And yet, rather than this I know that my Lord is different from the God that is preached in the churches.

The remembrance of that *fumie*, a burning image, remained behind his eyelids. The interpreter had placed before his feet a wooden plaque. On it was a copper plate on which a Japanese craftsman had engraved that man's face. Yet the face was different from that on which the priest had gazed so often in Portugal, in Rome, in Goa and in Macao. It was not a Christ whose face was filled with majesty and glory; neither was it a face made beautiful by endurance of pain; nor was it a face filled with the strength of a will that has repelled temptation. The face of the man who then lay at his feet was sunken and utterly exhausted.

Many Japanese had already trodden on it, so that the wood surrounding the plaque was black with the print of their toes. And the face itself was concave, worn down with the constant treading. It was this concave face that had looked at the priest in sorrow. In sorrow it had gazed up at him as the eyes spoke appealingly: 'Trample! Trample! It is to be trampled on by you that I am here.'

Every day he was taken out for inspection by the *otona* or some leading personage. The *otona* was the representative of the town. Every month he came with a change of clothes and then brought him to the magistrate's office.

There were other times, too, when through the *otona*

he was summoned by the officials and again brought along to the magistrate's office. Here he would be shown certain objects on which the officials were unable to pass judgement, and it was his job to state whether or not they were Christian. The foreigners who came from Macao had all sorts of strange goods in their possession, and only Ferreira or himself could immediately judge whether or not they belonged to the category of forbidden Christian objects. When his work was done, he would receive some cakes or money from the magistrate's office by way of recompense.

Whenever he went to the magistrate's office at Hakata, the same old interpreter and the officials were there, always greeting him with courtesy. There was never any question of humiliating him or treating him as a criminal. On the contrary, the interpreter carried on as though he had absolutely no recollection of what had happened in the past. And as for himself, he simply smiled as though nothing had happened. Yet from the very instant he set foot in the place, he was aware of a searing pain that told him of a memory that neither of them could touch but must always be avoided. This was especially so when he passed through the antechamber; because from here he could see the dark corridor some distance away from the courtyard. It was there on that white morning that he had stumbled along in the embrace of Ferreira. And so in embarrassed haste, he would turn his eyes away.

As for Ferreira, it was forbidden to meet him freely.

He knew that Ferreira was living in Teramachi, close to Saishoji; but they were not allowed to exchange visits. The only time they met was when they came to the magistrate's office in the escort of the *otona*. Ferreira, like himself, was thus escorted. Both of them wore the clothes they had received at the magistrate's office; they simply greeted one another in their strange Japanese so that the *otona* might know what they were saying.

At the magistrate's office he made a pretence of the utmost candor, but it was impossible to express in words his feelings toward Ferreira. Indeed, there was in his heart a complexity of emotions, such as reign in the hearts of two confronting men. Both of them felt hatred and contempt for one another. Yet for his part, if he hated Ferreira this was not because the man had led him to his fall (for this he felt no hatred and resentment) but because in Ferreira he could find his own deep wound just as it was. It was unbearable for him to see his own ugly face in the mirror that was Ferreira—Ferreira sitting in front of him, clad in the same Japanese clothes, using the same Japanese language, and like himself expelled from the Church.

'Ha! Ha! Ha!' Ferreira would cry out with his servile, laughing voice as he faced the officials. 'Has the Dutch firm come to Edo? Last month when I was in Dejima they were saying that they would.'

He would stare silently at Ferreira, taking in the sunken eyes and the drooping shoulders, listening to the raucous voice. The sun had fallen on those shoulders. At Saishoji, when first they met, the rays of the sun had beaten down on those shoulders.

His feelings for Ferreira were not only of contempt and hatred; there was also a sense of pity, a common feeling of self-pity of two men who shared the same fate. Yes, they were just like two ugly twins, he suddenly reflected as once he looked at Ferreira's back. They hated one another's ugliness; they despised one another; but that's what they were—two inseparable twins.

When the work of the magistrate's office was over, it was usually evening. The bats flitted across between the gateway and the trees; they flitted over the purple sky. The *otona* would wink knowingly at one another and depart to left and to right with these foreigners who had been entrusted to their care. As he walked away, he would furtively look back at Ferreira. Ferreira, too, would cast a glance back at him. Until next month they would not meet again. And when they did meet, neither would be able to plumb the depths of the other's solitude.

Chapter 10

EXTRACTS FROM THE DIARY OF JONASSEN,
A CLERK AT THE DUTCH FIRM, DEJIMA,
NAGASAKI

July 1644 (*June, the First Year of Shoho*)

3rd July. Three Chinese junks cleared the port. Obtained permission for the Lillo to depart on the 5th. Shall have to carry to her tomorrow silver, war supplies and miscellaneous goods, and finish all the preparation.

8th July. Settled the final accounts with merchants, coin-judges, house-owners, and Mr. Shiroemon. Wrote at the Chief's command orders for goods for Holland, Coromandel Coast and Siam to be supplied by the next voyage.

9th July. An image of the Virgin Mary was discovered in the house of a citizen here. The household was immediately sent to prison and cross-examined. Consequently the man who had sold it to them was searched out and examined. It is said that Padre Sawano Chuan, an apostate, and Padre Rodrigues, another apostate Portuguese, were present at the inquisition.

Three months ago a coin bearing the image of a saint was found in the house of a citizen here. Rumor has it that all the members of the household were arrested and put to torture to make them give up their faith; but they refused to apostatize. Padre Rodrigues, the apostate Portuguese, who was among the witnesses, appealed for mercy repeatedly to the Government but was not heard. They were sentenced to death. It is said that the man and wife and their two sons had half of their heads shaven and were paraded through the town on the back of lean horses for four days. I heard that the parents had been executed the other day by being hung up by the feet, and that the sons had been put into gaol again after witnessing this sight.

Toward evening a Chinese junk made port. Her cargo was sugar, porcelain, and a small quantity of silk textile.

1st August. A Chinese junk arrived from Fuchow with miscellaneous goods on board. Towards ten o'clock the guard recognized a sailing ship some six miles off the Bay of Nagasaki.

2nd August. In the morning started unloading the ship mentioned above and made good progress.

Toward noon the Clerk of the Governor and his Assistants called at my room followed by a group of interpreters, and questioned me for a couple of hours.

This was because Sawano Chuan, the apostate, who lives in Nagasaki, and Rodrigues, the Portuguese apostate priest, informed them that the decision was made in Macao to send priests to Japan by Dutch vessels from India. According to Sawano the priests would hide themselves in Japan hereafter, engaged in lowly work of the ship as employees of the Dutch. The Clerk warned us, saying that the Firm would fall into grave difficulties if such a thing should happen, and he advised us to be very cautious. If a priest should come to Japan hereafter by our ship, and, finding it impossible to smuggle himself into the country because of the strict vigilance, should try to leave by our ship and be caught, it would also be the ruin of the Dutch. He declared that, since the Dutch call themselves subjects of His Imperial Majesty and of Japan, they should naturally deserve the same punishment as the Japanese; and he handed me a statement in Japanese issued by the Governor, which is as follows:

Translation of the Statement

Padre Sawano, whom the King of Hakata had arrested last year, testified in Edo to the Supreme Authorities that there are many Roman Catholics among the Dutch and in Holland. He also affirmed that Dutchmen had called on priests in Cambodia and professed themselves of the same faith, and that it had been decided that priests should enter the Dutch firm in

Europe as workmen or sailors to sail over to Nagasaki, Japan, by ships of the firm. The Government could not believe it and suspected that he intended to put Dutchmen at a disadvantage by testifying against them, both the Portuguese and the Spanish being great enemies of the Dutch. But Sawano Chuan asserted that this was no lie but truth. For this reason the Governor commands the Chief to investigate whether or no there is any Roman Catholic among officers and crew. If there is, report it. In case a Roman Catholic should be found in future coming to Japan by a Dutch vessel without being reported to the Governor, the Chief would find himself in serious trouble.

3rd August. Towards evening finished discharging the ship mentioned above. The Governor asked today if there was a gunner in the same ship who could handle a mortar. Sent Paulus Ver, an assistant clerk, to the ship to make inquiries, but there was none. Reported to that effect. The Governor commanded me to make inquiry about this of every ship to come hereafter, and to report it if there was any such.

4th August. In the morning Mr. Honjo, a senior samurai at the Government, visited the ship and searched it closely even to every chest in the corners. He said that this cross-examination was due to the ex-priests in Nagasaki, who testified to the Supreme Authorities that there were Roman Catholics among the Dutch and that they might come over on board Dutch vessels. But for this new suspicion, said he, the inspection might have been more mitigated than the year before, and he explained this to the officers of the ship as well. In compliance with their request I went on board myself and in their presence advised the crew that, if anybody had hidden anything that had to do with the Roman Catholic religion, he should bring it out and he would incur no punishment. To this they all answered that they had nothing hidden, and I read aloud to them the laws and regulations the crew were supposed to observe. As Mr. Honjo desired to know what I had told them, I explained it to him in detail. Whereupon they left saying they would report this to the Governor and relieve his mind.

Towards evening a Chinese junk made port from Chüanchow. Her main cargo was gossamer, figured satin, crepe-de-chine and other fabrics, the estimated value of which was eighty *kan;* added to this were sugar and miscellaneous goods.

7th August. The two sons of the executed parents I mentioned elsewhere were bound and carried on the back of lean horses together with another victim, passing by the Firm, to the execution ground, where they were beheaded.

1645 (*November, December, the Second Year of Shoho*)

19th November. A Chinese junk arrived from Nanking with merchandise worth eight or nine hundred *kan* containing white raw silk, gossamer, figured satin, gold brocade, damask, and so on. She brought us news that three or four junks with heavy cargoes were due here in a month and a half or in two months. They told us that they could easily obtain permission over there to sail freely to Japan only if they paid their dues to the High Official, which amounted to between one hundred and six hundred taels in proportion to the quantity of their cargoes.

26th November. A small junk sailed in from Chang-chew (possibly Chang-chow) with a cargo of linen, alum and pots, estimated at more than two chests.

29th November. In the morning a couple of interpreters came to the Firm at the Governor's request, and showed me a Dutch verse printed under a picture of the Virgin Mary which read, 'Hail, full of grace, the Lord is with thee; blessed art thou among women (Luke 1. 28).' They said that the picture was obtained from a bonze near Shimonoseki and asked me what the language was and what it meant. They also told me that Padre Rodrigues, the apostate Portuguese, and Sawano Chuan said they could not understand the sentence because it was written in neither Latin nor Portuguese nor Italian. It was 'Ave Maria' in Dutch which was printed by a Belgian who shares our language. No doubt the picture must have been brought in by our ship, but I decided to keep silent until further inquiries were made. As for the figures I answered correctly since Padre Rodrigues and Sawano Chuan must have already explained it to them.

30th November. Fine. Early in the morning had the rudder and gunpowder carried on board and finished loading the rest of her cargo. At noon went to the ship, called the roll, handed over the documents. On returning to the Firm, entertained Bonjoy and his attendants with food and drink. Before dark the wind changed to the north-west and *The Overschie* did not depart.

5th December. Towards noon the interpreter came to ask me the places of purchase of the goods we import. I answered him that China and Holland are the main sources of supply. He wanted to see if there would occur any inconvenience in case the Chinese cease to come over.

I have tried to obtain information about the apostate priests ever since I arrived in Japan. A Japanese called Thomas Araki is said to have stayed in Rome for a long time, serving at one time as chamberlain to the Pope. He confessed himself a Christian several times to the authorities, but the Governor took him as insane because of old age and left him as he was. Later he was hung in the pit for a whole day and night and apostatized. He died, however, with faith in his heart. At present there remain alive only two: one is a Portuguese called Chuan who used to be the Provincial of the Society of Jesus here and is blackhearted; the other a priest called Rodrigues from Lisbon, Portugal, who trod on a holy image at the Office of the Governor. Both of them live in Nagasaki at present.

9th December. Offered Mr. Saburozaemon a small box containing the same assorted ointments as presented to the Emperor and Mr. Chikugo and other medicines, which was accepted with pleasure. The Governor is reported to have been overjoyed seeing the attached list explaining in Japanese the effect of each. A ship from Fuchow made port in the evening.

15th December. Five Chinese junks cleared the port.

18th December. Four Chinese junks cleared the port. Four or five of the crew of a junk from Nanking asked for permission to go to Tongking or Cochin on board another Chinese junk; but their request was refused by the Governor.

One of the house-owners in this island heard that Chuan the apostate was writing various things about the Dutch and the Portuguese, and sending it very soon to the Imperial Court. I almost wish death on that rascal who ignores God; our Firm will only get into trouble because of him. However God will protect us. In the afternoon two Japanese ships arrived in front of the Firm. We are to depart on board one, with the camels on the other. Towards evening the interpreters came to the Firm bringing with them servants to accompany us to Kamigata. One of them was a washerman who spoke same Dutch. I wanted him to come with us as a cook for the time being, but Denbe and Kichibe told me that the Governor had forbidden us to take anybody who spoke Dutch. I did not trust them, thinking that they were against his company simply because they wanted to have their own way in carrying on business. So I told them that the only indispensable languages for us were Japanese and Dutch, and that it was Portuguese, not Dutch, that was to be the most abhorred of languages. There had never been a single Christian, said I, who spoke Dutch, while I could name at once dozens of Christians who spoke Portuguese.

23rd December. A small junk from Fuchow cleared the port. Towards evening a big Chinese junk arrived at the mouth of the Bay and, on account of the cross wind, was pulled to Nagasaki at night by a number of rowboats. Many people were on board with silk streamers flying, and were making a great noise with drums and charamelas.

It is Nagasaki and the first day of January. A man walks around the streets from house to house, beating on a drum that looks like a tom-tom and playing the flute, while women and children give him pennies from their places at the windows. This is the day when two or three beggars from around Funatsu and Kakuibara form a group and, wearing braid hats, go around singing a song called Yara.

January 2nd. In the tradesmen's houses the first business of the year begins, and they decorate their shops from early dawn, putting new curtains at the door. The peddler of sea cucumber visits each house.

January 3rd. The elders of each town go to the magistrate's office to ask for the *fumie*.

January 4th. The *fumie* exercise is performed by the people. On this day, from Edo, from Imazakara, from Funatsu and from Fukuro, the *otona* and the leading citizens go to receive the *fumie* plaque and to check each house's observance of the practice of trampling on the *fumie*. Every household has joined in cleaning the road, and quietly they are now all awaiting the arrival of the *otona* and the leading citizens. At last, from afar the announcement rings out in a voice that is like a song: 'They have arrived. . .'; and in each house, in a room adjoining the entrance, everyone in the family is lined up, attentively awaiting the ceremony that is to come. The *fumie* is between seven and eight inches in length and between four and six inches in breadth; and on it is fixed an image of the Virgin and Child. The first to trample is the master of the house, then his wife and the children. The mother, clasping her baby in her arms, must trample too. If there are any sick in the house, they also, in the presence of the officials, are made to touch the *fumie* with their feet from their position in bed.

On January 4th he suddenly received a summons from the magistrate's office. The interpreter had arrived with a palanquin. There was no wind, but the sky was dull and cloudy; it was a rather cold day and (was it because of the ceremony of the *fumie*?) the sloping road was utterly changed from the previous day—for now it had become deadly still and quiet. At the magistrate's office of Honhakata an official dressed in ceremonial clothes was waiting. 'The magistrate awaits you,' he said.

The Lord of Chikugo squatted erect in a room in which was placed a single brazier. Hearing the sound of footsteps, he turned full upon the priest that face with its big ears. Around his cheeks and lips there played a smile; but there was no laughter in his eyes.

'Greetings!' he said quietly.

This was his first meeting with the magistrate since his apostasy; but now he felt no sense of disgrace in the presence of this man. It was not against the Lord of Chikugo and the Japanese that he had fought. Gradually he had come to realize that it was against his own faith that he had fought. But he could scarcely expect the Lord of Chikugo to understand a thing like that.

'It is a long time since we have met,' nodded Inoue, stretching his hands over the brazier. 'I suppose you are quite accustomed to Nagasaki now.' He then went on to ask the priest if he were undergoing any discomfort; and, if so, he should at once make it known. The priest saw at once that the magistrate was trying to avoid any mention of the fact of his apostasy. Was this out of consideration for his feelings? or was it simply the self-confidence of the victor? The priest would sometimes raise his lowered eyes to scrutinize the other's face, but the expressionless countenance of the old man told him nothing.

'In a month's time it would be good for you to go to Edo and live there. There is a house prepared for you there, father. It is a house in Kobinatacho, the place where I used to live.'

Had the Lord of Chikugo deliberately used the word 'father'? It cut bitterly into the priest's flesh.

'Moreover, since you are going to spend your life in Japan, it would be good for you to take a Japanese name. Fortunately, a man named Okada San'emon has died. When you go to Edo, you can take his name just as it is.'

The magistrate spoke the words in a single breath, rubbing his hands as he held them over the brazier. 'This man has a wife,' he went on. 'It would be inconvenient for you, father, to be always alone, so you can take her as your wife.'

The priest had been listening to these words with downcast eyes. Behind his eyelids arose the picture of a slope down which he kept slipping endlessly. To resist, to refuse—this was no longer possible. Whatever about adopting the name of a Japanese, he had had no intention of taking his wife.

'Well?' asked Inoue.

'Very good.' Shrugging his shoulders he nodded; and a feeling of exhausted resignation took possession of his whole being. 'You underwent every kind of insult; if you alone now understand my feelings, that is enough. Even if the Christians and the clergy look upon me as a blot on the history of the mission, that no longer matters to me.'

'I've told you. This country of Japan is not suited to the teaching of Christianity. Christianity simply cannot put down roots here.'

The priest remembered how Ferreira had said exactly the same thing at Saishoji.

'Father, you were not defeated by me.' The Lord of Chikugo looked straight into the ashes of the brazier as he spoke. 'You were defeated by this swamp of Japan.'

'No, no. . .' Unconsciously the priest raised his voice as he spoke. 'My struggle was with Christianity in my own heart.'

'I wonder!' A cynical smile passed over Inoue's face. 'I have been told that you said to Ferreira that the Christ of the *fumie* told you to trample—and that that was why you did so. But isn't this just your self-deception? just a cloak of your weakness? I, Inoue, cannot believe that these are truly Christian words.'

'It doesn't matter what you think,' said the priest, lowering his eyes and putting both hands on his knees.

'You may deceive other people, but not me,' answered

Inoue in a cold voice. 'Previously I have asked the question to other fathers: What is the difference between the mercy of the Christian God and that of the Buddha? For in Japan salvation is from the mercy of the Buddha upon whom people depend out of their hopeless weakness. And one father gave a clear answer: the salvation that Christianity speaks of is different; for Christian salvation is not just a question of relying on God—in addition the believer must retain with all his might a strength of heart. But it is precisely in this point that the teaching has slowly been twisted and changed in this swamp called Japan.'

Christianity is not what you take it to be. . . ! The priest wanted to shout this out; but the words stuck in his throat with the realization that no matter what he said no one would ever understand his present feelings—no one, not Inoue, not the interpreter. Hands on knees, his eyes blinking, he sat listening to the words of the magistrate in silence.

'You probably don't know,' went on Inoue, 'but in Goto and Ikitsuki, large numbers of Christian farmers still remain. But we have no desire to apprehend them.'

'And why not?' asked the interpreter.

'Because the roots have been cut. If from the four corners of the world men like this father were to come once more, we would have to apprehend the Christians again,' said the magistrate with a laugh. 'But we no longer have any fear of that. If the root is cut, the sappling withers and the leaves die. The proof of this is that the God whom the peasants of Goto and Ikitsuki secretly serve has gradually changed so as to be no longer like the Christian God at all.'

Raising his head, the priest looked into the magistrate's face where he saw a forced smile on the cheeks and around the lips. But the eyes were not laughing.

'The Christianity you brought to Japan has changed its form and has become a strange thing,' said the Lord of Chikugo as he heaved a sigh from the depths of his bosom. 'Japan is that kind of country; it can't be helped. Yes, father. . .'

The magistrate's sigh was genuine, and his voice was filled with painful resignation. With a gesture of farewell he withdrew together with the interpreter.

The sky was as ever dull and cloudy; the road was cold. Carried along in the palanquin beneath the leaden sky, he gazed out vaguely at the expanse of sea, gray like the sky above. Soon he would be sent to Edo. The Lord of Chikugo had promised him a house, but this meant that he would be put in the Christian prison he had heard so much about; and it was in this prison that he would spend his life. Never again would he cross the leaden sea to return to his native land. When in Portugal he had thought that to become a missionary was to come to belong to that country. He had intended to go to Japan and to lead the same life as the Japanese Christians. Whatever about that, now it was indeed so. He had received the Japanese name Okada San'emon; he had become a Japanese. Okada San'emon! He laughed in a low voice as he uttered the name. Fate had given him everything he could have wished for, had given it to him in this cynical way. He, a celibate priest, would take a wife. (I bear no grudge against you! I am only laughing at man's fate. My faith in you is different from what it was; but I love you still.)

Till evening he stood leaning against the window, watching the children. Holding the string attached to the kite, they ran up the slope, but there was no wind and the kite fell idly to the ground.

As evening came, there was a break in the clouds and the sun broke weakly through. The children, now tired of their play with the kite, knocked on the doors of the houses with bamboo sticks, singing:

'Let's beat the mole so that it will do no damage!

Bo-no-me, bo-no-me, let's bless this house three times.

Let's beat with a stick!

One, two, three, four.'

He tried to imitate the children's song in a low voice; but he could not sing—and this thought made him sad. At the house beyond an old woman scolded the children; it was the old woman that brought him food twice each day.

It was evening. The breeze was blowing. As he strained his ears, he recalled the sound of the wind blowing through the grove in the days when he had been confined to prison. Then, as always happened at night, the face of Christ rose up in his heart. It was the face of the man upon whom he had trampled.

'Father, father. . . .'

With sunken eyes he looked toward the door as he heard a voice that was somehow familiar. 'Father, father. It's Kichijiro.'

'I'm no longer "father",' answered the priest in a low voice, as he clasped his knees with his hands. 'Go away quickly. You'll pay for it if they find you here.'

'But you can still hear my confession!'

'I wonder.' He lowered his head. 'I'm a fallen priest.'

'In Nagasaki they call you the Apostate Paul. Everyone knows you by that name.'

Still clutching his knees, the priest laughed. It wasn't necessary to tell him this; he knew it already. He knew that they called Ferreira the Apostate Peter and himself the Apostate Paul. Sometimes the children had gathered at his door chanting the name in a loud voice.

'Please hear my confession. If even the Apostate Paul has the power to hear confessions, please give me absolution for my sins.'

It is not man who judges. God knows our weakness more than anyone, reflected the priest.

'Father, I betrayed you. I trampled on the picture of Christ,' said Kichijiro with tears. 'In this world are the strong and the weak. The strong never yield to torture, and they go to Paradise; but what about those, like myself, who are born weak, those who, when tortured and ordered to trample on the sacred image. . .'

I, too, stood on the sacred image. For a moment this foot was on his face. It was on the face of the man who has been ever in my thoughts, on the face that was before me on the mountains, in my wanderings, in prison, on the best and most beautiful face that any man can ever know, on the face of him whom I have always longed to love. Even now that face is looking at me with eyes of pity from the plaque rubbed flat by many feet. 'Trample!' said those compassionate eyes. 'Trample! Your foot suffers in pain; it must suffer like all the feet that have stepped on this plaque. But that pain alone is enough. I understand your pain and your suffering. It is for that reason that I am here.'

'Lord, I resented your silence.'

'I was not silent. I suffered beside you.'

'But you told Judas to go away: What thou dost do quickly. What happened to Judas?'

'I did not say that. Just as I told you to step on the plaque, so I told Judas to do what he was going to do. For Judas was in anguish as you are now.'

He had lowered his foot on to the plaque, sticky with dirt and blood. His five toes had pressed upon the face of one he loved. Yet he could not understand the tremendous onrush of joy that came over him at that moment.

'There are neither the strong nor the weak. Can anyone say that the weak do not suffer more than the strong?' The priest spoke rapidly, facing the entrance. 'Since in this country there is now no one else to hear your confession, I will do it... Say the prayers after confession... Go in peace!'

Kichijiro wept softly; then he left the house. The priest had administered that sacrament that only the priest can administer. No doubt his fellow priests would condemn his act as sacrilege; but even if he was betraying them, he was not betraying his Lord. He loved him now in a different way from before. Everything that had taken place until now had been necessary to bring him to this love. 'Even now I am the last priest in this land. But Our Lord was not silent. Even if he had been silent, my life until this day would have spoken of him.'

Appendix

DIARY OF AN OFFICER AT
THE CHRISTIAN RESIDENCE

The Twelfth Year of Kanbun, Water-Senior-Rat

AT present *Okada San'emon* is granted the ration of ten persons; Bokui, Juan, Nanho, Jikan, the ration of seven persons each. Submitted the following to Tōtōminokami on 17th June.

NOTE

1 Scibē. Age: 50. Cousin to the wife of *San'emon*. Ship's carpenter Fukagawa.
2 Gen'emon. Age: 55. Cousin to the same. Servant to Doi Oinokami.
3 Sannojō. Nephew to the same. With Seibē.
4 Shōkurō. Age: 30. Nephew to the same. Workman at Esashi-cho.
5 Adachi Gonzaburō. Reported to be an apprentice to Bokui, the handicraftsman. During the time of Hōjō's management.
6 Jin'emon. Uncle to the daughter of Juan. Lives in Kawagoe. Came once during the time of Hōjō's manage-

ment. Came to see Juan again on 26th April this Year of the Rat.

The First Year of Enpō, Water-Junior-Ox

9th November. Bokui died of illness at six o'clock in the morning. As examiners came Inspectors Kimura Yoemon and Ushida Jingobē with both Assistant Inspectors. Police Officers: Shōzaemon, Den'emon, Sōbē, Gensuke. Policemen attended: Asakura Saburōemon, Arakawa Kyūzaemon, Kainuma Kan'emon, Fukuda Hachirobē, Hitotsubashi Matabē. Cremated at Muryōin Temple. Posthumous Buddhist name: Kōgan Shōten Zenjōmon. Endō Hikobē and Sergeant Kidaka Jūzaemon examined the belongings of Tokuzaemon, the servant of Bokui, and sent him home after trying him by *fumie*.

The Second Year of Enpō, Wood-Senior-Tiger

FROM 20th January to 8th February, *Okada San'emon* is engaged in writing a disavowal of his religion at the command of Tōtōminokami. Consequently Ukai Shōzaemon, Kayō Den'emon and Hoshino Gensuke are released from duty to take charge of him.

16th February. *Okada San'emon* is engaged in writing a book. Kayō Den'emon and Kawara Jingobē are both to be released from duty to attend *San'emon* from 28th February to 5th March.

Okada San'emon is to write a disavowal of his religion from 14th June to 24th July in the Study of the Mountain Villa. Consequently Kayō Den'emon and Kawara Jingobē are to be released from duty to attend him.

5th September. Juan was sent to gaol. To be kept there for some time as a penalty for his perverse conduct. Those

288

who attended at the pronouncement were Rokuemon, Shōzaemon, Sōbē, Den'emon, Gensuke, Kawara and Kamei. Persons on monthly duty are Tsukamoto Rokuemon and Kayō Den'emon.

The Fourth Year of Enpō, Fire-Senior-Dragon

Kichijirō, the attendant of *Okada San'emon,* who came here following him, was also sent to gaol because of his suspicious behavior. On searching his pocket at the Enclosed Guardhouse, there was found in the amulet-case he wore hung from his neck an image to which the Christians pay respect, with St. Paul and St. Peter on one side and Xavier and an angel on the other. Summoned out of gaol, *Kichijirō* was asked about his native place and about his relatives. He is from Gotō and fifty-four of age this Year of the Dragon.

There is something suspicious about the faith of Hitotsubashi Matabē, who has been on familiar terms with *Kichijirō.* So Matabē is also kept in prison until *Kichijirō* explains himself. (Omitted.) As Matabē is friendly with *Kichijirō,* his faith is open to suspicion. Hence the above measure. When Kurōzaemon and Shinbē, who are said to have been in close association with Matabē, were examined, their persons were closely searched in the Study. Their clothes including both their outer sashes and loincloth, purses of pocket-paper, and amulets were examined without exception. (Omitted.) Tōtōminokami came here in person, summoned *Kichijirō* to the Study, and asked him from whom he had received the sacred object of the Christian. To this he answered, 'An attendant named Saizaburō, who visited this Residence three years ago, kept it with him. When he came here, he dropped it and went back. So we picked it up and I kept it. Tokuemon, the Gate-keeper, also knows this.' At this Tokuemon was called and questioned, and he said he had witnessed the scene one summer day when the airing of clothes had taken place. Questioned if he had not received it from *Okada San'emon, Kichijirō* said, 'There is no chance to get anything from *San'emon*,' which meant, as he explained, that there was no chance because *San'emon* was always attended by a couple of guards on duty whenever he saw him.

17th September. Lord Tōtōminokami came personally to the Mountain Villa, and summoned three attendants to the Study to examine whether or not they were Christians. *Kichijirō* and Tokuemon were summoned later and were cross-examined. He also commanded that all the tenements of the guards should be closely searched, and the three Official Residences and the Lodges as well. Even wives and children were told to undo their sashes and loincloth in front of the officer. The Buddhist images they kept with them were of course examined. And then, on searching the dwelling of Sugiyama Shichirobē, Kobure Jūzaemon discovered among old scraps of paper a note of Christian words, which Kayō Den'emon seized to submit it to the Manager. It read: Father, Archbishop, Bishop, Pope.

18th. Lord Tōtōminokami came personally to the Mountain Villa and heard the explanation from the three attendants in the Study. He also summoned Hitotsubashi Matabē to examine him. *Kichijirō* and Tokuemon were examined next. *Okada San'emon's* wife, his maidservant and boy were summoned and examined later. *San'emon* himself was also sent for and was questioned whether or not he had tried to convert *Kichijirō*, to which he answered he had never tried to convert him at all. So he was commanded to put his hand-print on the paper testifying that he had not tried to convert the same. Afterwards Sugiyama Shichirobē was summoned and was asked why he had kept that note of Christian offices that had been found the day before. Shichirobē said, 'During the time of Hōjō Awanokami's management his Chief Retainers told me to memorize these names as I was in charge of such matters. And so I received that note from Hattori Sahē, the Police Officer.' His explanation was admitted to be consistent, and he was sent back.

Tahē, an attendant to Kasahara Gōemon who serves the Minister Tatebayashi, and Shinbē, the guard who belongs as a porter to the Squad of Saitō Tanomo, both were called and brought face to face with *Kichijirō* to investigate about the image they had picked up. It turned out true that Shinbē picked it up. The same Tahē said that he had seen Shinbē hold it. Consequently both Tahē and Shinbē were sent back.

The same day. Hitotsubashi Matabē was hung within the gaol. The officers in charge were Hisaki Gen'emon, Okuda Tokubē, Kawase Sōbē and Kawara Jingubē. From this time on Matabē was tortured several times.

18th October. Fine. The Lord came personally to the Mountain Villa. The Inspectors Sayama Shōzaemon and Tanegusa Tarōemon also came and tortured Hitotsubashi Matabē and his wife on the wooden horse. Naitō Shinbē was summoned to the Study. Matsui Kurōemon was examined and has roughly confessed.

24th November. Had the notice board concerning informers of Christians nailed to the main entrance of the

Mountain Villa. Kawara Jingobē, Ukai Gengoemon and Yamada Jurobe saw to it. The same notice board was prepared at command of the both lords. It reads:

ANNOUNCEMENT
The Christian faith has been prohibited for many years. Everyone is encouraged to report suspicious persons. The following shall be given in reward:

> To the Informer on a Father: 300 Pieces of Silver
> To the Informer on a Brother: 200 Pieces of Silver
> To the Informer on a Retrovert: ditto
> To the Informer on a Catechist or lay
> Christian: 100 Pieces of Silver

Even though the informer himself is a catechist or a lay Christian, he shall be given 300 pieces of silver according to the status of the accused. Should anybody shelter such persons and be found out by information from others, severe punishment shall be inflicted upon him and his family and relatives, and even upon the Head of the place and the surrounding families. The above is our announcement.

10th December. Juan was sent to gaol. From both the Lords came the Managers Takahashi Naoemon and Hattori Kin'emon, and in the presence of the Police Officers from both the Lords, delivered to Juan the following statement:

Juan, who is always perverse, offered the other day an affront to Kayō Genzaemon, and proved himself to be a most insolent person. As a punishment for this, he is to be imprisoned. He is commanded to accept the above punishment.

Juan replied that it was his own desire and that he would accept it willingly. When led to the gaol, he produced his

292

purse and committed it to the officers. It was taken to the Guardhouse and he entered into prison immediately. The same purse was examined in the presence of the Managers and the Police Officers from the Lords and in it was found seventeen *ryo* and one *bu* in small coins. The rest of Juan's belongings were examined and recorded in the book. The Police Officers sealed it and put it into Juan's tenement.

Among Juan's belongings were a chain, two disciplines, two rosaries and an astronomical chart.

The Ninth Year of Enpō, Gold-Junior-Cock

25th July. *Okada San'emon* died of illness at 2-3 past the hour of the Monkey. Called on the Lord to report this with Ukai Gengoemon and Naruse Jirōzaemon. The Managers Takahara Sekinojō, Emagari Jūrōemon were immediately sent here from the Lord's. Had the corpse of *San'emon* constantly watched by three policemen.

The money *San'emon* had was thirteen *ryo* and three *bu* in small coins and five *ryo* in gold coins, which total twenty-eight *ryo* and three *bu*. His belongings were sealed by the attendants and the Lord's Managers, and were put into the Godown on 28th.

26th. The following six came to the Mountain Villa as examiners: Inspectors Omura Yoemon, Murayama Kakudayū, Assistant Inspectors Shimoyama Sōhachirō, Nomura Rihē, Uchida Kanjūrō, Furukawa Kyūzaemon. In the presence of the Lord's Managers, handed over to the Inspectors the statement as follows:

Okada San'emon, who had been in the Christian Residence, died at a little later than half past four in the afternoon of 25th. Born in Portugal, Europe, he was first placed under charge of Inoue Chikugonokami in the Year of the Ram thirty odd years ago, and then came into residence here in the Enclosed Building where he lived for thirty years until this Year of the Cock. He fell ill at the beginning of the month and lost much of his appetite, getting worse and worse in spite of medical treatment by Ishio Dōteki, the Prison Doctor, and finally passed away. The same *San'emon* was sixty-four of age. Except this there is nothing unusual here.

26th July.

The group of Hayashi Shinanonokami
Okuda Jirōemon
Ukai Gengoemon
Kawara Jingobē
Kawase Sōbē
Kayō Den'emon

After examination, the corpse of *San'emon* was buried in Muryōin Temple at Koishikawa. From Muryōin came a priest called Genshū. *San'emon*'s corpse was sent there on a vehicle, and was cremated. The posthumous Buddhist name of *San'emon* is Myūsen Jōshin Shinshi. Paid one *ryo* and two *bu* for the funeral service and one hundred *hiki* as cremation charge. These expenses of the funeral were paid out of the money *San'emon* had left.